# SKELMERSDALE

D0801152

| **AUTHOR** | **CLASS** |
|---|---|
| POARCH, C. | F |

**TITLE**  Lighthouse magic

# LIGHTHOUSE MAGIC

The waves rushed against the shore, singing a musical tune. Cecily was an independent woman, but right now she was glad Ryan was here. She wanted him here. She willed him not to move.

And suddenly she knew. This was the spot her mother had described. This was where her mother and father must have stood numerous times before. This was the scene that had meant so much to both of them.

Her heart beat against her chest. She could feel the rhythmical beat of his against her back. His arms tightened around her. She turned in his arms and looked up at him. His head hovered above hers. She wished she could see his eyes. It seemed eons passed before he lowered his head, hovered there a second. She felt the warmth of his breath on her face. Desire raced through her. It couldn't possibly be one-sided, could it? And then he kissed her. Cool lips touched the side of her mouth, her lips, and then brushed a tongue over her mouth. She opened her mouth and his hot tongue danced with hers with desperate need. The kiss started out as a slow, get-to-meet-you kiss, but swiftly deepened with need, with desire, with a need so intense it rocked her. This was one stemming from desire denied, desire shared.

**CANDICE POARCH**
**Publications**

Bargain of the Heart

The Last Dance*

Shattered Illusions**

Tender Escape

Intimate Secrets*

The Essence of Love

With This Kiss*

White Lightning*

NOVELLAS

"A New Year, A New Beginning" in *'Tis the Season*

and *Moonlight and Mistletoe*

"More Than Friends" in *A Mother's Touch*

Published by BET/Arabesque books

*indicates book is part of the "Nottoway Series."
**indicates book is part of the Coree Island Series."

# LIGHTHOUSE MAGIC

## Candice Poarch

ARABESQUE

★BET
BOOKS

**BET Publications, LLC**
http://www.bet.com
http://www.arabesquebooks.com

09048480 3

ARABESQUE BOOKS are published by

BET Publications, LLC
c/o BET BOOKS
One BET Plaza
1900 W Place NE
Washington, DC 20018-1211

All Kensington Titles, Imprints, and Distributed Lines are available at special quantity discounts for bulk purchases for sales promotions, premiums, fund-raising, and educational or institutional use. Special book excerpts or customized printings can also be created to fit specific needs. For details, write or phone the office of the Kensington special sales manager: Kensington Publishing Corp., 850 Third Avenue, New York, NY 10022, attn: Special Sales Department, Phone: 1-800-221-2647.

First Printing: February 2003
10 9 8 7 6 5 4 3 2 1

Printed in the United States of America

# ACKNOWLEDGMENTS

My sincere thanks go to readers, booksellers and librarians for their continued support.

Fervent thanks go to my sister, Evangeline Jones, who often accompanies me to book signings. Special thanks to my husband, John, for his continued support in my writing. I couldn't do it without him. As always, profound thanks go to my critique partner, Sandy Rangel, and my editors, Chandra Sparks Taylor and Karen Thomas.

# Prologue

"I wish . . . Oh, I can see your father's face," Marva Edmonds said from her hospital bed as her daughter, Cecily, held her hand. Then she chuckled and coughed around a smile. "Your father had the devil in him, you know." Her eyes were vacant as if she was thinking of a far-off place known only to her. "I can see his face as if it were yesterday when he'd lead me up the lighthouse steps."

"What lighthouse, Mama?" Cecily asked. Her heart was breaking in two. She'd lost her father only nine months ago. Now her mother was lingering on by a thread.

"In North Carolina."

"We've never been to North Carolina." Cecily wondered if her mother even realized what she was saying. But what did it matter? At a time like this she should be able to say anything she wanted to.

"He and I would go to the very top and gaze out the window. The winds on the coast can be ferocious. And sometimes Walter . . . He'd hold my hand like this." She squeezed Cecily's hand with a firm grip that belied her frail condition.

"Did you date Walter in college?" Cecily asked.

"We dated in college and married right after we graduated. Your daddy stayed on to finish his masters while I
taught."

"Mama, you married Otis, remember? He was a wonderful father and husband."

"It's true. Otis was a wonderful man—the best. But your
father was Walter Tolson. We loved each other, your daddy
and I. He called what we felt 'lighthouse magic.' I never
told him it wasn't the magic of the lighthouse that drove
me wild about him. It was the magic between us. He was
just that kind of man." She inhaled deeply and gasped in
pain.

"Mama?" Cecily called out anxiously.

"I'm okay, darling. Don't worry so. I'll be all right. But
I worry about you."

"Don't worry about me, Mama. Let's get you more pain
medication."

Marva lifted a hand and patted Cecily on the cheek. "No.
So much to say, so little time. I thought I'd have more
time." She paused a moment. "I loved Otis. I gave him all
I had to give. But it's only once in a lifetime when the heart
sings with delight. And that's where the magic comes in. It
was that magic with your daddy that I could never forget—
that lasted a lifetime."

"Where is this island?"

"South of the Outer Banks in North Carolina. Coree
Island. There's no place like it, Cecily. Go back to the island
and claim your inheritance. The lighthouse, the cottage.
It's yours. But you have to get there before the state takes
possession. You're a fighter. You're stronger than I was.
But if you ever need anyone, go to Pauline. Pauline Anderson. She was my one true friend there." Marva coughed
again. Cecily handed her a glass of water and guided the
straw toward her mouth. Drinking the water took a lot of
effort. Marva settled back on her pillow and seemed to rest
a few moments.

Cecily was in shock. All this was news to her. She had
dreams of a lighthouse sometimes, of beautiful ocean water.
But she thought they were a child's dreams or from books

her mother had read to her when she was a child. She had no idea she had lived on an island. Then she noticed her mother was watching her and wondered if the story her mother spun was mere rambling.

"My Sissieretta. I hate leaving you, my love. You've been a constant joy in my life."

"Who is Sissieretta, Mama?"

Her mother's clear brown eyes blinked. "Why, you are, my dear. Didn't I ever tell you that?"

Cecily shook her head almost choked on her words. "I'm Cecily."

"That's the name I made up after we left Coree Island. You were born Sissieretta. Sissieretta Tolson. Named for your great-grandmother. Go back, Cecily. They can't hurt you now. They have nothing to hang over your head."

"Why did you leave? What happened back there?"

Her mother closed her eyes briefly with a defeated sigh. "There was a hurricane. A relief fund was set up. Some money was missing from the fund and I was accused."

"Why did they accuse you?"

"I was in charge of the money along with three other women. I deposited the money that Saturday afternoon. Monday morning when I opened the vault it was gone."

"Who do you think stole it?" It was never a question that her mother took it. Marva was as honest as the day was long. Cecily wondered about the three women her mother had mentioned.

Her mother was quiet for a time as if she'd said what needed to be said and the subject was closed. It wasn't closed in Cecily's mind, however.

"I wasn't born on Coree Island as your father was," Marva said some time later while Cecily was turning this new information over in her mind. "But I grew to love the island. Ah, my darling, I can feel it now. The cool ocean spray on my face. Our favorite spot was near the lighthouse. When the full moon shone its brilliance and hit the window just right, the upper window would glow."

Marva laughed and it seemed sunshine had lifted the pall that lingered in the room. "Walter is chasing me along the wet sand. I scoop up water on him. We're laughing like kids. He catches me. And I'm laughing so hard I can barely stand. He picks me up and whirls me around. And then he kisses me. It's my island now. Mine and his together. And you are a product of our love. Go home, my darling daughter. Go home, if only for a little while.

"Take me there, Cecily. Take me home to Walter."

# Chapter 1

The early February evening was unusually cold. Cecily Edmonds stood at the door of the lighthouse keeper's cottage as the moon cast a shimmering glow on the North Carolina night. The whitecaps on the churning Atlantic waves were barely visible as car lights glanced flickering beams on them before they disappeared from view.

As the wind whined eerily, the chimes hanging on the porch tapped against themselves making beautiful music. But Cecily didn't feel the joy and peace the chimes and water usually brought. Her mind played on the disastrous events that finally ended.

In contrast to the cold outside, the inside was warm and comfortable. Earlier Cecily lit a fire in the fireplace, turning her tea shop into a toasty haven. Now she lowered the temperature on the thermostat, walked over to a corner, and picked up a teddy bear left from the pajama reading party for tots. A comfortable couch set away from the wall held an assortment of soft, colorful pillows and stuffed animals. A pile of books stacked on the table beside it was waiting for little readers to sink with into the overstuffed sofa cushions with feet dangling over the edge. The decorations she'd spent countless hours over resembled a scene in one of the books.

Cecily had hoped parents would be thrilled to bring their children. With optimism, she'd borne the expense of the autographed copies of books she'd handed out as gifts. The book sold out in stores. It was now in its second printing, which had not yet hit the bookshelves. Cecily tracked the author down in Raleigh where she discovered the woman possessed first-edition copies packed in boxes in her basement. Just three days ago she'd driven to Raleigh in a freak snowstorm to purchase the signed copies.

Only three children attended the reading party. Pauline Anderson brought her granddaughter, Ranetta, and two other kids with her. They were the only ones who received the autographed books.

"If it weren't for the weekend business from campers at the campground, we'd be staring at each other every day," Cecily said to her aunt.

"It will get better," Glenda Fayard said as she flipped the long braids from her cornrows to her back. They had fallen on her shoulder when she'd bent to swipe a cloth across the table near where Pauline Anderson had sat. "Trust me."

Cecily gave a self-deprecating smile, but surprisingly she trusted the woman whose skin and the spices she often used reminded her of nutmeg. Although Glenda stood four inches shorter than Cecily's own five-six, her personality made her seem much taller. "The islanders don't want me here, Glenda. They would do anything to force me to leave. I don't know why I'm torturing myself this way. Why I spent my last dime to refurbish this old building. I must have lost my mind."

"You're here, aren't you? Your on-line business is picking up. We sent out fifteen orders today."

"Fifteen orders isn't enough to keep us solvent. But I'm not giving up," she said as she lifted her chin. She'd make a success of this even if she was forced to depend exclusively on campers from the campground a few miles away. "At least not yet."

"That's my girl." Glenda finished with the table and collected the sugar and creamers. "You know, you need to get out in the community more."

"I don't have time to socialize."

"This isn't like New York where you can hang a shingle in the perfect setting, throw up a sign, mail a few coupons, and curiosity will bring crowds in off the street to see what's happening. Just about everyone here knows each other. And you have a past to live down. Your mother was a good woman, bless her soul, and my best friend, but you've got this mess to clean up. Whoever stole that money way back when hurt an awful lot of people. And though people talk a lot about forgiving, they aren't that quick to do so in real life. It wouldn't hurt for you to volunteer for some committees or do more than make an appearance at church. Start to get involved in things."

"Where am I supposed to find the time?"

"I'm a strong Christian. I believe God always makes a way." She held up a hand when Cecily started to say something. "I know you don't like for me to start my preaching and I won't. I'm just saying, stretch yourself a little and see what happens. The way I see it this town needs you as much as you need them. Three kids came tonight, but those three were very happy children. They asked questions galore. One sat on your lap the entire time. Sopped up every word you said like a biscuit dropped in gravy. Held on to that book as if it were an extension of herself. I'm thinking you touched a chord in those kids. Even though there were only three, three were enough."

Cecily nodded, though she had doubts. On the surface this island was a picture-perfect fantasyland. But beneath the surface lay secrets, envy, evil. Yet good people were there, too. An example was the woman who just drove away in a Lincoln with three charming little girls buckled into their booster seats with their books on their laps.

Cecily owed enormous gratitude to the woman she called Aunt. Six months ago, at her mother's bedside, Cecily learned that Glenda, who to this day treated Cecily like a beloved niece—who had uprooted her own life and moved hundreds of miles from her home in New York to Coree Island to help Cecily with her tea shop—had no blood connection to her. It was Glenda's kindness that made Cecily's life in Coree Island, North Carolina, tolerable. It was the decency of a beloved mother that kept Cecily here and determined to find the person responsible for her mother's flight twenty-six-odd years ago. Cecily was a fighter. She wasn't running from anything.

"You know people pass this shop on their way to the ferry in the mornings. It's easy enough for them to stop by for a boxed breakfast to eat on the ferry ride to Morehead City."

"Now, you're talking," Glenda said, chuckling.

"I'll call the paper and see if we can put an ad in the weekly edition."

"Sounds like a winner."

Cecily wasn't given much time to daydream. She heard someone walking up the stairs and assumed one of the kids finally remembered the stuffed animal she'd left behind.

But the face who appeared after the door nearly crashed against the wall wasn't Pauline's or either of the little girl's. It was the face of a stranger.

The windblown woman glanced around the room and settled her gaze on Cecily. Her nose was red from the cold and she shivered in her coat as she stood uncertainly by the French doors.

"Are you closed?" the woman asked. "I planned to attend the reading although I don't have any children. But an emergency at the clinic prevented me from leaving." She extended a hand. "I'm Ellen Grant. I just returned from vacation."

"You're the doctor here?" Cecily asked as she shook the woman's hand.

Dr. Grant nodded.

"It's nice to meet you. Come in and have a seat." Glenda hovered in the background. "This is Glenda Fayard, my aunt."

Glenda wore a pleased expression on her face, as if she

were mocking Cecily for her previous thoughts. Cecily ignored her.

"I just came by to introduce myself. I don't remember your father, but my grandmother remembers him very well. She made me promise to tell you she'll be here as soon as she returns from Charlotte. My mother and sister live there and Grandma is spending the month with her." Dr. Grant looked heavenward and shook her head. "My sister's having a time keeping Grandma away now that she knows you're here."

"I'm looking forward to meeting your grandmother." Maybe the older woman knew Cecily's father. What he looked like. Some of the things he did as a boy, his favorite meals.

"She's a distant relative. She said to be sure I told you that—that you have family here. So I guess we're relatives somewhere along the line."

Cecily looked closely at the woman, wondering if there was any resemblance between them. Dr. Grant was tall—about five-eight. She certainly wasn't emaciated. They were both somewhat rounded, skating between a twelve and a fourteen. They both wore their hair in ringlets in deference to the humidity and wind. But the likeness seemed to end there. Ellen was more statuesque. She was very self-assured. Probably accustomed to issuing orders. Her black eyes were lively and intelligent.

Glenda set cups of tea on a table, breaking Cecily's concentration. Steam curled into the air.

"The shop's closed but we have some soup left over," Cecily said at last. "Please share the dinner with us."

Ellen smiled. "Sounds like heaven. I skipped lunch today. But I'll pay."

"Next time. This one is on the house."

"Thanks," the doctor said and shucked her coat. "I hate to cook, so be prepared to see me often."

Cecily chuckled. "My kind of customer," she said, and hung Ellen's coat on the coat tree near the door. She liked this woman.

Glenda carried a tray laden with bowls of clam chowder,

sourdough bread, sandwiches, and a pot of tea to the table, all served on floral-patterned china, as if the occasion called for an extra-special touch.

Sharing dinner with Ellen Grant was almost like dinner with friends back home.

The two weeks since Cecily moved there had disappeared like a whirlwind. Pauline and her family welcomed her and some guy named Emery something called saying he'd stop by as soon as he could. Right now half his crew was out with the flu and he was working overtime. But most of the islanders failed to show the small-town hospitality that was mentioned by the chamber of commerce in brochures Cecily read on the area or the spirit her mother spoke so fondly of on her deathbed. Even though Cecily's father was born and raised here, her time away from the island made her an outsider. If she had roots, she didn't know how to claim them. Dr. Grant accepted her as if she belonged, as if returning wasn't a mistake after all.


By nine that evening Cecily had showered, rubbed on her favorite lotion, and donned a warm pink satin nightgown lined in flannel. She enjoyed reading before she turned in for the night, so she pulled out her Arabesque novel and placed it on the bedside table.

Her bedroom was painted a restful cornflower blue. A frilly gesture prompted her to cover the bed with a duvet of lacy blue-and-white-eyelet and top it with a dozen colorful pillows she was required to move aside each night.

She lived on the third floor of the keeper's cottage. She had only to look up to have a perfect view of the lighthouse and the light that shimmered from the top. Glenda lived in the second-floor apartment. The third floor was smaller, with a tiny kitchenette separated from the living room by a long bar and white shutters, but it was cozy and perfect for Cecily. The second floor boasted four nice size bedrooms, but she wouldn't consider forcing Glenda to climb an extra set of stairs.

Now Cecily crossed the room in her pink mules and

opened the curtains facing the ocean. As she gazed at the flickering light from the lighthouse, she wondered about the history of this old place—wondered about the secrets of those who'd lived on this floor during the last century—wondered about the ghosts. Wondered if children had slept here or if anyone had carried on a tryst. The upper floor was a secluded shelter, simply perfect for a tryst.

The Victorian cottage with its delicate-looking but sturdy shutters designed to withstand the ravishes of the ocean had been built in the late eighteen hundreds. But she knew nothing of the owners or the first keepers of the light, or how her father fit into the picture. She only knew that her father had some ancestor who'd donated the land to the island. That ancestor was the first keeper of the lighthouse in an area of the ocean deemed the Graveyard of the Atlantic. They were situated on the Crystal Coast, south of the Outer Banks. The closest land area city was Morehead City where the ferry made hourly trips until midnight and where the island's high school children attended school. She knew most of the workers on the island worked near or in Morehead City. A Marine base was located near there. There wasn't enough industry on the island to sustain the citizens. It was a secretive place and the islanders liked to keep it that way.

With the success of the campground, the word had spread anyway. Cecily lived there a short time and already she'd received many offers for her land. But she wasn't ready to sell. She'd never even consider giving up her land. She'd love to make a go of her tea shop. She'd love to make a living on this little island. She'd think again about strategies to tempt the islanders to her tea shop.

Mesmerized by the beam from the light, she listened to the incessant winds that were as common as sirens in New York. They blended in with her surroundings. She wondered about the existence of old pictures, old ledgers, old history that was suspiciously missing when she'd arrived. Was it destroyed because someone hated her mother?

Suddenly the phone rang, a stringent sound out of place in the otherwise quiet room.

She quickly answered it.

"Cecily, this is Ryan Anderson. I don't know if you remember me."

"I remember you," she said. He was Pauline's son, the one who seemed out of sorts most of the time. His voice, deep and sensual, sent a ripple of awareness through her. It was somehow incongruous with his touchy personality.

"I hope I'm not calling too late," he said cautiously. His voice sent her pulses spinning and she gripped the phone so tightly her hand began to cramp.

"I was still up."

"Good," he said with a lighter tone. "I'm designing a summer map and brochure for the campground and wondered if you'd like to place an ad for your tea shop. There's a small space left. Every camper gets a copy," he said. "It has directions, site locations, and ads from local businesses. It occurred to me you might want the exposure for your . . . shop."

"I'd love to," Cecily told him.

"We're on a tight deadline." He gave her the dimensions for her ad. "Can you get it to me in a week?"

"Sure. I'll bring it by. Would you like a disk or hard copy?"

"Both would be good." They talked another few minutes before they disconnected.

Cecily slowly put the phone on the hook and wondered at Ryan's story. He seemed withdrawn, as if he'd been through a few trials of his own. She wondered if his mother had convinced him to make the offer. When his family visited her tea shop, he seemed as if it took wild horses to bring him over and he disappeared soon after the introduction. His sister, Delcia Matthews, her husband, and her daughter, Ranetta, had stayed to dinner with Pauline and Clay Anderson. But Ryan had disappeared after ordering soup and a sandwich to go. Tall and well built, Cecily thought, as she approached the window and closed the curtains. She might live on the edge of the world, but she still couldn't sleep with her curtains open.

Ryan was a very attractive man and she found his nearness

disturbing and exciting. But the storms tossing inside him made taking a second look not worth the effort. His story must be one of *somebody done somebody wrong*. She'd been there so often that she didn't even want to know the lyrics.

"My goodness," Ruby Milford said the next afternoon after church. They met in a building that previously served as a one-room school. After a larger school had been built, the church purchased the property and the buildings were joined. Before that, church dinners were eaten outside. Now the hunger relief committee met to decide what they'd serve when their time was due. They served once a month after forming cooperation with other churches in the area.

"Business was very brisk last weekend with all the tourists in town," Taylor Blackwell said. "Any of you take your kids to that tea shop last night?" she asked.

Ruby, a medium-sized woman, looked pleased as several people around the room shook their heads.

Pauline Anderson was spitting angry at Ruby and her entourage of witches—livid with the way they bad-mouthed Sissieretta, but she couldn't help the young lady by spewing her fury. She regarded the three ladies who sat together like a flock of vultures—Ruby, Shelly, and Taylor—at the table as if one couldn't act or think without the other. Long ago they'd been dubbed the three witches. Pauline wanted to jump up and pound on the silly womens' heads, but she contained her emotions. A person could catch more flies with honey than with vinegar, she'd always believed, at least until they plucked her last nerve. And she was very close right now.

"Pauline, I heard the campground was pretty full," Taylor said.

Pauline pasted a fake smile on her face. "Ryan said they turned down more than a hundred reservations," she said. "He's adamant that they expand soon to keep up with growth."

"Business from the campground is really good for the island," Taylor agreed. "I must have sold two hundred duck decoys. Ryan must be beside himself that he couldn't buy the lighthouse property. He'd planned to expand the place. I know Cecily is going to be difficult about it."

"We don't know what she'll do or her reason," Pauline said. "If she decides not to sell, she would certainly be within her rights. After all, it is her land."

"Cecily's got a whole lot of nerve coming back here after what her mama did," Ruby lamented.

"I think it's wonderful that Sissieretta is here. This is her home," Pauline responded loudly enough for everyone to hear. She thought Sissieretta was a lovely name and it shouldn't be shortened to Cecily. Besides, her mama and daddy named her Sissieretta and that was the way it should be. "It's where she belongs."

"Pauline, you always were a soft touch, too nice and trusting of people. I know Cecily's mother was your friend, but I don't know how you could forgive that woman for walking away with a couple hundred thousand dollars of our money. Islanders needed that money to rebuild after the hurricane. And she took half of it and skipped town."

"It didn't quite happen that way. Remember, it was never proven that she stole the money."

"It sure didn't disappear into thin air. Maybe that's how Cecily could afford to make the repairs on that old building," another woman said. "Off the money her mama made by fleecing us."

"That was twenty-six years ago. I didn't believe her mother stole the money then, and I still don't believe it. Why, any number of people had access, even you, Taylor, Ruby, and Shelly." She looked at each of them in turn.

"I wasn't guilty of anything. She was the last one with the money. Pauline, even you saw her close the pouch. If she was so innocent she woulda faced us head-on. She wouldn't have run," Taylor said.

Several heads nodded in agreement.

"She was afraid. The town gathered like a hunting party. She had a daughter to think of. A person can't always prove their innocence," Pauline retorted. "This conversation is going absolutely nowhere. We have a meeting to get on with. I won't be part of anything that will crucify that girl. And I'll fight anyone who tries to run *her* out of town."

"Came back here all snooty. Even you have to agree she doesn't have the island spirit. She hired outsiders to make the repairs on the building. She should have hired someone right here."

"My son turned her down," Maisy Plunkard said. "She needed the work done right away and he had contracts to fulfill on other projects."

"Humph."

"I for one will not be attending this grandmother, grand-daughter tea that she's planned. Who ever heard of such? Didn't take my granddaughter to that reading thing, either," Shelly said.

"I took Ranetta. Sissieretta gave them autographed copies of Jaciah's new book. The one that sold out in the bookstores just before Christmas."

"Hattie said they aren't even available yet." Hattie Dever-oux owned the island's only bookstore. "I tried to get one for my daughter," someone said. "How did she get them?"

"I don't know, but Ranetta and the two children who went with her received signed first editions. Sissieretta gave the books to them. All of the children had a wonderful time." Pauline noticed the envy on Shelly's face and continued. "I think I just might help Sissieretta with that program. It's certainly needed."

"You're retired now."

"Being involved keeps the mind young."

"Humph."

"I think the tea is an excellent idea," Pauline continued. "I bought the most beautiful dress for Ranetta to wear. She's never attended a tea before."

"I saw that dress," her sister-in-law, Willow Mae, said. She'd snored lightly beside Pauline the last 15 minutes. "I was with Pauline when she picked it out. Ranetta's going to look like a precious little angel in it. What have y'all decided on?"

"You're going to spoil her rotten," Shelly said with an envious smile, ignoring Willow Mae's reference to the meeting that should be under discussion. But the conversation had finally turned productive. Pauline knew that Shelly would now try to outdo her. Wild horses couldn't keep her away from that tea.

"Spoiling is what grandparents are for," Pauline murmured.

"How is Delcia feeling these days?"

"Wonderful."

"When is that baby going to drop?" Wanda said. Along with her partner, Wanda owned the local restaurant and bar.

"Not for another three months."

"Summer pregnancies are no fun."

"That's for sure."

"You should invite her to become a member of our group. We could use more young people like her," Taylor declared.

"Why don't you ask her, Pauline?"

"Between the baby and the camp I don't see how she'll have the time. But I'll ask her." *If we ever get out of this meeting,* Pauline thought. Now she remembered what she didn't like about small islands.

But there was so much to love, too. Controversies reared their ugly heads everywhere. There was no escaping that. But she hoped Sissieretta would remain. What on earth could Pauline do to make her feel more welcome? Marva had been her best friend before she left. Pauline felt as if she sent her daughter home for Pauline's safekeeping, and she wouldn't let her old friend down again. She should have done more to keep Marva here, to convince her not to leave town all those years ago. It was too late to help Marva, but not too late to help her daughter.


Now that the state wasn't taking possession of the property adjourning the lighthouse, Ryan thought of ways to convince Cecily to sell it to him. He felt he stood a much better chance with her than he did with the state. Island property was prime real estate; almost none was for sale, and large developers would more than likely end up with it instead of islanders. Developers had been trying to convince islanders to sell to them for years with no success. Cecily owned more than three hundred acres. A developer could build scores of million-dollar homes on that acreage.

He maneuvered his truck on the dark road toward the tea shop. By now Cecily had had enough time to settle in, and if he didn't approach her soon, the property wouldn't be ready for the summer tourist onslaught *if* she decided to sell.

As Ryan parked his truck and headed to the front door, he pulled his coat snugly against him to cut the biting wind that tried to whip through him. He took the wide steps two at a time.

A tiny light shone in the tea shop. The window display was pretty, he had to admit, with the flowery teapot sitting on a little table with delicate cups and saucers and gold spoons. Must be a doll's table because two porcelain dolls sat in little chairs as if they were discussing juicy gossip. Just like a bunch of busybody women, Ryan thought and chuckled, a hollow sound that seemed to echo in the night. She'd depicted women exactly the way they were—at least some of them.

He'd gone into her shop only once, but the place was so frilly, he felt like a big klutz sitting in the dainty chairs. His parents had made certain he was acquainted with the finer things, but here, he felt as if the cup handle would crush in his hand. This was an island, for chrissakes. Sturdy people—fishermen—people who lived close to the land—close to nature. They'd never feel comfortable in this little shop. He supposed no one took the time to tell her that. It was obvious she hadn't done very much research before she made the decision to open it.

The shop was closed for the evening and it was dark on this side of this island, except for the light beaming from the lighthouse. Not very safe for two women living alone. His sister, Delcia, would rap him on the head if she heard him make such a sexist statement. She'd lived alone in her house for years after her husband died. He slept a lot easier when she married Carter.

He skirted the house to the back and climbed the steps

to the third level. Lights from inside glowed around the curtains, so at least she was still up. He rapped on the door.

Cecily answered, wearing a bathrobe and pink fuzzy slippers that managed to look cute and comical at once. And—he hated to admit it—sexy. He realized he was staring.

"Sorry, didn't realize it was so late," he said.

"It's not. I dressed for bed early. Please, come in."

He entered, expecting to encounter the same frilly room as the tearoom downstairs, but he was pleasantly surprised. True, the living room was very feminine with roses and whites and blues, but the overstuffed couch was comfortable and sturdy; so was the rest of the furniture. Knickknacks were all over the place, but at least he didn't feel like a bull in a china shop when she motioned him to the overstuffed couch and he sank into the soft cushions. It smelled feminine, too, like the jasmine that released its scent in springtime. His mother had planted it by the house.

"Be right back," she said.

He nodded. This was his first opportunity to relax all day and he wasn't totally at ease now. His gaze traveled over her backside as she left the room. Cecily's sweet scent lingered in the air and something intense flared in him. From the first moment he'd spotted her, a homing device activated inside him, tuned in to her wavelength. He didn't trust this homing device. He'd made the worst decision of his life three years ago when he'd married LaToya. And he'd paid for that mistake every day since.

Cecily returned, having exchanged the robe for jeans and a powder-blue sweater that outlined her rounded breasts.

She curled up in a chair across from him. With the fire blazing in the fireplace casting a sensual light on her brown face, the room was much too cozy.

"May I get you tea or coffee?"

Ryan shook his head. "I came to discuss the land adjacent to the lighthouse."

"The estuary."

"Well, part of it is. The other part has just overgrown over the last few years."

"What about it?" she asked cautiously.

"I'd like to buy it, except for the few acres attached to this house and the lighthouse."

"It's not for sale," Cecily muttered with such finality, Ryan was momentarily stunned.

"I realize that. Do you have plans for the land?"

"No. It brings me peace and the people who visit my shop seem to like the view. How had you planned to use it?"

"We want to expand the campground."

She frowned. "A campground so close would interfere with my privacy."

"We wouldn't build right up on your shop. The part we could actually use isn't in the shop's view."

Cecily shook her head. "I'm sorry I can't help you. But I just arrived and I'm not ready to make any decisions yet."

Ryan nodded, disappointment tightening his throat. "You'll keep my proposal in mind then?" He was well aware that she probably received many offers and for more money than the campground could possibly afford. But they needed that land.

She nodded, her tone cautious as she said, "I won't make any promises."

At least she left the window open. After she'd been here awhile, he'd approach her again. But she was an enticing sight sitting with her legs tucked under her, curled up like a tabby cat. He should have left right then but he found himself prolonging his stay. His mom had hammered him with the fact that he'd turned antisocial lately. Telling him to put LaToya behind him and move on with his life. Well, he'd done that. But he wasn't looking for another city lady to take her place. The cost was more than he was willing to pay.

Still, he found himself asking, "How have you found our island?"

"It's a very peaceful place."

"Ranetta, can't stop talking about your reading get-together."

"I'm glad she enjoyed it. She's a lovely little girl."

He chuckled, talking about a topic he loved. "I admit I'm

prejudiced when it comes to her. I'm the consummate doting uncle.''

Cecily's first genuine smile illuminated the room and Ryan wanted to see more of it. It set fire to him, too, as heat curled through his body. But suddenly he stood. It was time to leave. Cecily was a city girl. She wouldn't be here long before she tired of the laid-back island lifestyle—the lack of theaters, opera, fancy clubs, and what people stuck their noses in the air about and called ''culture'' as if plain everyday, hardworking people weren't good enough. Just like LaToya, he thought. If his divorce taught him one thing, it was that you couldn't make people into what you wanted them to be. They were who they were. If a person wasn't comfortable with living in your world, you'd best steer clear of her and accept that fact.

Still, the island was small and he found himself offering, ''If you ever need help, I'm in the phone book. If you can't find me at home, I'm usually at the park.'' He wrote his home number on a business card and handed it to her.

Why did she look surprised? They might not have a whole lot of culture on the island, but they were generous spirits.

''Thank you,'' she said, as she walked him to the door and handed him his coat.

''Have a nice evening,'' he said. He left and was halfway down the stairs before he heard the door close behind him. When she was ready to leave for the city, she'd sell the land, he was sure. In the meantime, they had slots for about twenty cabins. They were working on them now to ready them by mid-March for spring break when college kids would arrive in droves.

But it wasn't campsites that stirred his blood that moment. It was his body's response to Cecily. Hadn't he learned his lesson? Evidently not, because LaToya had stirred his blood to boiling. She knew how to pry what she wanted from a man. Some women were deceitful. LaToya had taught him that well. After they'd dated for years, LaToya had decided she wanted him to move to Triangle Park. After debating the issue for months, Ryan finally called the wedding off. He couldn't be someone he wasn't. He wasn't a city guy. He loved his work on the island. He loved the small community atmosphere. He loved his home and his job. He wasn't willing to move and start over in a job he knew beforehand he'd hate.

But after a month, LaToya had come back to him, apologizing for trying to change him. Assured him she wanted him happy. To do what made him happy. She could adapt to island life because she loved him.

Believing that lie had been his first mistake. Eloping with LaToya had been his second. The marriage hadn't lasted six months. But it had cost him every single penny, every CD, every share of stock he'd accumulated over the years. The only saving grace was that after a hefty mortgage on his house, he'd finally paid her off. And he still owned his half of the campground. But after more than ten years of saving, he was broke.

He wasn't about to look at another woman right now, regardless of how attractive, how beguiling she appeared to be. What he needed was to expand the business so they could accommodate more campers, giving him the opportunity to rebuild his finances. He'd never been so broke and it felt odd that he was so close to destitute. The only money left was the portion the park kept for repairs and expansions. He'd convinced Delcia and Carter to use part of that to expand the campground. But if he couldn't buy the land from Cecily, he couldn't expand.

Ryan started his truck with its CAMP COREE sign stenciled on the side and headed for home.

Both Ryan's parents' cars were in the yard when he arrived home. They'd lived in Asheville for only a few years after their retirement before they grew homesick and returned home. They'd moved away in the first place because of the ferocious storms and occasional hurricanes the island was famous for.

When they left, they'd sold him the house. They were now building a smaller home. But it wouldn't be ready for at least another couple of months. Until then, they were staying with him. He'd gained three pounds since they moved in. His mother's meals were delicious and he was eating too much. Maybe he'd take a run along the beach.

"I'm so angry with those women," Pauline Anderson was saying as he entered the house.

"Who're you angry with?" he asked as he hung his hat on the coat tree.

"Ruby's group."

"What did they do now?" Those women were always into something. Kept the town buzzing.

"They want to run Sissieretta out of town."

He looked in the fridge, took out a bottled water and unscrewed the top. "All they have to do is wait. She'll leave soon enough on her own."

"I certainly hope not. Why on earth would you think that? This is her home."

"She was raised in the city, Mom. She's not going to adapt to country life." He took a long swallow of water.

"Life here is more than a passing phase. It's in the blood. Your father and I are perfect examples of that."

"You grew up here. She didn't."

"Son, you're not going to be able to outtalk your mother in this," Clay Anderson said.

Ryan sighed. "What's all the gossip about anyway? That little tea shop isn't a threat to anyone."

"They're a bunch of hens always gossiping about something," his dad said. "Cecily's mother was accused of running away with half the relief fund way back when you were a baby."

"I've heard talk about it."

"She didn't do it. They never caught the thief," his mother said, adamantly.

"It's not going to stop the talk."

"This family is going to do everything we can to make her feel welcome so she'll stay, aren't we?"

His dad patted his mother's hand. "Sure we are, honey."

"Ryan?"

"Yeah, sure." He didn't know what all the to-do was about, though.

"Honey, you can start by taking me to the Romantic Valentine's Dinner at her restaurant next Friday night. I'm going to see if I can round up some more women to talk their husbands into taking them."

"I thought we were going to the mainland," his father said.

"I've changed my mind."

"Oh."

"Ryan?"

"Yeah?" he said, glancing at his mother cautiously.

"Get some of your old friends to take their wives."

"That's women's work. Guys don't do that stuff."

"What's wrong with being romantic? Besides, you need to find someone to take that night."

"At the last minute?"

"Any number of young ladies would love to go with you."

Ryan shook his head. "Might give them the wrong idea."

"Find someone."

"There isn't anyone and I'm not getting stuck with someone who'll be nagging me months after the dinner."

"You can be such a disagreeable son."

He gave her his irresistible lopsided smile. "But you love me anyway."

She rolled her eyes at him. "I'll talk to Carter and Delcia."

"I'll baby-sit."

"No, you will not. If you can't find a date, go by yourself."

"I'm working."

"Calm down, honey," Clay said to his wife. "Cecily's not a baby. The gal's going to be fine."

"Talk to Harry and Willow Mae, Clay, will you? Never mind. I'll talk to Willow Mae."

"Good idea. That ornery cuss doesn't have a romantic bone in his body."

"He's your brother."

"That's how I know. I'm ready for bed, honey. We can celebrate Valentine's Day early." He rose from his chair and approached her. He eased his arms around her ribs, kissing her on the neck.

Ryan laughed at his parents' foolishness. He watched his mother and father together. He had hoped for a relationship much like theirs. They were in their sixties and had more of a romantic life than he did at thirty-four. There was something definitely wrong with that picture.

But his father successfully took his mother's mind off of Cecily and her tea shop.

"It is getting late," she said around a fake yawn, as if he didn't know what would happen once they reached their bedroom. Good thing it was located at the opposite end of the house from his.

"Supper's warming in the oven, Ryan," his mother said, swatting his dad's hand as he urged her toward the hallway. "We tried to wait for you but you were so late."

"That's okay," he said, as his father maneuvered her on. Watching them, Ryan felt left out. Not that he wanted to be the center of his parents' attention. He'd hoped to share that kind of intimacy with a special woman. He and LaToya had never gotten beyond the hot sex.

His mind flashed back to Cecily in the sexy bathrobe. He really needed that walk. The moon was bright that night. "Think I'll take a jog before I eat. See you in the morning." Yeah, he really needed that jog tonight. He headed to his room to change into sweats.

# Chapter 2

Mrs. Anderson arrived early at the tea shop the next morning with Ranetta in tow. The little girl was dressed in a pair of green pants and a cute green-and-white sweater top. She clutched her book close to her chest and glanced up at Cecily with scene-stealing brown eyes.

"We decided to give Delcia a morning off," Mrs. Anderson said as Cecily settled the little girl in the booster seat. "Ranetta and I are going to treat ourselves to your delicious blueberry scones."

"See my book?" Ranetta asked. She'd barely let the book go long enough for her grandmother to pull her navy coat off.

"I most certainly do," Cecily said, and tweaked her cold little nose.

Pauline looked fondly at her granddaughter. "We can't get her to put that book down. We wanted to save it since it's autographed, but she won't part with it."

"Let her enjoy it." Cecily was pleased the little girl was enjoying the book. She believed books were to be read, not to sit on a shelf to collect dust. "I'll give you another one for safekeeping."

"We'll buy it from you."

"I'd planned to give them away. I took four to the library."

"We really appreciate it," Pauline said.

Cecily handed Pauline a menu, and a crayon and a small coloring book to Ranetta. "May I get your drinks while you decide on your order?"

"Ranetta would like orange juice and a cup of hot chocolate with whipped cream, and I'll take English Breakfast tea."

Cecily left to get their drinks, and glanced at the two other tables occupied in the room. The customers sat with backpacks on the floor near their feet. Must be campers, she thought. High school kids worked at the tea shop on weekends, but she didn't have enough business for extra help on weekdays.

Maybe it was good that it was quiet this morning. Cecily wanted to talk to Pauline about the three women her mother had mentioned on her deathbed.

It was time that Cecily began to search for the person who stole the money. She wanted to clear her mother's name. Her mother failed to mention the women's names, but she was sure Mrs. Anderson knew their identities.

She carried the drinks to Pauline's table, took their orders, and finished up with the two other tables.

Ranetta and her grandmother ate their meal of eggs, bacon, and scones. Cecily watched the door for customers who never appeared. When the ladies finished, Cecily asked Glenda if she would entertain Ranetta while she talked with Mrs. Anderson. Ranetta was eager to go to the children's corner and have her book read to her.

"Mrs. Anderson, I'd like to speak to you about something," Cecily said as she settled in the seat Ranetta had vacated.

"On her deathbed, my mother mentioned three women who might have had something to do with the relief fund theft, but she died before she told me their names. Do you know who those women could be?"

Pauline frowned. "I might. Did Marva mention why she thought these women might be responsible?"

"No. She didn't have time. She had so many things to tell me. And then . . ." Cecily's throat clogged. She mentally pulled herself together—closed her eyes to stop an onslaught of tears. Some days she was okay. She could go an hour or two without remembering. Other days grief clutched her like a vice.

She felt Pauline's hand patting hers. Cecily opened her eyes. Only then did she realize her hands were closed into fists.

She and her mother had been so close, at least she'd thought they'd been. It was only on her mother's deathbed that Cecily realized she didn't know her mother very well at all. That hurt. There were so many secrets her mother had kept from her. Things she would have wanted to discuss with her. At times, irrational anger tumbled Cecily's world. The instability of her emotions since her mother's death made her wonder if she'd ever get a grip on reality. Her mother should have told her about the past years. The knowledge would have given Cecily a chance to learn about her father and about her roots, gather information about the past they'd shared together. But her mother wasn't here for Cecily to talk to any longer. Cecily slowly unclenched her fists. It was left to her to piece together details on her own. She hoped her mother's closest friend on the island would help her.

"Yes, I know the women," Pauline finally said. "You're setting yourself an impossible task if you plan to gather evidence after all these years."

"Wasn't there some investigation?"

"Sure there was, but it was hushed up after your mother left. The police did a little digging, but your mother was gone. Unfortunately she was their only suspect. There was little they could do. She did a wonderful job of disappearing."

Cecily pressed her lips tightly against her emotions. "Who are these women?"

Pauline paused. "Cecily, I hesitate to tell you. Right now,

spend your time getting acquainted with the islanders, and giving them the opportunity to get to know and accept you.''

Cecily shook her head. ''I don't think they will accept me until the person who really stole that money is uncovered.''

''Honey, you're not going to get your answers after all these years,'' Pauline said with worry creasing her forehead. Then her face cleared. ''Tell you what. I'd like you to come to dinner tomorrow night. You and Glenda. You close early on weekdays so it shouldn't present a problem. I'd like you to meet some of the islanders. Delcia has wanted to throw a party for you but she isn't up to the preparations right now.''

''That's very sweet of her, but not necessary.''

''At least have dinner with us.''

''All right.'' Cecily smiled. ''Thank you for inviting us.''

''Good.'' Pauline patted her hand. ''I'll expect you around seven?''

''Sounds good. And the three women?''

Pauline sighed. ''You aren't going to leave it alone, are you?''

''I can't.''

''All right then. The three women have been a tight clique since high school. They are Ruby Milford, Shelly Giles, and Taylor Blackwell. Years ago I searched my mind to see how they could have taken the money but I couldn't prove anything.''

''I'm going to prove it,'' Cecily said with a conviction Pauline didn't miss.

Pauline reached over and patted her hand again. ''Be careful, dear. You're home now. I know what happened to your mother was despicable and tragic. But there are many good people on this island. Not perfect, but no place is. It's a wonderful place to raise children with values that will carry them into healthy adulthood.''

Someone had taken that away from Cecily and her mother.

''I'm glad you're back.''

Cecily smiled. ''So am I.''

* * *

Talking with Pauline about her mother brought back the old memories, so later Cecily walked along the blacktopped road toward the graveyard. On one side of the road was the marsh where tall grass grew toward the Sound. On the other side the ground was more solid. Gnarled scrub oak and pines reached toward the sky and undergrowth grew thick and rich. On the crest of a small hill, almost a mile from the tea shop, the family graveyard stood in a clearing surrounded by an intricately carved wrought-iron gate. Many of her ancestors were buried there and the designs of the stones had changed over time. The oldest stone was dated to 1805.

Six months had passed since her mother died, but the pain that hung heavy on Cecily's heart ripped through her as she lifted the latch on the gate and entered the peaceful grounds where her mother and father lay side by side. Cecily had found an identical stone to her father's for her mother. She placed flowers on both graves. She first stood at her mother's and spoke of the three women, but she sought peace. Somehow being there helped her feel closer to her parents. But now she stood at her father's grave and wondered what kind of man he'd been.

She knew nothing of her father. Had never seen a picture. Where had her mother put them? She must have saved something of him. What traits did she take from him? Was her hair like his? Were her eyes? How tall was he? What kind of personality did he have? Did he like sports? Was he handsome? He must have been a good man, because her mother still loved him decades after he died. They must have had a powerful love. Cecily wondered what it would feel like to love like that. Since her father hadn't been around, perhaps his good traits had mushroomed in her mother's mind.

Cecily felt as if a part of her were missing. A huge part, since now she felt she must learn about her mother as well as discover the father she never knew.

Since her mother and Mrs. Anderson had been friends,

she wondered if the older woman had pictures of Cecily's parents. She'd ask her tomorrow night at dinner. She must have at least one picture of her father.

Cecily left the graveyard, pulled her coat tighter around her, and returned to the tea shop. Only a couple of people had come by. None that Glenda couldn't handle alone.

"I'm going to take some brochures to the campsite," Cecily said to Glenda. "Valentine's Day is on a Friday this year. Perhaps they'll have campers who want to celebrate."

"I don't know who would want to freeze their tushes off at a campground on what's supposed to be a romantic day."

"The average temperature is fifty-six degrees in February here," Cecily reminded her.

"During the day, but at night it drops to the thirties."

"Campers are a breed in and of themselves. Actually, it'll be fun to snuggle in those sleeping bags together."

"Give me a soft, comfortable bed and plenty of heat, thank you very much."

Cecily grabbed a stack of brochures, the disk, and a hard copy of the ad and headed out. It was only a short drive to the campsite. Grass grew tall and gold along the water's edge. The island was small and it didn't take very long to reach the campsite. She was surprised to see so many campers in residence, but even more mobile homes. The owners tucked in as if they'd settled in for the winter.

She'd passed by when she first arrived on the island and toured the town but she never drove onto the site. Now she pulled into a parking space in front of a log cabin. She knew Ryan worked with his sister and brother-in-law at the camp. For a moment she wondered if he would even be there, but knew that he would. In the short time she'd been there, she'd learned that he was a workaholic. She could appreciate that. She was one herself. But his work ethic wasn't what suddenly accelerated her heart rate, she thought as she left her car to go inside.

He was leaving the office. He stood over six feet tall and had incredible dark eyes, black eyes a person could lose herself in, and a medium brown complexion. His handsome face and muscular build were disturbing to her in every way, though she wouldn't admit it even under threat of torture.

He should be in an ad for those jeans that emphasized the force of his thighs and hips, giving her a glimpse of the powerful man beneath.

Then he looked at her and smiled. The smile seemed to light up his face. Gone was the taciturn man she was familiar with and that was even more dangerous.

"Hi," he said as he approached her. She hugged the brochures to her chest, for a second forgetting the purpose of her trip. *This is downright stupid,* she thought. But his slow southern drawl appealed to her. It wasn't too slow, but just enough to add a sexy timbre.

"Those for me?" he asked.

"Oh, yes," she said, feeling silly. "Ah, they're the brochures for the Valentine's dinner. I hoped you would hand them out to your guests."

"Be happy to," he said, taking them from her and giving them a cursory glance. "I'll even mention the dinner on our Web site. May bring in some customers."

"Think so?"

He shrugged. "Never can tell."

"Well, thanks," she said for lack of anything better. "The ad is here, too. I hope it isn't too late."

"It's not. Want to take a look around?"

"Sure."

He turned to a woman at the desk. "Barbara, I'll be out for a while," he said.

The woman merely smiled and said, "Sure."

Ryan pressed his hand against her lower back, leading her deeper into the building. "During the summer months, this area is part of the camp store. In the winter, business is slow and we close the reservation building." He took her through the camp store, then outside, pointing out one of the shower areas. A few mobile homes were parked near the sound. A few cabins were located in the center of things.

Through the tour, Cecily was very aware of him beside her, the awareness flowing through her like a pleasing wine warming her insides. He handed her into a pickup truck and they rode around the grounds. The campground was impressive. One summer she camped in the mountains, but it wasn't nearly as upscale as this. The showers had been only mildly warm, even if you were one of the first to shower in the mornings. Here, she imagined the water was steamy hot. The place was excruciatingly neat and the buildings were well maintained. Not a sliver of paper marred the still-green grass. They passed a swimming pool, food stand, miniature golf area, swings and slides for kids and picnic tables for each site. Each road was clearly marked with neat orange and white signs. Cecily realized that if she allowed him to use her land, he wouldn't erect a dump in her back yard.

The look of the place said a lot about the man—the people who owned it. Ryan loved his job. He took pride in his work and saw that it was done well. She respected that in a person.

And then the tour was finished and they returned to her car.

"I'll pick you up tomorrow just before seven," he said, opening her door.

"I can drive." She knew she'd enjoy her time at the Andersons', but Cecily wanted the freedom of her own transportation. When she was ready to leave, she'd prefer not to have to depend on anyone. She was depending on him to hand out brochures. That was enough.

She climbed into the car. Ryan shut the door after she settled in her seat.

"I'll be there before seven to pick you up," he repeated, then turned and jogged toward the camp store.

Cecily opened her mouth to call after him, then thought better of the gesture. *Why make a federal case out of something so small?* she thought, started her motor and drove the short distance to the tea shop. On the way she thought of her tactics for searching out the embezzler. She'd spoken to Glenda earlier. She, too, thought it was too early to muddy the waters. Cecily's natural inclination was to jump right in and get things done. But both Mrs. Anderson and Glenda had many years of wisdom on her. She wasn't waiting very long, she knew. To her mother's chagrin, patience had never been her virtue, but she'd give serious thought to her next move.


As promised, Ryan arrived to pick Glenda and Cecily up at six-fifty. Since Cecily didn't know what to expect, she dressed carefully in a black dress that hit just above the knees, with white jade jewelry to set it off. She finished the outfit with a spritz of perfume.

"Don't you look snazzy?" Glenda said. She wore a long dazzling top over shimmering royal-blue slacks.

"You look stunning yourself," Cecily said, making clicking noises.

Glenda posed. "I'm not too old to strut my stuff when I want to."

"I know that."

They heard a car drive into the yard. Glenda peeped through the curtains. "Guess we won't be riding in the camp truck this time."

"What are you talking about?" Cecily approached the window to take a look.

"Got a shined-up SUV. That's a pretty one, but I prefer the truck. Give you a chance to snuggle up to him on your way over."

"Don't even go there."

"Won't hurt you to take a look at him."

Cecily didn't need to hear that. She observed him more than she wanted to.

"He's a mighty handsome man."

"I've noticed."

"It's about time. If I were thirty years younger, I'd give you a run for your money."

"Oh, please," Cecily said with an assurance she was far from feeling.

"I heard he wasn't dating anyone. The field is open."

"And he's been waiting for dear old me to come along and knock him off his feet." Cecily rolled her eyes at Glenda and settled comfortably on the sofa.

"Yes, he has."

Cecily chuckled.

By that time, Ryan was at the door and Cecily was pretending a confidence and poise in opposition to her tumbling
insides. When he entered the apartment, he seemed to be as
disinterested as she tried to appear but she didn't miss his
obvious examination and the approval he couldn't conceal.
He looked at her as if he were photographing her. Cecily's
heart fluttered.

After a brief greeting, they were driving to his home. He
kept up polite conversation on the short trip. This was
Cecily's first visit there and she found something sleepy and
soothing about the two-storied structure more designed for
a family than a single man. Several cars were parked in the
yard. Light flashed on a swing hanging from ropes thrown
over a thick tree branch sturdy enough to hold an adult. It
reminded Cecily of old romantic movies where the hero
pushed his heroine on a warm spring day, or a parent pushed
a child. She thought again that this home was made for a
family.

Pauline Anderson met them at the door and Cecily handed
her a floral china teapot with a container of English-breakfast
tea with two matching cups, saucers, and dessert plates as
a hostess gift.

"You shouldn't have," Pauline said, but she looked
pleased as she opened the gift. "This is absolutely beautiful.
And look at this. My favorite blend. I won't have an excuse
to spend mornings in your shop."

"Oh, yes, you will," Cecily said around a laugh.

"You better believe it. Thank you, dear." She kissed
Cecily on the cheek.

A crowd of people was milling in the room, and after
handing their wraps to her husband, Clay, Pauline took
Cecily and Glenda around the room introducing them to
people. Cecily steeled herself for the animosity she'd become
accustomed to but these people were welcoming and open—
at least for the most part. There was Pauline's daughter
and son-in-law, Delcia and Carter Matthews. Ranetta was
playing with Clay's brother, Harry. There was a layer of

hostility coming from Willow Mae, Harry's wife, that the older woman couldn't quite conceal.

"Emery Cleveland, meet Cecily and Glenda. Emery owns a fleet of fishing boats. They take out scores of tourists each week and catch lots of fish in the Atlantic."

"It's a pleasure to finally meet you, Cecily."

Cecily extended her hand but he hauled her into his arms. "Your daddy and I caused a lot of mischief when we were boys."

"I want to hear all about it," Cecily said as the man patted her on the back and then released her.

"We'll have plenty of time to catch up on old times," he assured her. Then his gaze settled on Glenda and his eyes lit up. When he wasn't watching, Cecily caught Glenda's perusal of him. "Emery is your distant cousin on your paternal grandmother's side of the family."

"I'm finding I have more relatives than I realized," Cecily said.

"You've got plenty on the island. Now you're the only one on your daddy's father's side of the family. You're the last Tolson. But you've got plenty of kinfolks," Emery assured her.

Clay opened the door to more late arrivals.

Dr. Grant came through the opening. "Doc, come on over here," Emery said.

"Hi, Emery, Pauline. Sorry I'm late. Last-minute emergency."

"I know how it is. Dr. Grant is the only physician on the island." Pauline said.

"We've met," Cecily said. Finally she began to relax. Knowing she was among family lifted some of the lonely weight. Feeling alone in the world wasn't pleasant. Although she never felt quite alone with Glenda around.

"I hope you have pictures of my father," Cecily said to Emery.

"I have more of your father, but I have pictures of both your mom and dad," Emery assured her.

"What does he look like?"

"You've never seen his pictures?" Emery asked.

She shook her head.

"Marva left so quickly, she didn't have time to pack anything," Pauline said. "Clay and I saved most of them. As soon as we go to Ashville, we'll bring them back with the rest of our belongings. But I believe we have an album with pictures." She glanced around the room searching as if they might be on a coffee table. "Don't worry. We'll find it before the night is over."

"Thank you," Cecily said.

"I've got pictures of your grandmother and lots of relatives. I'll get them together and bring them by your shop," Doc offered. "I'm so glad I can purchase my tea on the island now. I always have to go to the mainland to get good blends."

Cecily smiled.

"I'm looking forward to that romantic Valentine's dinner," Pauline said.

Emery flashed a quick glance at Glenda, who was looking in another direction.

Many guests talked about her father—telling her things like how he won the regionals on the debate team, or how he and Clay had sneaked out for some mischief. Clay didn't look too comfortable when that bit of information was revealed. The conversation continued over dinner.

Dinner was delicious island fare of clam chowder, fried shrimp, coleslaw, hush puppies and fries.

After dinner was over, Clay found the photo album. Everyone else talked in the family room. But he called Cecily to the living room so that she could look through the album with him. When he pointed out her father, a tight knot lodged in her throat.

"We played on the football team," he said. "Your dad was the quarterback."

It was a snapshot of him throwing the ball. He looked tall, very handsome, and serious.

There were pictures of Clay and him on dates with Pauline and some woman who wasn't her mother. "That's Ruby," Clay said.

Ruby? Could this be the same Ruby her mother had suspected?

"He and Ruby didn't date very long. They went out a couple of times, but your father went to Greenville, met your mother in college, and fell head over heels in love."

"And then they settled here."

Clay settled back on the couch. "Not at first. Your mother worked while he completed his master's. They had you a year after he graduated."

"I see." She thought of Ruby again. Could Ruby have stolen the money for revenge for her mother stealing her father from her?

They talked for about an hour and then they wandered into the family room to mingle with the other guests. Like a sponge, she soaked up every scrap of information. She couldn't get enough about the past. But finally guests began to leave and Cecily still sat with the album.

Finally Glenda came in peering at her watch.

Cecily glanced at her own and was shocked at how late it was. "You're ready to go?"

Glenda waved Cecily back. "I'm taking her home," Emery said. "You just sit there and enjoy your pictures. I'll go get your coat, Glenda." He reluctantly tore his eyes from Glenda and walked off.

Cecily approached Glenda. "Why didn't you tell me you were tired? I can get Ryan to take us home."

"Are you crazy?" Glenda whispered, looking around to make sure no one could overhear. "I've been trying to get him alone all evening."

"You've been ignoring him, even though he went out of his way to talk to you."

"Didn't want to act like I was desperate. Can't be too easy. Let him do the work."

"There you go, playing games."

"It's not a game. Planning a strategy is a science."

Emery returned with Glenda's coat and helped her into it as if she weren't a capable woman. But this was the South where men were taught gentlemanly behavior from the time they were in diapers. Cecily found his actions enchanting.

Of course she could do for herself and did. But she found courtly behavior to be nice and romantic.

Cecily watched them leave. She picked up the album and continued to peruse the treasured pictures. Her eyes filled. As she studied a younger version of her mother with her father, she sucked in a breath and tried to keep her emotions in check, but still, tears streamed down her face.

She was in the room alone and then suddenly Ryan sat beside her. He took her trembling hand in his much larger one and she sucked the pain even more. She was looking at a picture of her father and mother together in front of the lighthouse.

She could hold the tears no longer. Before she could stop them, she was enveloped in Ryan's arms, sobbing.

# Chapter 3

An hour after Glenda left, Ryan took Cecily home. The treasured photo album she'd pored over for hours went with her. They'd finally told her to keep the album. But Cecily planned to have copies made of the pictures and give the original back to them.

She had mixed emotions about all this news. First, she'd loved Otis Edmonds, who had raised her as his own daughter. In all the years they were together, she'd never doubted that he was her natural father. He had loved her as much as she'd loved him. She couldn't suddenly forget the experiences they'd shared through the years. He'd pitched her her first baseball. As a surprise he'd purchased tickets and taken her to see *The Nutcracker* one year. Just the two of them. He'd sat patiently through the ballet—she with her heart in her eyes, and he with the indulgence of a father basking in his child's pleasure. He'd gone to father-daughter gatherings with her. He had soothed her first heartbreak with a boy when she was twelve.

So many precious memories they'd shared. How could she replace those memories with a man she'd just met? In a sense she felt that by needing to know her natural father, she betrayed Otis's importance in her life. Yet, this man, this new face with eyes like hers, with hair like hers, was her natural father. A man she knew nothing about, whose face she last glimpsed when she had been little more than an infant, and certainly couldn't be expected to remember now.

A lump clogged her throat, even after the crying jag. She didn't know if the crying was for so much she'd lost in the last year. Otis had died months before her mother died. She and Glenda had endured enormous losses this last year. She felt too consumed with loss to even deal with that, much less all this new information that had suddenly sprung up.

Sometimes she wondered if she should have waited to move here. Perhaps she'd been too hasty in closing the door to her life in New York. It was often said that one shouldn't make huge plans or moves soon after a traumatic experience. *Wait, a few months. Give yourself time to grieve. Then make changes,* many said to her, Glenda being one of them.

Cecily believed her hasty decision prompted Glenda to move with her, without being asked to do so. The older woman knew the changes Cecily was going through were as poignant to Cecily as they were to her. Glenda was one constant left in her life. Thank God for her.

Suddenly, it was quiet and Cecily realized she'd ridden all the way home without once thinking about the daunting man beside her.

He brought the SUV to a stop in back of the house. The low beam of the living room light still shone in Glenda's apartment so it was obvious she was still out.

"Thank you for the ride," Cecily finally said. She should open the door and get out right now, she thought, but something stopped her.

"Any time," Ryan said. He leaned back in his seat with one hand thrown comfortably over the wheel. He turned the car lights off but left the radio playing. It was a soul station playing oldies, casting a romantic mood. The scenery lent enough romance without the music adding to it.

Ryan should just get out of the warm truck and escort Cecily to her door and say good night. But watching her pour over those pictures tonight, witnessing the sorrow on her face and her tears stirred something deep and elemental in him. There were deeper layers to her than LaToya. When was he going to stop comparing every woman to his ex? he wondered.

He'd been fighting this attraction to Cecily from the first time he'd met her in her little tea shop. Right now the slight scent of her perfume, the atmosphere begged him to prolong the evening.

"Want to walk on the beach?" he said in the silence.

"Now?" Cecily asked.

"Sure." He glanced toward the horizon as far as he could see. "Night's clear. Not too cold."

He'd changed from slacks to jeans and sneakers before he left to bring her home. Perhaps subconsciously he had this all planned. He'd been steering very clear of her lately.

"But it's cold," she said.

"What's a little cold? You've got sweats, don't you? Go in and change."

"I shouldn't," she said, but the idea seemed to appeal to her.

Ryan waited in the living room with a cup of tea that seemed always to be handy while Cecily changed out of her dress. He wasn't a tea drinker but he grudgingly admitted that the brew was tasty.

He perched on the end of the couch. Her prized photo album lay on the table in front of him. He opened it and looked at the photos, most of which were black and white. He thought of his memories of his family which he pulled out to play in his mind at odd moments and knew that the album would never fill in all the blanks. But they evidently offered some solace for Cecily.

He glanced around the room—wondered why the hell he was here, sitting on her couch, waiting to take a late-night stroll with her. What a stupid decision, he thought, wishing he hadn't made the offer in the first place. But when she entered the living room wearing hot-pink sweats and looking warm and cuddly, he knew he'd made the right decision. He was also glad they were going outside in the cold. It had

been more than a year since he'd been with a woman. LaToya
had played a number and a half on him. But he seemed to
be waking up again and his system missed the loss of intimacy. It was this woman that stirred his blood.

"Ready?" he asked.

"Just about."

She donned a knit hat, a jacket, and gloves and they went
out into the night.

Cecily was grateful they kept to a leisurely pace. Glenda
might have cried fatigue when she left the Andersons', but
she still was suspiciously missing. And now Cecily and
Ryan walked on the cold wet beach. True, it was cold, but
the cold was invigorating as the wind slapped her in the
face. A full moon was out. The lighthouse looked eerie in
the night with the cottage that resembled a forlorn Gothic
structure. Tiny lights beamed from faraway ships.

"Stop," Ryan said softly, "and look up."

Cecily did. The beam from the moon danced on the water
and cast an unusual glow on the lighthouse window. It was
beautiful, it was eerie, it was surreal, and she shivered.

Suddenly, she felt Ryan's arms close around her from
behind. His fingers closed on her arms that had wrapped
themselves below her breasts. The heat from his body spread
through hers. She no longer felt the cold. Or the aloneness
that had pierced her thoughts only minutes before.

The waves rushed against the shore, singing a musical
tune. Cecily was an independent woman, but right now she
was pleased Ryan was here to share this moment. She wanted
him here. She willed him not to move.

And suddenly she knew. This was the spot her mother
had described. This was where her mother and father must
have stood numerous times before. This was the scene that
had meant so much to both of them.

After months of second-guessing she finally knew. She'd
made the right decision in moving back to this island. She
needed to know, to experience what they had before she
could go on with her life. Even if the island wasn't meant
for her. Even if the tea shop never realized a profit. Her
presence here was much more than her tea shop.

She was here to discover her roots.

Southern men could be such gentlemen at times. Not that she'd had much experience with southern men. Ryan was the only one of her acquaintance. But Cecily wanted him to step out of that gentlemanly role right now.

Her heart beat against her chest. She could feel the rhythmical beat of his against her back. His arms tightened around her. She turned in his arms and looked up at him. His head hovered above hers. She wished she could see his eyes. It seemed eons passed before he lowered his head, hovered there a second. She felt the warmth of his breath on her face. Desire raced through her. What she felt couldn't possibly be one-sided, could it? And then cool lips touched the side of her mouth, her lips, and then a tongue brushed over her mouth. She opened her mouth and his hot tongue danced with hers in desperate need. The kiss started out as a slow, get-to-meet-you kiss, but swiftly deepened with desire, with a need so intense it rocked her. This was one stemming from desire denied, desire shared.

His hands moved over her back, pressing her closer to him. Hers inched beneath his short jacket, worked the shirt from his jeans and felt naked, hot skin beneath. She felt the ripple of muscles, the smoothness and hardness at one, and inhaled his pleasant masculine scent. He held her close, tasted her deeply, then strung kisses on her cheek and down her neck.

For a space of time, she forgot about loneliness, of all she'd lost. Forgot about the cold. She thought of the pleasures to be discovered in Ryan's arms. The roaring of the tides became the roaring of the blood in her ears.

And she wondered if her father had kissed her mother on this same stretch of the Atlantic beach. She wondered if the first ancestor who had moved here more than a century ago had found his ladylove and shared a special intimacy with her, too. Had built the Victorian cottage as a romantic tribute of their love.

Ryan's lips stopped moving. He held her tightly against him, his breathing shallow and labored. Her own heartbeat had accelerated. What was happening to her here? It was just a kiss, she tried to tell herself. Nothing special.

She'd left Raymond back home waiting for her although she'd told him not to. She didn't know what her future entailed and she didn't want him waiting in limbo for her.

This wasn't right. She'd never felt these intense feelings for Raymond. Was this that first adrenaline rush of attraction that died down to nothing as so many emotions did when the first rush of desire evaporated?

Cecily pushed away from Ryan.

"I didn't mean to do that," he said.

"I know," Cecily said. "Let's go back. I have an early morning."

They walked back to the cottage in silence, but Cecily was very aware of Ryan and aware of the attraction that had begun to bud like a fresh rose in springtime.


Back at the Anderson house, Clay leaned back in his chair, his hands behind his head, the way Pauline had said made him look sexy, and watched his wife as she poured lotion into her hands and rubbed it on her neck and shoulders. Pauline had a sexy way about doing things like that. Her delicate hands glided along her collarbone and then her shoulders leaving behind a shimmer from the lotion. He wondered if she rubbed her skin that way to catch his attention. It worked.

She rubbed more lotion on her hands and smoothed it down one arm and then the other. Graceful moves, he thought just before he caught her eyes on him in the mirror. She had that devilish, wickedly sensuous look in her eyes as she spread the lotion between her breasts.

They'd been married so long he wouldn't know what to do with himself without her. Every day his love deepened and intensified.

"I think the dinner went well, don't you?" she asked Clay. Clay was halfway out of his seat before he realized she'd spoken.

"I do," he finally said and settled back again to watch

her show. "She's a lovely young lady. Make some young man a good wife one day." But he didn't want to talk about Cec—no, Pauline called her Sissieretta—He didn't want to talk about her right now.

Pauline sighed, looked worriedly at him through the mirror. "I wish Ryan would consider her."

Thinking of his son and the witch he'd married put a damper on his amorous thoughts. "I wish he'd never gotten mixed up with that ex-wife of his."

"If he'd just waited awhile."

Clay leaned his elbows on his knees in a weary gesture. "We can't run their lives for them." Lord knows he'd butted in more than he should have in his children's lives. He'd almost lost his relationship with Delcia by their estrangement when she'd gotten pregnant without the benefit of a husband. Then his son had gone and married the wrong woman. He had tried not to get involved when he saw Ryan running headlong down the road to disaster, although he had thrown many hints that hadn't done a thumbtack's worth of good. Now he could only stand by and be there for his son when he needed him. But there was nothing he could do to take the hurt away. And Ryan had closed himself off to anything good that could possibly come his way.

"I'm still furious with LaToya. She was only after his money. And now she has it. Every dime."

"Worse than that, the woman he dates next is going to have to wade through the garbage of hurt he experienced with LaToya. But at least he got out of it."

There was pain in Pauline's eyes when she looked at him through the mirror this time. "But he's scarred, not physically, but mentally. Broken bones are so much easier to heal."

"Unfortunately. But it isn't too late for him. Now he's free to find a nice young lady."

"Like Sissieretta?" Clay asked.

"Like Sissieretta. I think she'd be good for him."

"Better stay out of it. Let them find their own way if it's meant to be."

"I don't know, Clay. A little push wouldn't hurt."

Clay shook his head. "Oh, no, you don't. He won't thank you for it."

"He hasn't come back yet. He's had plenty of time to return."

The hope in her eyes tore at something inside Clay. "Let's hope he's not at the campground."

"He has no reason to go there. He works too long and too hard as it is."

"It's an escape."

"He needs a good woman. Then he'll have a reason to come home at night. Every man needs that." Pauline sighed. "He lives in this big rambling house all alone. We'll be moving soon and he'll be all alone again."

Clay chuckled. "Better not let him hear you talk like that. He's a man, sweetheart. Not your little baby anymore."

"He's my youngest," Pauline said in that stubborn voice that let Clay know it was time to change the subject.

Clay had lived long enough to know it was a self-defeating act to come between a mother and her chicks.

"Yeah," Clay said to be agreeable. "You must be exhausted." He hoped she wasn't too exhausted, because watching her primp in the mirror had stirred his blood.

"Actually, I'm not. Thank you for suggesting that I get help for cleaning up after the party."

"Your heart's always in the right place, but you worked so hard putting this thing together. Didn't want you wiped out afterward."

"All I did was rest and enjoy the company. You're such a thoughtful husband, I think I'll keep you forever," she teased.

Clay chuckled. "You better believe it."

The sexy mint-green nightgown with tiny spaghetti straps boasted an enticing V that ended low between her breasts. The skirt fell to the floor in a soft pool of fabric.

"You don't think it's a little warm in here?" Pauline asked as the furnace kicked in.

"Not a bit." Clay had turned up the temperature for a reason. Pauline covered herself up from neck to her toes when she was cold. He wasn't having any of that tonight.

He'd just have to give Ryan a little extra for the heating bill. On second thought he'd just go on down to the office and pay it. Ryan wouldn't accept money from him. But seeing his wife this way was worth every dime he paid.

"You weren't this cold-natured before," Pauline said as she ran the brush through her hair.

"Blood must be getting thinner." Clay's voice dropped a couple of octaves and he cleared his throat.

She glanced at him from the mirror with a wicked grin. "You've got a lot of good years left yet."

"Think so?" His pants were tightening around him.

She gave him a slow once-over, sending his heartbeat into overdrive. "I know so."

She stopped brushing her hair, picked up a bottle of perfume, and spritzed on the scent he loved most on her. He whiffed the delicate scent drifting over to him. Not too overpowering, he thought as his gut tightened.

When he gazed at his wife, he didn't see wrinkles that hadn't been present when he'd married her at twenty-two. Or imagine the breasts that had been firm and plump that had now turned soft with time. He wasn't put off with the estrogen patch she wore on her left arm. He glimpsed the mother of his children, the receiver of his affection, his confidant, his partner in all things. This was the beautiful woman he married—whose beauty transcended time, and was elevated for all that they had shared.

And now as he watched her prepare for bed his memory took him back in time to the night that they'd married. She'd been a virgin, nervous and unsure. They'd fumbled their way through intimacy. Each time they came together had been better than the last time. And through the years she'd learned the touches that pleased him just as he'd learned her sensitive spots—the little touches that pleased her.

Pauline was his soul mate. Delcia had found hers with Carter. He prayed Ryan would find his, too. Clay couldn't fathom life for his children without what he and Pauline had shared through the years.

Right now he gazed upon his wife who heated his blood

like a radiator blowing direct heat through his system. It was Pauline warming up his system.

Clay moved out of his chair and closed the distance between them with three long strides. He wrapped his arms around her beneath her breasts. Ran his tongue along her neck. Damn, she smelled delightful, tasted as exceptional as fine wine.

"All I could think about tonight was getting you alone," he whispered in her ear before he swirled his tongue around the lobe.

"Ummmm" she murmured and he felt the quickening of her heartbeat. "I think we've still got the house to ourselves. Ryan hasn't returned."

"It's a good thing too," Clay said, running his hands between her thighs. "Tonight, I want to hear your song loud and clear." His voice had gone husky and deep.

Pauline's breath caught, breathed out in a shaky puff. "His bedroom is at the other end of the hall." Her fingers tightened on his thigh.

"For good reason." Clay twisted the chair to give him better access; then he urged her out of the seat. And finally kissed her full lips. Tasted the sweet essence of her. He was a man who'd been deprived for far too long. He closed his eyes on the struggle and desire within. He could never, ever get enough of Pauline.

Her fingers stroked his chest, unbuttoned his shirt. She ran her fingers through his gray-and-black-peppered chest hair, eliciting a deep groan from him. "Baby, your touch is like fire in my blood."

"I live and breathe for your hands on my body," she responded.

He raised his head. Her eyes were luminous and soft. He traced his fingers on her smooth brown shoulders, slid the straps off, letting them hang on her arm for mere seconds before gravity pulled at it. Then he kissed her softly on the shoulder. The gown pooled to her feet, and she stood gloriously naked before him. His wife. His breathtakingly beautiful wife.

He placed her across the bed in the center of the spread

and kissed every inch—touched every millimeter of her body. She moaned and swayed to his touch.

And then he was on his back and her delicate hands were undressing him and gliding over his body. She knew what pleased him, knew the spots that raised his temperature. It was what he loved about loving her. At this stage there wasn't any guessing. They knew each other like the backs of their hands. He knew where to touch her to send her soaring, she knew where to touch him to arouse him most. And yet, coming together was new all over again. He strained against her and then he was inside her feeling the heat and contours of her body. They moved like beautiful, well-tuned instruments playing sweet melodies. They danced a well-choreographed ballet. And at the pinnacle they cried out and he exploded inside her. They stood on that precipice for a heartbeat until he lowered his head to hers and kissed her tenderly.

Then he slid to her side, gathered her close to press her back against his chest. Wrapping his arms around her, he tucked her head under his chin. And his hands rested across the soft pouch of her stomach. An embrace so familiar, so necessary. Comfort and peace settled over him as he held his wife of thirty-eight years. A woman who knew him well—who loved him like no other. A woman he trusted above all others.

If only there were such a woman for his son.

As he closed his eyes to settle down for the night, he realized he hadn't heard Ryan's SUV return. Realized he couldn't put too much stock by that because in the heat of things a 747 could have parked on his roof and he would have thought it was his desire blowing the top off. But he still hung on to a thread of hope that Ryan was getting to know Sissieretta and they both saw something special in each other.

The next morning, while readily acknowledging her foolish mind-set, Cecily continued to feel a warm glow from the night before. Both from Ryan and the pictures of her parents. She carried the album to the tea shop so that she could sneak peeks at the pictures during the frequent lulls of her day. But there hadn't been very many. The phone rang off the hook with grandmothers making reservations for the grandmother, granddaughter tea. Many promised to stop by.

Glenda had been late returning home that night, considering that she'd left the Andersons more than an hour before Cecily had. The walk with Ryan along the shore had ended. The warm memory of his sweet kiss had left a relentless flame. And his SUV had disappeared long before the high beams of Emery's car had led with a shaft of light toward the cottage.

Glenda had been suspiciously silent about her late evening with Emery, and Cecily had sworn she'd pretend nothing out of the ordinary had happened. But the cheerful glow on Glenda's face, and her relentless humming as she prepared sandwiches and ladled soup, hinted at a story that was just itching to be exposed.

And Cecily's willpower disappeared as quickly as a light from a snuffed candle. "So tell me about last night," Cecily said, anxious to know all the juicy details and a little peeved because Glenda hadn't been forthcoming.

A sparkle heated her face. "Your cousin showed me around the island. That's all."

"Half the night?"

"You know how it is when people start talking."

Cecily watched Glenda struggle to maintain a disinterested tone.

And Cecily pursed her lips and raised her eyebrows. "Yeah? How?"

"None of your business," Glenda added with a smile of defiance.

"It's like that."

"Darn right," she said. "He's a nice man. Showed me one of his boats. I got so cold out on the water, he took me by his cabin and made the best coffee with a touch of chocolate to warm me up. By the way, I think you should get one of those espresso machines before the summer crowd comes. Emery told me they don't have one at the camp-ground or at Wanda's diner."

"I'll think about it. Now back to last night."

"The wind was sharp enough to cut right through you, wasn't it?"

"Humph. Good reason for you to stay in tonight. Won't have to worry about getting cold."

Glenda's outraged eyes threw sparks at Cecily. "Don't get smart with me." She sniffed, placed a tomato on the sandwich, and topped it with lettuce. "He's coming by to show me the portion I couldn't see at night. It was mighty dark last night."

"Even with the full moon?"

"What time did you get home, Miss Nosy?"

"Earlier than you, obviously."

Cecily took the sandwich from Glenda and carried it to the customer. "Enjoy your meal," she said to the woman and went to the cash drawer to prepare a deposit.

Half an hour later after the woman left, Cecily said, "I'm going to the bank, Glenda."

"No problem. We aren't likely to get a rush while you're gone."

"Unfortunately," Cecily said, walking out the door and almost bumping into Emery, who looked past her to the bowels of the shop. For heaven's sake. The man had parted with Glenda just a few scant hours ago.

"Thought I'd bring some pictures by for you to see." A shoe box was tucked under his arm. "All the pictures are labeled. But I see you're on your way out."

Cecily started back inside. "It can wait."

"No need. Glenda in there?" He anxiously scanned the interior.

"She's in back somewhere. I'll—"

"You go on. I'll find her. I'll leave the pictures with her."

Cecily shook her head. The man was so anxious he was about to jump out of his skin. "Okay."

Cecily stifled a chuckle on her way to her car. Emery had been quite taken with Glenda. And Cecily was thrilled. It was time that something good came into Glenda's life.

Cecily frowned. She never remembered Glenda dating anyone serious for as long as she'd known her. She dated casually and Cecily wondered why. Had she been hurt and left too afraid to try again? Glenda was too strong to let one hurt determine the rest of her life. Cecily shook her head and continued on.

The wind was biting today, making it seem several degrees colder than the temperature actually was. In the car she let the motor run several minutes to warm up the engine, and then started on her way.

The bank was downtown. On her way she passed the campground and almost drove off the road while watching to get a glimpse of Ryan. They didn't know each other well enough for her just to drop by.

So she directed the car from the shoulder and accelerated toward the bank.

Once inside the small brick building, she stood in a short line. While she waited she perused name tags. The only one she could see from the distance had MARGARET emblazoned on it.

All the tellers seemed too young to have firsthand details of the robbery all those years ago. So Cecily scanned the people sitting at desks. A woman her mother's age sat at one desk, helping a younger woman. A young man sat at the other desk talking on the phone. The woman was too far away for Cecily to read her name tag.

When Cecily first arrived, she'd expected an older building to house the bank, but the construction was fairly new, resembling any other bank in suburbs around the country.

For the most part, gone was the era of the old family-owned bank. This one was part of a huge chain. She wondered if this was the bank it had always been or if it had been smaller but now garbled up by a huge conglomerate.

"May I help you?" the woman said. Cecily had been so deep in her thoughts she hadn't realized the line had moved. She approached the window.

"I'm making a deposit." Cecily handed the pouch to the woman.

A woman named Janice helped her.

"Has this bank always been Threadeau?"

"No. Threadeau bought Last Savings ten years ago when Mason retired. His family had run the bank since the thirties."

"Pretty soon, small businesses will be a thing of the past."

"Tell me about it. I was scared to death they'd fire us all and bring in their own people. But most of us kept our jobs, except for a few people. Some had worked here thirty years, since graduating from high school. They were offered a nice retirement package. Taylor opened a little shop with hers. The rest of the old geezers are sitting in their rockers or fishing."

"Sounds like fun if you can manage it."

"Guess so. Thanks for the book. My little girl went with Ranetta to the read-a-thon a week ago. She's been talking about that book ever since. My mom's taking her to the tea. Every morning she asks me if this is the morning of the tea. And every night she asks me if the tea is tomorrow."

Both women chuckled.

"I'm glad she's looking forward to it," Cecily said, warmed all over.

"Now all I have to do is talk my husband into taking me to the Valentine's Day affair."

"I'm not biased, mind you, but I hope you're successful."

Janice chuckled and handed Cecily her receipt. "So do I," she said and Cecily walked away feeling pretty darn good on a cold day in February.

# Chapter 4

Ryan stared at the group of reservations he more than likely would not be able to honor come spring break in mid-March. So far he had sixty reservations for college students and professors from several locations in the country who wanted to study the success of the estuary. More calls were coming in daily. This was an unusual year.

Problem was, the campground was already full for that weekend. The first huge fishing convention of the year was scheduled. Regulars knew how quickly spaces filled up. Most lots had been reserved a year in advance.

Ryan glanced out the huge window where he glimpsed several mobile homes in the distance. Many retirees liked to winter on the Carolina coast. In his wildest imagination he would never have guessed the campground would grow as large or as rapidly as it had. Initially it was his sister's idea to open a campground. They owned the land together, and he decided to go into business with her. Only he grew to love the camp. Liked the flow of people who returned year after year. Many were like old friends. And many lasting friendships had grown among the campers. More than a hundred clubs had formed. Clubs like the ones arriving on Valentine's weekend were what kept the campground operating during the lean winter months. Business was nothing like Memorial Day through Labor Day, but it was enough to keep a few islanders employed full-time.

Many campers had favorite campsites that they'd grown attached to.

He and Delcia had improved the campground, offered more each year. He'd left only long enough to get his accounting degree.

Delcia's first husband had worked at the campground. He'd died five years ago. But Delcia had fallen in love all over again almost three years ago when Carter Matthews came on the scene looking for his foster brother's murderer. That was when they had learned the foster brother was a twin and that the twin had been murdered. The twin and Delcia had Ranetta together before his death. And that had caused a breach between their father and Delcia. It was mere days before the wedding that Clay Anderson finally came around.

That time had been particularly painful for Delcia. She and Dad had always been close.

"You seeking divine guidance from staring at those papers?" Carter said, coming into the room looking too chipper for so early in the morning.

"I wish."

"She won't budge on selling that land, huh?"

"Nope. And the convention is less than a month and a half away."

"Guess we have to turn them away," Carter said flipping through mail.

"I hate to do that."

Carter glanced up from his letter. "Do you have another alternative?"

Ryan shook his head. "Can't think of anything—yet."

"Guess you better let them know. Maybe they can find other arrangements."

"We'll see. I'll think on it another week."

He dropped the mail on the desk. "Don't take too long."

"I won't. I've been wondering if she'd rent it to us temporarily. Just for that weekend—or the year."

"Not that easy. Showers, bathrooms have to be installed. And then there's readying the campsites. A lot of work for just a weekend arrangement."

"We'd lose money on it in the beginning. But if she continues to let us use the land, we'd make a profit. She might even decide to let us buy it."

"Are you sure she doesn't have plans of her own?"

"She says she hasn't. I think she's thinking it will interrupt her customers at the tea shop."

"We'll be far enough away for her to have her peace."

"True. But it won't be quite the same. Still, it'll bring in more business for her."

Carter rubbed his chin "That crowd will be more accustomed to the kinds of things she sells there."

"Think you'll go along with the extra expense of installing the bare necessities for an experimental site?"

"I'm game, man. I'll talk to Delcia."

"About what?" Delcia asked. She looked bigger and bigger every day.

Carter reiterated their conversation.

"Okay with me," she said

"What are you doing here? You're supposed to be taking it easy," Carter muttered.

It was ironic that Carter was asking the questions this time. Ryan had to stop himself, reminding himself that Delcia had a husband to see after her. She'd been alone during her last pregnancy and Ryan had taken it upon himself to look out for her.

"I can't stay in the house twenty-four-seven. Besides, Ranetta is at day care."

"Only half a day. She'll be home and you'll be ready for a nap."

"So will she. I appreciate your concern, but I'm not a baby. I'm *having* a baby. There's a difference." Delcia pulled Carter close and kissed him. He rubbed against her protruding belly. Ryan tore his gaze from the intimate gesture.

"Besides," Delcia said when she came up for air, "I need to keep my mind active."

"You'll have plenty to keep you busy soon, with two babies running around."

"Don't forget I have a husband to run after those babies, too."

"That's for sure. Right now, I'm running after a toddler and a wife." Carter rolled his eyes toward the ceiling; that got him a whack from Delcia. "Give a man a break, will you?"

Delcia shook her head. "New fathers. What can I say?" She headed for the door. "It's your turn to pick up Ranetta. I'm going over last night's accounting figures."

"Guess you're in charge of the store," Carter said to Ryan. "I'm checking on the new cabins. The contractor said he'd run into a problem."

"Sure." Ryan wasn't alarmed. There were always snafus on construction jobs.

Most of the expansions and repairs were done during the winter months when business was slow. Most of the time, they also performed the physical labor, but not this time. The twenty cabins they were erecting were more elaborate than the plain shells they usually built. These were fully equipped with kitchenettes, bathrooms, televisions, heat, air conditioning and phones. Since the island had no hotels, and since many people loved the creature comforts of hotels, they'd decided to explore something a little different. Getting the permits had taken months, but now they had them and construction should be finished by spring break.

Carter kissed Delcia warmly.

"The two of you do live together, don't you?"

"Yeah." Carter smiled and rubbed Delcia's tummy like Aladdin's lantern.

Ryan shook his head but he was pleased with his sister's happiness. As he walked to the store with six customers milling about he thought of Cecily and the untimely kiss that had heated him to his toes. He thought about his stupidity in taking that walk with her in the first place. He'd give her a year on the island before she packed up and headed back to New York. He knew she was leaving, yet he'd kissed her anyway. What was it about his gluttony for punishment? No more foreigners. To him a New Yorker was a foreigner—talked too fast, moved too fast. Unwilling to settle for the slower pace of the South. When he was ready to venture out again, he was settling for an island woman.

Had his mother spoken to Cecily? If not they might have a huge problem on their hands.

Just then Ruby's daughter, Hazeline Milford, entered the store. She'd been making a pest of herself lately. He looked heavenward. He must have done something really bad to displease the Man above because He either had a great sense of humor or else was doing a terrific job of playing tricks on him.

"Hey, Ryan," Hazeline said, straightening the too-tight nurse's uniform.

Ryan fixed a tight smile on his face. "Hazeline."

"Mama sent me by to pick up the order you were supposed to get her."

"Hasn't arrived yet," he said.

"That's too bad. She was counting on it."

She worked at the hospital in Morehead City. When Dr. Grant didn't hire her on because she already had enough nurses at the clinic, Ruby had put up a big fuss. "On your way to work?" he asked.

"Yeah. Working the evening shift today."

"It's a job."

"And I like it, except for working the evening shift. Miss out on too many dates that way."

"I work late myself more often than not."

"Maybe I can stop by some evenings on my way home," she suggested.

"I don't work that late," he amended.

Her smile faded. She was pretty enough, but she had too much of her mama in her for him to stomach. She seemed false somehow and pushy. And when he was thinking about an island woman, he certainly wasn't thinking of Hazeline.

"You enjoy your vacation with your mama?"

"Yeah, it was nice. Got tired of the cousins though."

Probably took some of the attention away from her, Ryan thought. Hazeline liked being the center of things.

She scanned the tea shop brochure on the countertop. "A Valentine's Day affair. That sounds real nice."

"Yeah," Ryan said. "I'm going."

"You've got a date?"

He nodded. "Yeah."

"Oh," she said with a crestfallen look that had Ryan feeling like a dog for disappointing her, but she wasn't the woman for him any more than LaToya had been. He wasn't about to walk headlong into another whale-size mistake.

He hated to admit it but there wasn't one thing he liked about Hazeline. She had gone to high school with him. Back then she was pushy, nosy, bad-mouthed people like her mama just to be mean, and wasn't above hurting anybody who got in her way. He couldn't stand her in high school. She hadn't gotten any better through the years.

"So who're you taking to the Valentine's affair?" the nosy woman asked as if she had a right to his business.

He was about to tell her to mind her own business but thought better of it. Since everybody knew everybody on the island, he couldn't come up with a plausible lie so he settled on, "Cecily."

"Her?" Hazeline's nose wrinkled up, her fish eyes popped, and her mouth looked as if she'd sucked on a lemon.

"Yeah," he said so heatedly, Hazeline stepped back.

"Well, to each his own." She jerked her purse straps onto her shoulder.

"I'll call your mama when that order comes in," he told her. He was sick of her coming by every day trying to weasel a date out of him.

"You do that," she said, throwing a malevolent glance at him before she made her hasty retreat.

*Damn it.* Now he was stuck with asking Cecily to an affair that she couldn't very well attend. She was working. But Hazeline had such a big mouth the news would be all over the island by morning. And his own mama had been sending signals that he should take Sissieretta out since the day the ferry had brought her to the island. She'd never let up now. At least the news should quiet her—for a little while anyway.

But he didn't want to like Cecily any more than he already did, darn it. The more he was around that woman, the more he wanted to be. His hormones started raging like crazy. He acted as if he'd lost his mind over her, just as he had over LaToya. But this foolishness with Cecily was more intense. LaToya had worn on him. His attraction to Cecily had snuck up and hit him like a shark—sudden and relentless.


When Cecily left the bank she paused and scanned the street in both directions. Just a scattering of cars passed on the almost desolate avenue. Across the way were cute little tourist shops. But down the end and off to itself was a lone brick building. A sign displaying SHERIFF'S OFFICE swayed in the wind. Cecily had yet to go there to gather information on her mother's case.

Normally she would have walked just for the exercise, but the wind was pushing hard, making the temperature seem colder than it actually was. Cecily got in her car, drove the short distance, and parked in front of the sheriff's office. Inside were two officers and a secretary.

One of the officers spoke to her. "May I help you, miss?" he asked. He looked as if he may have played football a long time ago. What must have at one time been muscle had now turned to fat. His potbelly protruded over his belt. Cecily could imagine him with a six-pack of beer on Sunday afternoons in front of the tube watching the Panthers and the Redskins.

"My name is Cecily Edmonds," she said.

Officer Derrick, the man said extending his hand for a shake.

"I'm looking for information on a robbery that occurred after a hurricane twenty-six years ago." The information on the case was public.

"Edmonds." He seemed to turn the name around in his mind. "You're Walter's girl?"

"Yes," she said. It took some getting used to being

referred to as Walter's daughter when she'd thought Otis was her father all her life.

"Your daddy was a Tolson. You're the last of the line. Heard you were back. Guess I'm gonna have to make it over to that tea shop. I'm a coffee drinker myself."

"We serve coffee, too. Soon we'll have an espresso machine."

"Now you're really getting fancy." He scratched his chin.

He appeared to be about the same age as her father would be had he lived.

"I worked that case," he said.

"Then you can help me."

"I can. But I don't see what good it would do. There wasn't very much to go by. You see, your mother was the only one alone with the money. She was supposed to drop it into the depository that night. She was one of the people who collected it Monday morning. No one else was even alone with the money. At the bank or the fire station where it was collected."

"Well, I'd still like a look."

"Young lady, I'm gonna speak to you like I would to my own daughter. Me and your daddy played on the football team together. Leave it in the past where it belongs. Don't go around stirring up trouble. The town recovered. Your mother got off scot-free. Most people have put it in the past."

"Not everyone."

He nodded. "It's a small island. Some never forget. They, just like you, are gonna have to live with it." His focus turned inward as if he had his own secrets he'd like to be forgotten.

"My mother didn't steal that money."

He focused on Cecily again and the subject at hand. "Like I said, it's way back in the past. And I looked into the situation. Did a thorough job of it."

"I'm sure you did, but I'd like to see the information anyway. You must have interviewed the volunteers who worked with my mother along with other bank personnel. I would like a look at that information."

He scratched his chin thoughtfully. "Not everything is on computer here, especially not that far back. We're a small office here. It'll take some time even to get to the files." He patted her on the shoulder. "Tell you what. Call me in a couple of days."

"Thank you," Cecily said. "I will."

Cecily didn't like this officer one bit. She hated being patronized. In New York she would have given him a few choice words. This was North Carolina, though. And she had enough enemies.

She stopped by the newspaper office, placed an ad for the next edition and headed in the direction of the tea shop. The farther she drove from town, the more lighthearted she felt. She slowed again when she passed the campground and glanced toward the reservation building wondering if Ryan was there and somehow knew that he was.

Suddenly a car sped out in front of her. She slammed on the brakes and missed hitting the car by no more than five inches. Cecily came to a complete halt.

The driver gave her the finger and burned rubber as she sped away.

"Back to you!" Cecily said in the silence of her car over her adrenaline pumped heartbeat. What on earth had made that woman so angry and reckless? She'd expect such actions in New York where the pace was frantic. She hadn't encountered it here.

Shaking her head, Cecily drove the rest of the way home without incident.

Emery was just leaving the tea shop and she waved to him as he passed in his truck.

As soon as she entered, Glenda met her. "If it's not busy, I'm getting off a little early."

Cecily glanced pointed around the empty room. "Emery's going to show you around the island again?"

"We've got a sense of humor today, don't we?"

Cecily told her about her rude mishap coming from town. Glenda clucked about, then went to the kitchen to bake fresh scones. Cecily thought that was peculiar, since she always baked them first thing in the morning. But Glenda said she was baking some for Emery. They were his favorite item on the menu.

By the time an old woman whose face was leathered with sun, ocean winds, and age entered the shop, the delightful aroma of baking scones wafted in the air. The woman sniffed appreciatively. But once she saw Cecily, she regarded her so keenly that Cecily almost fidgeted. It was a dark face, one that wore the ravages of years, even a kind face in many ways. The dress she wore was long, covered with a short black wool coat. Doc hovered in the background with a shoebox in her arm. This woman must be her grandmother.

Suddenly, the old woman held out heavy arms. "Come here, child," she said in a gravelly voice, though it wasn't a smoker's voice—but a voice tinged with age.

Cecily walked toward her and stopped a foot away. The woman lifted her hands to Cecily's face. Tears swam in the woman's midnight eyes, eyes that seemed to peer into Cecily's soul. Cecily felt uneasy with the close scrutiny. "Welcome home, child." Then the woman embraced Cecily in strong arms.

Cecily inhaled the cold sea air mixed with a touch of vanilla for perfume. As much as the first two weeks had been unwelcoming, this week had been the complete opposite. Glenda had begun a budding romance with Cecily's cousin. The party Pauline had given had brought in more customers and had made her more accepted in the community. For the first time since returning to the island she began to understand what her mother had loved so much about this place.

After rocking Cecily for what seemed forever the woman finally stood back. "You should never have left your home, child. But now you're back. With family." She nodded. "We're going to keep it that way."

Cecily smiled. "It feels good to be here. But come. Have a seat." Cecily led her to the couch in the back room which allowed them a measure of privacy. Cecily helped the woman out of her coat and hung it on the coat tree while the woman settled into the soft sofa cushions. Doc handed Cecily the shoe box and told her she'd have lunch while Cecily and Granny visited.

"What can I get you to drink?" Cecily asked Granny.

"Whatever you're having."

"Can I get you scones or little finger sandwiches?"

"Doll baby, that would be nice."

When Cecily went to gather the things, Glenda waved her on, indicating she would bring a tray over.

Cecily joined the woman and sat sideways on the couch beside her. She wanted to get a good long look at this woman. She wondered where she fit in her father's life.

"All that bad stuff is in the past, thank the good Lord." Her heavily lined face cracked into a smile. "I wish your daddy could see you now. He'd be so proud. Oh, listen to an old woman carry on. You don't even know who I am. I'm Granny Grant. Your daddy's grandmother and I were sisters on his mama's side of the family. I'm your great-aunt."

"All my life, I thought I had no relatives except for a distant cousin who moves around constantly. Now I'm finding I have many relatives."

"It's a bit much to take in all at once, I know. But we're never in this world alone, child. You remember that." Granny Grant put her purse on the floor by her feet.

"I know you want to know about your daddy. And we'll get to that little by little. There's a whole lot of history between Sissieretta and your daddy. I'm gonna give you a chance to settle in and get to know the place."

Disappointment crowded Cecily. She wanted to know right then.

"When Doc told me about you, I wanted to pick up and come home right away. But I don't drive anymore. Almost took the bus. The kids had a fit as if I can't handle myself alone anymore."

Cecily wondered just how old the woman was.

"My ninety-fifth birthday is coming up," she said and looked off into a place only she knew of. "I knew Sissieretta and Hannibal Moore. I was twenty-three when Sissieretta died. Hannibal died years before. They'd been together so long, Sissieretta never recovered from his death. It's that way with some people who love so hard they become an extension of each other. It's rare, but it's a beautiful thing to witness.'' Granny was quiet for a spell as if giving respect to the dead. "It's a rare kind of love."

Cecily wanted to know more, but wouldn't push. She'd let Granny Grant take her time and tell her story in her own way. Glenda brought the tray and set it on the huge clock coffee table that must be a century old. Cecily fixed Granny a plate and poured her tea.

"Sugar?" Cecily asked.

"Just a spoonful." Granny sipped her tea and held the cup in her hand.

"They had an odd sort of relationship. Hannibal's mother hired Sissieretta on as his cook when she came back to the island. That woman couldn't stand the island. Came down from Philadelphia. His daddy had always lived right here. Wouldn't move from this island even when it meant losing his wife. Anyway, the story goes, Justin, Hannibal's dad, and Joyce, they met when he'd gone up north on a business trip. The old man owned a factory right on this land you own now. You got a lot of history in your family. Anyway, it sat next to the water. They needed a lot of water. And it had easy access to the ships that pulled in here. The ships would go off to major ports in places like Baltimore, Philadelphia, New York.

"Anyway, he built this house for his Philadelphia ladylove so she could catch the ocean breeze in the heat of summer. Now most folks don't know that we don't get that many hot days in the summer because of where we are. The breeze round this island often keeps the bugs away too.

"Anyway, he built this house so she could look out at the beauty of the ocean he loved so much. To his way of thinking, how could she not love it as much as he did? And we have to give her credit, because for a time she pretended to like it. She stayed here several years, but this island isn't for everyone. Either you love it or you hate it.

"She loved art, the museums, and mixing with the society crowd she ran with in Philadelphia. Came from one of those hoity-toity families. But while she was here they had one son. Finally she couldn't take it anymore. She longed for home. And when the boy was two, she left, taking him with her.''

Granny was silent then. Took a sip of her tea and a bite of scone that had cooled. Cecily sipped on her own drink that had grown tepid, but she was too full to eat anything. She topped their tea from the pot sitting on the table.

"The old man wasn't the same after that," Granny continued. "Losing his son and wife just sucked the life right out of him. Kinda turned mean and surly. But Hannibal loved it here and she let him visit in the summers.

"This land," Granny said, looking out through huge lenses. "People aren't shy about their feelings for this place.

"Well, the story goes, when Hannibal finished college, he came right back here. His father was getting on in age. And there seemed to be one hurricane after another hitting the island that year. The white folks moved away for the most part. Black folks couldn't afford to. You could buy an acre of land for little more than a dollar back then. And lots of us used the tiny bit we had and bought up most of the island. A few whites held on, even though most of them didn't live here anymore. They built little summer cottages so their families could spend the summers on the beach.

"Justin Moore hadn't been a young man when he married Hannibal's mom. She was thirty-nine, too, when she had Hannibal. He was in his late forties. But when everyone else left the island, he refused to leave. It was late eighteen hundreds, and the factory was little more than a memory. Justin was closing in on seventy. The building was old. The machinery just about useless except for a few pieces. The waste had nearly destroyed the water and marshland. And the barrage of hurricanes didn't help matters. Hannibal sold off what little he could from the factory.''

"What did he do for income then?"

"He didn't need the money. His mother's people had money, lots of it. He had an inheritance from her folks."

"Was the lighthouse here then?"

Granny shook her head. "No. It was little more than a

light stuck up on a pole. We had a lighthouse crew, but not an official lighthouse. Anyway, a couple of years after his daddy died his mother took sick. He went up to Philadelphia and brought her back here. Sissieretta's mom was a nurse. She looked after the care of Hannibal's mother. Sissieretta didn't like a lot of blood and stuff but Hannibal needed a cook and somebody to help look after the house. Sissieretta did that. 'Ceptin' she figured the house was a bit too big for one person to keep. She hired on help for the cleaning and she did the cooking and bossing. He gave her the top floor of the house. I think he musta fallen in love with her the moment he set eyes on her. His mama was here, so it kept things respectable. And her mother wasn't going to have any hanky panky going on with her daughter so he was sure to keep his feelings to himself.

"The place her folks owned was more inland and she shared a room with her two sisters. They were good folks though—a close family—good people." Granny looked up. "Sissieretta loved living up there on the top floor, though. I remember her saying she could see the world from way up there."

"Grandma."

Both women were pulled immediately out of their fascinating world. Doc stood in the doorway.

"My granddaughter brought me over here. She's got to get back to work."

"I'll be happy to take you back."

"No need. I'm tuckered out."

Cecily helped Granny up out of the chair and went to get her coat. "Thank you for the information," Cecily said, holding the coat while Granny slid her arms in. She was in her nineties but she didn't appear frail for a moment. She looked very capable.

"Baby girl, I've got a whole lot more to tell you."

"And I'm looking forward to hearing every word. I want to know everything about my father and mother."

"I can tell you about your father. But it's best to leave trouble in the past where it belongs."

The warmth swept out of the room. Granny approached

her granddaughter and the two walked out of the shop to the Honda parked in front.

Cecily rubbed her arms. She was left with mixed emotions. She loved her mother with all her heart and soul. Yet the people here hated her. Even if they didn't say it, they felt it. She could feel it coming from them. She wondered how they could hate someone so important to Cecily and yet accept her with equal fervor. It was as if they saw only one side of her, the father she never knew. Perhaps this was their way of coping. Or maybe it was the only way they could accept her—at least until she found the person who had stolen the money, and cleared her mother's name.

It never occurred to her that her mother could lie to her— at least not about that. She had revealed the information on her deathbed. She sent Cecily back to her roots. Back to a new way of life. Sometimes Cecily wondered what she'd do with that life and if it was truly for her.

She was born in the city, just as Hannibal's mother had been. Would she one day find the island too constraining as Joyce had? With her quest to clear her mother's name, had she overlooked the fact that this island might not indeed be for her?

Cecily shook her head. Of course she wouldn't move. This was her home. She'd uprooted her life, and Glenda's life, to move here. She couldn't decide on a whim to start over again. She'd made her decision and she'd stick with it.

There was something intimately appealing about this island. She loved the third floor of this house every bit as much as the first Sissieretta had. She longed to find out more about her namesake. She wondered if there were any secrets up there yet to be uncovered. She wondered what else she and Sissieretta might have in common.

# Chapter 5

It was late as usual when Ryan parked his truck in back of the tea shop. He still found it difficult to imagine the keeper's house turned into a delicate tea shop. But in certain ways the building fit the image of romance and Victorian charm with its lacy curtains, ornate trim, and warm coziness. Cecily's decorating ability helped to foster that impression, he thought.

The news had spread around town that she was looking into the theft. Although he'd be the last to say it, he believed her mother took the money and skipped town. Money didn't just disappear into thin air.

But he admired the way Cecily fought for her mother against all odds. That appealed to him more than he wanted it to. He liked fighters, women who weren't afraid to stick up for what they believed in, just as much as he hated simpering deceitfulness. This one act didn't advertise her whole character but it was a good character reference.

Ryan left the truck.

Outside, back stairs led from the first floor to the third. He knew that those stairs had been added in the late eighteen hundreds after Sissieretta moved in. They weren't part of the original design of the building. In fact Old Man Hannibal, as it was told, added the stairs to make his access to Sissieretta easier and less obvious. As the story goes, his excuse had been to give Sissieretta privacy in her comings and goings from the house.

Ryan liked the idea of the privacy stairs. He didn't have to disturb Glenda to see Cecily. He could imagine Hannibal sneaking out the front door ostensibly to take a walk along the coast and instead heading for the back. And just as Ryan was rounding the building right now, the man climbed the same stairs one floor at a time until he reached the top. Ryan turned to view the ocean. This portion of the land was on a corner almost—with the ocean on one side, the sound on the other. Both the front and the back of the house allowed spectacular views of water.

Ryan knocked on the door and imagined that Hannibal's knock had been much softer than his own—if the door had been locked at all. Like a vision, Cecily opened the door, the reflection of the room's warm light behind her. She was breathtaking and he wished again that he were here to see her for reasons other than business. He thought of Hazeline, who had given him a personal reason for coming.

Cecily smiled and motioned him in. Crossing the threshold, he glimpsed a floral china teapot and tray on the table by the chair. A delicate matching cup on a saucer was beside it. A soft, delicate throw was draped near a book on the sofa. Fire glowed and snapped in the stone fireplace.

Aroma from the tea drifted into the air along with the steam. The lights he'd seen had not been lamps at all, but dozens of candlelights flickering around the room. They cast a surreal beauty. Suddenly Cecily was in front of him, peering up at him from gleaming velvet-brown eyes. She was saying something but he didn't hear. Forgetting the purpose for his trip, he lifted his hand to her chin and tilted her head upward. He lowered his head and kissed her, slowly. She tasted sweet and fresh like the tea. And she didn't stop him.

He pulled her warm body close to his. He could only tell how warm she was by touching her back. He still hadn't shed his thick coat. He took one hand and unzipped his coat, then pulled her close to him, hoping she wouldn't push him back. She didn't and he deepened the kiss, tasting the sweetness within her mouth. Their tongues dueled in a wild dance.

"I've wanted to do this since the moment I saw you," he finally said, then bent and kissed her again, not giving her an opportunity to speak with anything except her tongue meeting his. He felt her fingers on his back beneath his coat, loving the touch of her hands on him. They stoked his temperature up a whole twenty degrees at least.

Damn, thinking about Hannibal climbing those stairs for the same purpose he'd wanted to was driving him nuts. Was he crazy kissing her like this out of the blue? Was she going to think he was out of his mind? But she tasted too damn good to let go. But he did let her go. He came here for business reasons, not to make out. And not to give her the wrong impression, that he was using this attraction to get what he wanted out of her. He didn't stand a snowball's chance in hell of getting what he wanted anyway. But he would try. Getting this land had two purposes—it would get his finances back in shape that much quicker and it would expand the park which had stretched as far as it could.

But his erratic thoughts barely put a damper on this intense need to have her. He released her anyway and moved back from the temptation she presented. His gaze roamed her soft, damp mouth and collided with her bemused eyes. He stood electrified by the loveliness of this woman with passion-kissed lips.

He inhaled a deep breath, put his hands on his hips. "I didn't mean to do that," he finally said as he tore his gaze from her, lest he kissed her again. He wiped a hand down his face, went to the window, and peered out. He saw the outline of the moon outside.

"You said that the last time."

"Can I blame my craziness on the moon?" he asked.

"If you need to," she answered him in a soft voice from across the room.

He turned in her direction. She folded the throw with trembling fingers and smoothed it on the back of the sofa.

She placed her book on the table, presenting her back to him. Then he realized, she was as uncertain as he felt. He approached her. Wrapped his arms around her from the back. Ran his hands up and down her arms.

"Kissing you wasn't because of the moon," he whispered softly. "It wasn't because I'm crazy—maybe just a little crazy."

He chuckled and so did she, easing the mood a fraction.

"It's because I've been wanting you for what seems like forever. I don't want to deny it any longer and I don't think either of us is ready for . . . well, the time isn't right."

"You're right," she said. "I've got so much going on, too much to learn, too much to uncover to get involved in a serious relationship."

"What I feel for you—and by your kiss, I'm thinking, what you may feel for me—doesn't necessarily wait for when we're ready. It never seems to happen according to schedule, when everything in our lives is perfect, does it?"

"Maybe not."

Reluctantly, he released her and returned to the window. Then he realized he still wore his coat and he took it off, placed it over the arm of a chair. He was too hot and he ran a finger along his collar.

"I didn't come here to kiss you."

"Why did you?" She held her arms facing him. "Why don't we sit?" She sat and poured a cup of tea for him, handing it over.

He was too agitated to sit but he did anyway and took the tea from her and sipped. She remembered how he liked it. She was in the business to remember, he realized.

"I'd like to present a proposition to you."

Her lips tightened and the uncertainty in her eyes changed to determination. "I'm not going to sell you my land."

"I realize that. I was thinking of something on a temporary basis."

"How temporary and how intrusive?"

"College students and professors throughout the country are interested in your estuary for research. They want to use their spring breaks to study nature, marine animals.

"Right now I have reservations for one hundred twenty campsites for professionals who want to study here. I think the land can be useful. Some animals are on the endangered species list. Because of Hannibal's care, this estuary has been brought back to life. It's the only place like it in the country. At one time, species that are almost extinct thrived up and down the eastern coastline. I think the sites here can be used to make studies so that other areas can be improved and brought back to life. They are on wetlands on other parts of the island, but not parts as fluent as here." Ryan paused. "I don't think my mother informed you that she gave them permission to do so before you arrived."

"No, she didn't."

"Do you have a problem with the research?"

"From what I've heard, bringing the land back to its glory was Hannibal's quest. I wouldn't want that to change."

"It won't change. We can have locals trained to lead these groups to make sure nothing is damaged."

She seemed to mull the idea over in her mind. "Give me a few days to think about it."

"That's fair enough."

"What will happen if I refuse?"

"The campground is full that weekend. I'll have to turn them away."

"Spring break is little more than a month away. How will you get everything ready in time?"

"Remember, this is a campground we're talking about. It won't take long to install bathroom and shower facilities. We'll outline plots. There will be only minimum electricity. We won't put a store here. All that will be at the main campground. This will be earmarked strictly as a research site, but your tea shop is close enough to handle their need for food and coffee."

Cecily nodded. "I'll get back to you soon."

He paused a moment, before he said, "There was another reason that I came tonight, other than business, that is."

"Why?" she asked.

"Valentine's dinner. Any chance of us getting together?"

"I don't know, is there?"

"I'd like to take you to the affair, but I imagine you'll be working."

"I will. But you can come afterward." Then she paused, narrowed her eyes at him. "Are you trying to romance my land out of me?"

He smiled, took on the face of an innocent kid. "Who, me? I wouldn't do that." With his smile, he looked younger, more carefree, and the look shouted that he would very well do just that.

Skeptical, Cecily raised her eyebrows.

Ryan couldn't very well tell her that he was doing it to keep from taking Hazeline out. "My whole family is going. I don't have a date."

"Not for lack of opportunity, I'm sure."

"So I'm kind of picky."

"I see." She imagined she should feel honored, but his reluctance left unanswered questions.

He shifted to his other foot. "Are you going to make a big deal out of this?"

"Since you so graciously offered, I'll accept," she finally said.

"Good." He nodded, glanced at her one last time before he left.

Cecily was left wondering about the strangeness of the offer, of the man in general.


Friday night arrived. Valentine's night. The many chores that lay ahead of Cecily occupied her mind. And the shocker of it, the thrill of it, was that she'd sold out for that night's reservations for Valentine's dinner.

What had once served as the living and dining room Cecily used on a regular basis. But now, the doors to what were previously a music room, library, and large downstairs bedroom and glassed-in breakfast room were also used, the couch and clock table had been moved aside in the library to make room for tables.

Tables set with romantic candles, and brilliant chrysanthemums with ferns and baby's breath created a romantic illusion. Cecily took one last stroll around the rooms, straightening chairs here and there, smoothing a crease out of a tablecloth, twisting a napkin just so, aligning a knife handle—in general, assuring herself everything was in place.

Ryan's cousin, Mark Anderson appeared wearing the tux he'd rented for the occasion. After helping to seat the guests, he would take pictures of the couples settled comfortably at their tables.

She made her way to the kitchen, where everyone was darting around like ants. "Everything on schedule here?" she asked.

"Everything in here is under control. Go on out before you drive yourself into a nervous wreck and me along with you," Glenda said, beating something in a huge chrome bowl. With everything seeming to be under control, Cecily left the room.

Only minutes away from a packed house, Ryan's kiss crept into her mind. It kept creeping back at odd moments. It was the one thing she didn't need to think about right now. Worse, she was anticipating his visit after dinner was over. Not that she'd have an appetite.

Even with all the work ahead of her and although they had both said this wasn't the time to begin a relationship, she hadn't been able to get him off her mind since she last saw him two nights ago. That night he'd sent an earthquake-like shock through her. She replayed his touch and his words over and over in her mind.

The officer had not called back yet and Cecily wondered why it took so long to find those files. Her impatient nature was rearing its head. It wasn't as if the sheriff's department was hopping with crime. She imagined the notes were stacked in some dusty file box in the bowels of the building.

In this morning's newspaper, the fact that somebody's dog had run off with Mr. Warren's favorite fishing line had been the highlight of the crime page. Customers who had come through her shop had hemmed and hummed about it. Back in New York it took a grizzly murder to warrant that much attention. These islanders lived in a world of their own, unlike anything Cecily had ever encountered. It brought back images of *The Cosby Show*. Although the setting had been New York, the story was a slow-paced family folksy setting.

The island was wearing more and more on her. After Granny had regaled her with her story, Cecily thought often of Sissieretta and the fact that they had probably slept in the same bedroom, glanced out the same windows on the top floor. She often wondered about Sissieretta. Her hopes for the future, knowing that as long as she was here, and the time period in which she lived, her future was very limited. Had she made do with the best that she had? Had she loved Hannibal or had she settled? With the factory closing, many local jobs more than likely were lost. Even now, most islanders worked on the mainland in factories and on the marine base. The cost of living in Coree was very low compared with the rest of the country. Cecily wondered at the changes that moved Coree to what it had become today.

"Look spry. Seems like your first customer's coming in," Glenda said, narrowing her eyes toward the door. Her chef's hat was tilted sideways. She was dressed in all white.

Cecily refocused her thoughts back to business. She had hired extra help tonight along with the entertainment she hoped would thrill her guests. She had gone all out for this extravaganza. Dressed in a long flowing gown of turquoise, she sailed across the room, skirting tables that reflected beautifully in the waning light. She wanted everything about this affair to be as elegant as she'd planned. At the prospect of seeing her shop full for the first time, Cecily greeted the first couple and she escorted them to their table.

Two hours later, a menu of rack of lamb, shrimp Newburg, and beef burgundy had been well received. The gaiety of couples filled the tea shop. Doors to the banquet rooms had been thrown open to handle the overflow. Mark roamed from table to table snapping pictures, later handing them to customers in the frames Cecily had ordered for the occasion.

And then it was game time. Cards passed to all the players were being completed by couples.

"No cheating." Ryan heard Cecily's voice on the loud-speaker as he entered the building wearing his suit. Everyone was so intent on her, only Mark noticed his arrival.

"Dinner's over." He frowned as he peered closely at some ledger. "I don't have a reservation for you."

"Moonlighting?" Ryan asked before he told his cousin, "There isn't a reservation for me." He noticed his parents sharing a table with Delcia and Carter. All were scribbling something on a card and joking with each other. Then he saw Carter throw down his nub of a pencil and push the card aside, shaking his head.

"There aren't any tables left," Mark continued. "Besides, it's for couples only. Where's your date?" he asked, trying to figure out a solution for the dilemma. "Maybe I can get the people in the kitchen to fix up something for you."

"Don't worry about it," Ryan said and noticed his mother motioning him over. He strolled toward their table. Mark followed him.

"Get Ryan a seat, please, Mark," Pauline asked.

"He doesn't have a reservation."

"Don't worry about it, dear."

Within moments, Mark returned with a chair from the lobby. Ryan slid into a space between his mom and Carter.

"Carter, you have to finish the card," Delcia said in menacing tones. Her protruding stomach kept her from sitting close to the table.

"Help me out here, man," Carter was saying. "If I don't answer these questions correctly, I'll wind up sleeping on the couch tonight. It's too cold for the couch." He pushed the card away. "No way."

Delcia picked up the pencil and thrust it at him with a warning that promised retribution once they left. "If you can't answer these few simple questions about me, you deserve the couch."

Ryan and Clay chuckled.

Carter sighed like a man who was in way over his head and knew it. He took the pencil and started scribbling.

"You should have come earlier, son. You missed dinner," Clay said.

"I know."

"Maybe they'll fix you a plate," his mother muttered as if she couldn't bear the idea of her child going without a meal.

"I've got plans to eat later," Ryan said.

"Oh. Are you're going out with someone?" She smoothed his lapel. "You're looking very handsome. Be a shame not to. Maybe . . ."

"Give him a break, will you, Mom? He's not eight and on his first date."

Feeling like a fifth wheel, Ryan said, "The evening's young yet. We'll see."

"Is everyone through?" Ryan heard Cecily's voice again over the loudspeaker, then caught a glance at her when she walked in with a microphone in her hand. He only just caught himself from doing a double take. She was stunning in her straight gown that shimmered like diamonds against her gorgeous brown skin. A huge scoop showed off half her magnificent back. The V in the front was respectable at least. He found he couldn't take his eyes off her as she stood between the openings that joined another room.

"Now, pass the cards to your partner. Partners, check the answers to see how well your partner knows you."

Delcia was very quiet as she checked Carter's answers.

"Clay, you don't know that I like lilacs best?" Pauline asked.

"Of course I know. Just trying to get a rise out of you. It worked."

"You old devil. I know you too well." She continued checking, narrowing her eyes at him every time he checked one of her answers wrong.

"Everything okay over there?" Carter asked Delcia.

"Very funny."

"I don't know. You've got four wrong so far. Looks to me like *you're* gonna be sleeping on the couch. That king-size bed's going to be mighty lonely tonight."

"You wouldn't put your baby on the couch, would you, honey?"

"I'd put my wife there. In a heartbeat."

"You scoundrel."

Then he heard Cecily's voice again, and saw a tuxedoed person in the room. "Now let's see a show of hands for anyone who got all of them correct."

"How about if they got them all wrong?" Carter called out.

"You're in serious trouble," Cecily said and Delcia hit him on the shoulder.

"I didn't get all of them wrong."

"Let me take a peek at yours."

She pushed him away and reluctantly raised her hand. "We've got a winner here. Any more winners?"

There was joking and ribbing around the room.

"You are our grand prize winner." Cecily brought a gift box to the table and handed it to Delcia along with an envelope.

"That's my gift. I got them right, not you," Carter teased.

Ryan wasn't surprised that Carter won the prize of two free dinners. Then Delcia uncovered the box top to expose beautiful Moroccan tea glasses stenciled with gold and an ornate teapot. They were also given a picture frame sized to fit the photos. Mark took their picture and inserted it into the frame.

"Do I get a kiss?" Carter asked.

"Am I sleeping on the couch?"

He pulled her close. "All night long," he whispered and claimed her lips.

Everyone clapped. Ryan caught his mother looking warmly at the couple and then she turned a sad gaze to him. Ryan hated that she worried about him.

He focused on Carter and Delcia. Carter had scooted closer to her and whispered, "I might let you sleep in the bed, after all." Then he winked and she blushed.

When Carter had first arrived on the island searching for his brother, he'd been serious, and isolated and a recently retired Navy SEAL. He'd changed over the last three years to show a more carefree and relaxed personality. While it hadn't totally been his sister's doing, her love had relaxed Carter, and creating a loving home had given him a joy he hadn't experienced before. The intimate moment was forgotten when other prizes were called out.

The customers had left, thrilled with their experience, especially the women. The employees had cleaned up the shop. Ryan had left hours ago and Cecily and Glenda were sprawled on the couch waiting for him to return.

"I'm almost too tired to eat," Glenda said.

"So am I," Cecily murmured. "But I was too nervous to eat a thing most of the day. I can't wait to take a shower, then relax." The scent of food still lingered in the air.

Cecily started to stand but before she could haul herself off the couch, the door to the kitchen opened. Out came Ryan and Emery. Each man carried a vase of beautiful cut flowers.

Ryan looked sexy with a towel wrapped around his waist and still wearing his suit pants. Gone was the jacket. The tie was missing and the top two buttons of his pristine shirt had been undone, showing a splattering of black hair.

First Emery approached Glenda, executed a courtly bow that had them grinning and clapping. It reminded her of the old singing groups her mother used to talk about. The tapes she watched of the Temptations, and the Stylistics. They had smooth moves that one rarely saw any longer. He set the vase of lilies on the table in front of Glenda. Cecily saw the heat rising in Glenda's face. This was the kind of thing Glenda loved, and happened too infrequently.

Ryan didn't have that old southern courtly way but he was handsome and smooth nevertheless when he placed his vase of pink roses in front of her and lifted her hand to his lips. His warm breath on her skin nearly stopped her heart.

"Happy Valentine's Day."

She hadn't thought to get him a thing. She hadn't thought that one kiss had taken them that far. Still, he was mesmerizing her with his eyes.

And the mood wasn't broken until Emery pulled him aside. "We'll be right back, ladies."

Cecily glanced at Glenda, whose smile hovered on her lips. "You planned this, didn't you?"

"I knew Ryan was coming, but not Emery. Emery is my surprise." She fanned herself. "Girl, I think I'm having a menopausal moment. I'm hot all over. Did you see him move? Oh, Lawdy. I'm wondering what he's like in bed."

"I thought you were a good Christian woman." Truth be told, she'd wondered the same thing about Ryan.

"I can wonder, can't I?"

"Guess you can." But they wondered more when the men returned with a cart bearing heaping plates of food and set them on the nearest table along with a bottle of wine chilling in an ice bucket.

They started to get up, but the men motioned them back. "We'll bring it all to you," Emery said.

"You're spoiling me," Glenda said.

"You're made for spoiling."


On Monday morning Cecily snipped the ends of the fragrant roses, hoping the magnificent petals would last longer. She then stuck them into fresh water and admired them as she called the police station.

"I was just going to call you," the officer said. "I've found the files you want. You can stop by any time."

"I'll be right over."

Outside the day was calmer than usual. And the tide was gently flowing to shore. The temperature hovered above 60. Cecily was still riding on her Valentine's good humor although the message she had received over the Internet this morning was disturbing. It warned her to leave the island. She wasn't wanted here. She decided to leave a copy of it at the police station. If some weirdo was trying to get her to leave her island, it wasn't going to work. At least not until she was good and ready to go. Or *if* she ever decided to go. Word had gotten around that she was seeking information about the relief fund. Perhaps the person who stole the money felt threatened. One never could tell.

When Cecily climbed into her car she looked up at the

lighthouse. The stately black and white building was a sym-
bol of history. With modern technology many lighthouses
were symbols of the past. When she'd visited the island the
first time and toured it, walking the many steps to the top,
she'd thought of opening it for tours. But getting the cottage
renovated into the tea house required all her time. Now, she
wondered if perhaps she should proceed with those plans.
It really didn't require very much work. And in its given
form, it would give tourists a look back in time at the history
of lighthouses. She'd talk to Glenda about it.

Glenda was still riding high with her budding relationship
with Emery. Even though Cecily hadn't ever remembered
seeing Glenda so satisfied and happy, she sensed that the
older woman was holding something back. Before they
moved to the island, Glenda had mentioned that she might
go back to New York after Cecily got her shop up and
running good, but if things started rolling in the right direction with Emery, Glenda just might change her mind about
leaving.

Cecily thought about that a moment. She'd miss Glenda.
Despite the fact that Glenda wasn't her blood aunt, nothing
could change the love and experiences they'd shared through
the years from the very first day her mother had settled in
New York.

Although pleasant feelings buoyed her emotions about
Ryan, the questions—if he'd kissed her, given her roses to
win her confidence—still flowed through her mind, despite
his denial that night.

Cecily arrived at the station, and asked to speak to Officer
Derrick. She informed him of the note, leaving the copy
with him. He promised to check into it and get back with
her.

She read the information in the folder he handed her. It
didn't offer anything she didn't already know.

On her way home she was left with a sense of disappointment. She'd expected more. Now she knew she'd have to
do the research on her own.

She stopped as another car backed out of the slot. Then
she started on her journey home. The ice cream parlor had

a CLOSED sign in the window. A few doors down, she passed the newspaper office. The tiny sign swinging in front indicated it had been in the same family since 1935.

She hit the brakes. No one was behind her so she backed up and pulled into the parking slot. Somebody with a camera came tearing out of the building, then went back to turn the sign to closed.

"Excuse me," Cecily said.

"Yeah?" The man looked harried.

"I'm interested in seeing old copies of your paper that date back to the seventies."

"We've got 'em but you have to come back later. I'm on the trail of a hot story." He hurried to his beat-up SUV.

Cecily followed him. "When would be a good time?"

"Any time but now." He thrust a card at her. "Boyd Thompson. Call me." Then he shut the door, started his car, and backed up so fast he almost backed into a driver.

Cecily read the curse words on the man's mouth although she couldn't hear him. Then he shook a fist at Boyd. The editor waved a hand of regret and burned rubber as he hurried down the road.

She wondered at his hot news. She read the paper every day and hadn't once come across what she considered a hot news article. Her breakfast ad was printed in Friday's paper. Cecily wondered at the results to come.

Cecily started her journey home, thinking of the shop's meager sales, though business had increased.

And then she thought of Ryan's plans for the estuary. It would bring more people to the tea shop year-round if more wanted to do research. The research could be done any time of the year. Even if Ryan had tried to romance her land out of her, she was going to lease it to him temporarily—with conditions. Her ancestor had worked to bring the land back to its formal beauty. She wouldn't, during her keeping of the land, see it go back to a wasteland.

Cecily lowered the window to smell the ocean breeze. From a distance, she spotted the tip of the lighthouse. She was like a homing pigeon, beaming in on her lighthouse.

This was beautiful country, Cecily thought. She planned

to give the land the reverence it deserved. And she was so eager to hear more of her ancestors. Especially about Sissieretta and her father. How had such a woman ended up staying permanently at the keeper's cottage? And when had it turned into a keeper's cottage? Obviously it hadn't originally been so. The home had been built years before the lighthouse, when the shining beacon of light had merely been a lantern perched on a tall pole.

# Chapter 6

The shop closed at five on Sundays and was closed on Mondays—until tourist season. That evening Cecily and Glenda went to dinner at Wanda's place.

Wanda's was bustling with business, mostly locals who watched them closely, especially the three wicked ladies who sat only a couple of tables from their corner booth. Practically every table was full. The waitress took their drink orders and left to get them while they perused the menus.

"So where are you going on your vacation?" they heard Taylor ask Ruby.

"Just to Raleigh. I'm going to spend a couple of weeks at my brother's place. We might go to the mountains, do some skiing."

Taylor barked out a laugh. "You don't ski."

"I'll drink hot chocolate and watch," Ruby said. "The kids and my brother love to ski."

"That should be nice," Taylor said, "except I like to get away sometimes. I'm thinking about taking a cruise. I've never done that. Be nice to tour the Bahamas and not worry about food and things. Get pampered. After all these years of hard work, I think we deserve it, don't you?"

"This is the time for it," Shelly said.

"You ladies should take a cruise with me," Taylor said.

"I think I'd like to go with my husband," Shelly told them.

"What about you, Ruby?"

Cecily peered above her menu to see Ruby shake her head.

"Too expensive for me. Don't have the money."

"What in heaven's name do you do with your money?" Taylor snapped. "I keep telling you to put some away. Stop messing around with no-account men. All they do is spend your money and run you into debt. Then leave you."

"Well, if I didn't date a no-account one now and then, I wouldn't date at all. There aren't that many to choose from, after all."

"I'd rather be by myself than deal with nonsense," said Taylor.

"I get tired of being by myself all the time. And the foreigners moving here are taking our men, leaving nothing for us." She threw a heated look toward Cecily's table.

Obviously, she considered Glenda and Cecily to be foreigners.

"At least I can afford to take a vacation now and then," Taylor said.

"Well, so can I, Taylor. And I'm going on one next week." Ruby emptied her glass of white wine.

"To your brother's house. Never off on your own."

"I enjoy spending time with my brother. Some families like to spend time together. We live at different places. We don't get to see each other very often. And I thank the good Lord I have him."

"You go there two or three times a year."

"What's wrong with that? They visit me and enjoy the ocean. His children love it here and I like for them to visit."

"Nothing if you don't mind sponging off other folks."

"We're family. We don't consider it sponging."

"Ladies, must we always get into an argument?" Shelly cut in.

"I didn't start it," Ruby said, throwing a narrow glance

at Taylor. "Taylor's always got something to say about everybody's business. Always talking about how much money she's got. Like nobody else can ever do anything. Nobody wants to hear about your money. Other people have lives too. That doesn't include her."

Taylor sniffed. "If the truth hurts."

"I got enough money to do the things I enjoy. That's all I need." Ruby placed her napkin on her plate and pushed back from the table, walking down the narrow aisle to the cash register.

Shelly sighed, and mumbled something to Taylor. Then the other ladies picked up their checks and followed her.

"Well, I guess things aren't so hot in paradise," Glenda said. "If only we can get some of these customers," she added, looking around.

"If only," Cecily said, finally concentrating on her menu. She had hoped for a glimpse into who may have stolen that money. It always came back to the three witches. Taylor seemed to be on a better financial footing than the others. But if she had stolen the money, would she talk so freely about it? Wouldn't she try for a low profile to keep the information a secret?

"Hi," the waitress said. "My name is Aleka. Are you ready to order?"

"I think I'm going all out," Glenda said. "I'll start with the New England clam chowder and the fish special. Those hush puppies sound delicious."

"They are. Very. It's my grandmother's recipe."

Cecily had expected a suspicious glare, but the waitress was very friendly. "Are you ready to order?" Aleka asked Cecily.

"I'll take the same," Cecily said.

She took their order and took drink orders from new arrivals, spoke to other guests. Then she refreshed Glenda's and Cecily's drinks and hesitated a moment. "I was talking to Delcia the other day. She's thinking about joining our book club, but she said she's going to wait until after the baby comes and they settle down. Some of my friends and I started a book club a few months ago. We've been meeting in homes each month. Each person brings a dish. I'm think-ing it might be nice to meet at your place. Then we wouldn't have to worry about cooking supper for family, then having to come up with something for the group. I hate to cook.''

"We can certainly accommodate you," Cecily said.

"My sister's husband took her to the Valentine's special. She enjoyed it. I wanted to come, too, but I had to work."

"It turned out better than we anticipated. We were very pleased."

"She won the free dinner for two. She was in seventh heaven. She couldn't say enough good things about the tea shop. I think her husband was pleased, too, even though he'd die before he admitted it."

"I'm glad she was pleased," Cecily said. "Our library had couches and chairs where everyone can sit and be com-fortable, or you can use one of the meeting rooms if you'd like more privacy. In there you can sit around a table."

"The couch sounds comfortable to me. It'll almost be like we're sitting in a living room. Maybe I can come by for menus. Talk it over with the group."

"Stop by any time. We'll be happy to work out something for you, especially for your first time."

"Good. I better get back to work." She blew out a breath. "It's a zoo in here."

"Things are beginning to pick up," Glenda said.

"Word travels." Cecily replied.

"You and Ryan seem to be hitting it off okay."

Cecily contained a blush. "I never know what to think with him."

"Is that what you call it now?"

"He wants to lease some of the land near the estuary." Cecily described Ryan's plans.

"It sounds like a good idea to me."

"Me too. But I want it carefully planned to make sure the land isn't overused."

"You and Ryan will work something out."

"I've made up my mind to let him use it. I'm not ready to sell it, though."

"It's gorgeous land. I've been more at peace here lately

than I've been in a very long time. I feel a sense of freedom here."

"Are you sure that isn't because of Emery?"

"Well," Glenda said, taking a sip of her lemonade, "it just might. But tell me, how is your research going?"

"Very slow." Cecily chose her next words carefully. "Glenda, I hope you don't feel that I love Otis less because I found out about my natural father and need to know things. I hope I haven't hurt you. I'd never intentionally cause you pain."

"I loved my brother. He was the best. But I've always felt he and Mavis should have told you about your natural father when you were old enough to handle the news."

"Why didn't they tell me?"

"I think, God bless his soul, Otis didn't want you to know. You were his only child. He wanted you to think of him as your real father. And your mother was always afraid the people here would find her and prosecute her."

"But she didn't do it."

"I know she didn't. But she was still afraid. More than for herself, she was afraid of what would happen to you if she went to prison."

"Did you know her story when she first came to you?"

"No, it was years later when she told me. After she married my brother. We met in a restaurant. She needed a job and I was the restaurant manager at the time. She was desperate and my heart went out to her. I lived in an apartment down the street. I don't know what made me take you both in. Because I didn't know who she was. I just knew I couldn't leave her to the mean streets. She didn't know anyone in New York." Glenda shook her head. "It was very hard for her in the beginning."

"I imagine it was."

Glenda had taken her mother in just as she kept Cecily in her heart right now.

"I still love Otis as my father," Cecily continued. "He's the only one I ever knew. But I need to know about my roots."

"I know that. You do all the searching you need to. Don't give me a second thought."

"I do think about you, Glenda. You're my family."


The next morning a couple of people were waiting on the porch by the time the tea shop opened.

"You need earlier hours if you're gonna get fisherman business," an older man said. "Saw that ad in the paper."

"My granddaughter let me taste that blueberry biscuit she brought home from the Valentine's do. It was mighty good. You got any ready?"

"Sure do," Cecily said.

"I don't drink tea," the man said. "Good strong coffee will do me."

"Scone and coffee. Coming right up," Cecily said.

"You couldn't make apple, could you? I love apple anything."

"We can certainly add it to our menu."

The man nodded.

"I'll be back tomorrow."

"I'll see what I can do," Cecily said.

He settled back in his seat. Ordered another scone before he paid for his breakfast and left.

A half hour later, Emery arrived. The little crowd had left. He and Glenda exchanged warm glances before he said. "I'd like to talk to you about a business proposition," he said to them both.

"What proposition?"

"I offer lunch on the charter boats. Would you be willing to pack lunch boxes for them?"

"Just tell us what you want," Cecily said.

They discussed menus and prices, then he kissed Glenda and left.

That morning they had several times the business than they usually had.

Cecily had called the newspaper office, but the editor said it wasn't a good time yet. He was trying to get the weekly paper ready for publication.

By the time Pauline arrived an hour later, Cecily was thumbing through the pictures that Granny had lent her. In one picture her father wore a football uniform and held the helmet in his hand. In another he wore a cap and gown. She wondered if he had dated any of the girls in his class. She smiled at the thought, but put the shoe box beside the album Clay had loaned her so that she could greet Pauline.

"I haven't looked through that album in ages. I was a junior when Clay and your dad were seniors."

"Did you date Clay even then?"

"Oh, yes. I'd known since my freshman year he was the one for me. It took him a while longer to come around. Men are usually slow on the uptake that way. I joined the cheerleading squad just to be close to him."

Pauline took the book and thumbed through the pages. "Here I am." She positioned the book for Cecily to see.

Two guys were holding her in a pyramid.

"You were a thrower."

"To my mother's fear. Let me order tea and scones and I'll tell you about some of your dad's friends."

"And girlfriends?" Although now that Cecily knew he had been her mother's first love—and last—it was strange thinking of him with someone else. But this was before he even met her mother.

Cecily heated up a blueberry scone and poured breakfast tea for Claire and herself. Adding a pat of butter on a dish, she took the tray to the library. She and Pauline sat next to each other so they could share the book. There were no other customers in the shop.

Pauline forked off a bite of scone and chewed as she flipped pages. "Your father used to date Rosolyn," she said, pointing to a picture of a cheerleader in Claire's group.

"He and Clay had a thing for cheerleaders didn't they?"

"Not necessarily. He also dated Ruby Milford."

Cecily thought of the woman fussing last night. What on earth could her father have seen in her? "You're kidding, right?"

Pauline flipped pages. "There she is."

Cecily had to admit she wasn't bad looking, but her personality left something to be desired.

"She married Emery a year after your father and mother married. Emery was younger than she. Their marriage only lasted a couple of years."

"When did she date my father?"

"Right after he broke up with Rosolyn. He didn't love either of them. I don't think they took him too seriously. Both relationships were short-lived."

Cecily began to worry about Glenda. A two-year marriage didn't seem very stable. "I wouldn't want Glenda hurt by Emery."

"Emery is a wonderful man. He and Ruby just couldn't work out their problems. He wouldn't talk about what happened. I don't think Ruby really loved him. But he remarried a couple of years after he and Ruby divorced. He and his second wife were together for almost twenty years and were very happy together."

She saw pictures of Taylor and Shelly. "Did Ruby remarry?"

"Yes. Her second husband died in the same hurricane as your father."

"Were many people hurt?"

"No. Although there was plenty of property loss, they were the only casualties."

"Did Taylor ever marry?"

"Shelly is married, has been for many years, but Taylor never did. She worked at the bank until she retired. Then she opened an antique shop in town. It's been very successful although business comes to almost a standstill during the year. She makes enough during the summer to survive the same way most of the small businesses do here. For the most part people aren't rich, but they do well enough. I wanted to talk to you about the reading group. Have you thought about having a Friday night reading group for tots? I know the first one wasn't very successful, but I think it would be a lovely idea. Lots of people have told me they wish they had brought their children. I would be willing to choose the books and read them if you don't mind. I'm a retired teacher and I miss children. I think it would be wonderful for Ranetta to associate with other children. I want them to love to read at young ages.''

"It sounds like a wonderful idea, Pauline. Just let me know when and I'll have everything set up for it.''

"How about next Friday? I'll choose a book and put up flyers in the grocery store and churches. If you wouldn't mind, I'd like to get a teenage book club going, too. It would be nice for them to meet once a month.''

"That's a lovely idea, Pauline.''

"You're the one who initiated it. Ranetta still walks around with that book. Always wants someone to read to her. She loves to be read to but that night I think you built a little fantasy world that impressed her more than anything I could have done.'' Pauline patted Cecily's hand. "I can't thank you enough for that.''

Cecily smiled, imagining the room filled with little tots with books on their laps, eagerly looking toward the front as the story was being read. It was an impressive image. Pauline was single-handedly making her fall in love with this place.

"My visit had dual purposes. I'd like to invite you and Glenda to dinner Monday evening. I know you don't work Mondays. We'll get to relax and talk.''

"I can't answer for Glenda, but I'd love to. Thank you.''

"Let me know if Glenda can make it.''

Later that day Cecily called Ryan, telling him that she would lease the land to him. Soon after the call, a truck delivered the delicate tea sets Cecily had ordered for the little girls to use at the grandmother, granddaughter tea. Reservations were still coming in. Before the Valentine's affair the reservations had only trickled in; now the phone was busy with them. She debated whether she needed to order additional sets.

"I think we're going to do well for the tea,'' Glenda said. "I overheard a few people talking about it in the grocery store yesterday.''

"I do, too," Cecily agreed. She'd looked at her account balances and it wasn't pretty. A message popped up on her computer screen. She opened it to scan it. She groaned.

"What is it?" Glenda asked.

"Delilah's coming for a visit."

"What is she up to this time?"

"She didn't say." Every time her cousin Delilah came, trouble followed. She only came when she needed something. The last time they were together, she stole Cecily's boyfriend. Cecily thought about Ryan. They weren't actually dating, but he had mentioned that he had feelings for her. She liked him too. But if Delilah decided she wanted him, he was all hers. But then again, Cecily didn't plan to play the role of a sleeping dog this time. The last one she didn't care about, not really. This time . . . She didn't love Ryan, but she thought they were working up to something. She didn't respond to Delilah's e-mail.

"Tell her she isn't welcome. She doesn't need to come until things are right between you and Ryan."

"It's a little late for that."

"That's just like Delilah. Send you a message too late for you to respond. She knows she's not welcome. But you're so softhearted, you'd invite her anyway," Glenda said.

"She is family." Delilah was Marva's second cousin's child.

"The kind you can do without."

"That's the way it is with family."

Glenda looked at her skeptically. "When is she coming?"

"Tomorrow."

"Keep her away from Ryan."

"How am I supposed to do that?"

"I don't know, but you know she's man hungry. She'd snatch her own mother's husband if she were alive."

"I'm not going to worry about Ryan or Delilah. If he falls for her, then he isn't right for me."

"Don't be such a saint. You better fight for your man."

"He's not my man," Cecily said as she scanned her other messages.

"He could be," Glenda said.

"You better keep her away from Emery."

"Emery isn't mine anyway."

"That man has a smile on his face every time he comes here. I'm his cousin. But does he ever come to see me? No. It's you."

Glenda wrung the dish towel in her hand. "Do you think he's getting serious?"

"What's wrong with that?"

"I can't have a serious relationship. Nothing permanent anyway. I'm going to call it off."

"Are you crazy? All my life, you've never been with anyone who treats you kindly. Anyone you can develop a lasting relationship with. Now you've come across someone who's genuinely kind. And you want to turn him away? Why, Glenda?"

"I'm not one of those women cut out for lasting relationships."

"If I told you that, you wouldn't believe it for a minute. What's going on?"

Glenda turned away from Cecily and walked toward the window and shook her head. "I just can't, that's all. If he calls again, tell him I'm not available."

"I'm not going to do that. You deserve someone nice. I can't think of any good reason why you should. Unless you don't like him."

"That would be a convenient answer."

"But not true?"

"It just can't be."

"Why?"

Glenda didn't say anything, merely continued to peer out the window.

Cecily was a little hurt by Glenda's actions and concerned too. "Don't you trust me?"

"More than anyone on earth."

"Then why?"

She shook her head. "It just can't be. He's such a nice person. I couldn't bear it if . . ."

"What is it, Glenda?" Just then the message bell popped,

indicating someone had e-mailed her. Cecily flipped through it and read it.

Glenda merely shook her head and refused to answer.

"I can't believe it," Cecily said finally.

"What?" Glenda showed interest for the first time in the last few moments.

"This is the fourth message I've gotten from this crazy man."

"The one about you trying to get away from him?"

"Yes. I took a copy to the police station yesterday. He said he'd look into it." She printed out the message but refused to respond. She'd already told him he had mistaken her for someone else, and if that hadn't stopped him, responding again certainly wouldn't.

"I'm glad you did. There are some real crazies out there. You can't be too careful." Glenda leaned over her shoulder. "Think you should stay with me for a while?"

"I should be okay. But to be on the safe side, I'm going to give the police this one too."

"The address for the tea shop is advertised on the Internet. He can come directly to your place."

"Who can come to her place?"

They looked up to see Ryan. On the heels of the eerie message, Cecily's heart was beating rapidly.

"Cecily has been getting threatening e-mail messages."

"What does it say?" He leaned over Cecily's shoulder and read the message.

"Let me handle this." He pulled Cecily up and sat in the chair.

"You can't do any more than I've done," she said.

Ryan started typing into the screen.

*Leave my fiancée alone. If you don't, we'll report you to the police.*

"Do you think it's a good idea to antagonize him?" Glenda asked.

"Some weirdos who frighten people over the Internet are

cowards. Hopefully this will do the job. Have you taken this to the police?"

"Yesterday I gave Officer Derrick the last message I received."

"Do you have a copy of all of them?"

"Yes."

"We'll stop at the library and make Xerox copies, then give him all the messages."

"Sounds like a winner to me," Glenda said. "I'm feeling a mite spooked. We're in the middle of nowhere out here."

"Both of you are welcome to stay at my place. My parents are there."

"Thanks, but we'll be fine," Cecily said. "Chances are this person is hundreds of miles away." At least she hoped he was.

"The offer stands if you change your mind." Gathering the papers, he stood. "Let's take a trip to the station."

"You don't need to go with me. I can drive to the station."

"Will you be okay, Glenda?" he asked as if Cecily hadn't spoken.

Glenda waved a hand. "Go ahead. I'm fine."

"Really . . ."

"Let's go." He put a hand under Cecily's elbow and urged her to get a jacket.

"I don't like being forced."

"I'm not being overbearing. I'm concerned about your safety."

Cecily got her coat and they left for the station. She heard Glenda's chuckles behind her.

Ryan had parked at the edge of the parking space closest to the water. As soon as they got into the SUV, Ryan started it but left it in park. Then he leaned toward her, pulled her into his embrace, and kissed her.

He smelled fresh and intoxicating.

"Is this a thank-you for the land?" she asked.

"Don't make me any more angry than I already am. I missed you," he said against her lips and kissed her again. "This has nothing to do with the land, the camp, your store. It's about me needing to hold you in my arms." His gaze was as soft as a caress. He kissed her again, gentler this time. He brushed his tongue over her lips, nibbled at the corners. Ran his hands beneath her unbuttoned coat and gathered her close to him. She seemed to be drifting along on a cloud. He tugged at her sweater and she was powerless to resist. His hand felt wonderful against her bare skin.

She ran her hands beneath his sweater, felt his springy chest hairs against her palms. He pulled her closer and deepened the kiss. At the base of her throat a pulse beat and swelled as though her heart had risen from its usual place.

Then he stopped and moved away from her. His shoulders tensed and his hands gripped the steering wheel in a death grip before he looked at her with such a serious expression Cecily wondered if something was gravely wrong.

"I have a confession to make," he said. "I don't want to move into anything too quickly. Let's just take our time, okay? Give us time to really get to know each other. I don't know where this is going to lead. I know there's some . . . chemistry between us."

That was putting it mildly, Cecily thought.

"Seems reasonable."

He blew out a long breath. "I've got some more explaining to do, I know." He was silent for a long moment. Seagulls squawked across the ocean. He seemed mesmerized by them.

"I was divorced from my wife a year ago. The marriage lasted six months but it died long before that. The divorce merely completed what had been a bad union from the start. It was nasty. I lost everything except the house and my share of the campground. I had to mortgage the house, so I'm starting off from scratch. I'm flat-out broke. Is that going to be a problem for you?"

"I'm starting from scratch, too, with a business that's not exactly exploding with customers. I'd say we're in the same boat."

"I'm not making any promises."

"Me either. You might not like my hosiery hanging over the bathtub. Or my eyelet pillows on the couch. Too feminine for your masculinity."

He seemed to relax. "What, eyelet sheets too?" he asked.

"A lady's got to keep some secrets."

He chuckled out loud this time. Cecile realized she'd never heard him laugh before. She'd seen many sexy smiles, but not one outright laugh.

"How did I live so long without you?" he said, and kissed her again. His hands edged around and caressed her breasts through her bra.

Cecily moaned. He maneuvered his fingers beneath the bra and tugged on a nipple.

Cecily tore her mouth away. "You're driving me insane."

"I'm already there, baby." He kissed her again and she stroked his erection through his jeans.

His groan was deep and elemental. And the kiss grew frantic with need. Then they heard a car approach and he released her.

Their breathing was labored as they pulled themselves together.

"Look at me," he finally said, swiping a hand across his face. "A grown man about to make out in the car in broad daylight in the parking lot." He shook his head and chuckled. "You drive me crazy, woman."

Cecily tugged her clothes into place. "I don't know what came over me. In a car in front of my own store. What are you doing to me?"

"Whatever it is, it's reciprocal."

Cecily blew out a long breath.

Ryan leaned back in his seat and clenched his hand on the steering wheel. The windows steamed, wrapping them in their own secret world. He activated the defogger and in seconds the world came into view.

"I was concerned about approaching you intimately at the same time as I talked to you about the land. I was worried you'd get the two confused. I don't play games. I like you a hell of a lot. But I'm leery, too. I wonder if this island would be enough for you. If you'd decided it's not. I'm worried that you'll want to move back to New York one day. But this heat for you spreading in me won't let me ignore you. I can't get you out of my system."

"Is that what you're trying to do? Get me out of your system?"

"It wouldn't work if I tried." The heat in his eyes seared her as if a flame had touched her. "I want you in every possible way I can get you."

"Good."

"Good what?"

"I want you as much as you want me."

"Good," he said and put the truck in gear. "Then we understand each other."

"Does this mean we're dating?"

"Very much so."

A thrill shot through Cecily. The look he gave her was full of heat and male possessiveness. His eyes held her as if she were in a trance. He leaned over and kissed her quickly. Leaving her with a thrill, he backed up and they were off. There was nothing reassuring about that kiss. It was designed to set every nerve tingling in her body.

# Chapter 7

The next week passed in a flurry. With only two lawyers on the island who also worked out of offices in Morehead City, it wasn't easy tracking one down. There were too few businesses on the small island to support them, but they were raised on the island and like many others, loved island living. Cecily met with Marsha Petty to have her draw up the lease so that Ryan would have access to the land as quickly as possible to begin constructing a minimal campground. Marsha assured Cecily she would get back with her within a week, which she did, and now construction on the campground had begun and her peace was already shattered with the invasion of machinery to build a cesspool and a well for water.

Cecily peered out her window. Although she could hear machinery, she couldn't see anything. Was Ryan there? She was eager to see what had been done to the campground. She almost hated for the natural sight to be ravaged with campsites. This land had so much to offer and she had grown to appreciate it, probably as much as the islanders did.

She had gotten into the habit of daily walks and decided to go in that direction, knowing very well she was going there to see Ryan. She really didn't need an excuse. But part of her was still grappling with his confession that he was attracted to her. The thought sent warmth flowing through her and even the brisk wind didn't cool what she didn't know if she was quite ready for. But life rarely waited for a person to get ready. Ryan was here, now. So what was she going to do about it?

Finally the phone rang. It was the editor telling her he was available.

"Glenda, do you think you can handle things alone for a while?"

"Sure I can. Where are you going?"

"To the newspaper office to look through old papers."

In the kitchen Cecily boxed up four scones and fixed a large cup of Earl Gray to take with her.

"You plan to be there a long time?"

"These are a gift."

"Smart. Really smart. Take your time."

Cecily arrived at the office in just a few minutes.

She met Boyd inside. He wore a long-sleeve shirt, no tie with jeans. The shirt was wrinkled as if he hadn't hung it up when it came out of the dryer.

The man extended a hand, enclosing Cecily's hand in a firm grip.

"Sorry I was so rude the other day, but I was rushing out to get information for our lead story."

"I understand," she said, offering the box of scones and container of tea to him. "I brought you a gift."

He opened the box immediately and took one of the scones out and bit into it.

"If I'd known the food was this good, I'd have come by your place sooner," he said, taking a second bite.

"What was this hot story?" Cecily asked.

He wiped the crumbs from his mouth and hastily swallowed. "It's coming out in tomorrow's paper. About the hit-and-run that took place in Morehead City. The man was one of Emery Cleveland's employees. Have you met Emery?"

"I have. He told me he was a distant relative. How is the man?"

"He'll survive. Still in the hospital, unfortunately. Be out of work a few months. But there wasn't very much information. I interviewed some of the people who saw it happen. The police haven't gotten anything concrete yet."

Cecily remembered the camera that had been hanging around his neck. "Are you a one-man show?"

"We have a full-time person that deals with the ads, distribution, and other odds and ends. And a couple of part-timers—high school kids who write articles on the local games. Now," he said, plunging his hands into his pockets. "What can I help you with?"

"I want to read some of your old articles that date back to the mid-seventies."

"Everything's on microfiche now. We make the film in one-month increments," he said as they passed the table with the camera above it.

They climbed a rickety set of stairs to an open loft. He led her to an area where papers were stacked to the rafters. And from there to filing cabinets that were filled with micro-fiche.

"Everything is labeled, so it shouldn't take you very long to find what you're looking for. I'm going to be downstairs if you need me. Eating those delicious scones you brought. Hey, mind if I interview you for our next issue?"

"Not at all."

Cecily pulled off her coat and hung it on the back of a chair. Then she started reading the labels on drawers until she located the microfiche she was interested in.

She located the date of the hurricane, then she turned on the machine and started to read. She'd gone through several sheets of fiche before coming across an article on her mother and the theft. There were suspiciously few articles. After she had left town, a couple of articles came out on it and then nothing. The three witches, as Pauline called them, were interviewed. Their assessment of her mother had been horribly skewed. After that, the articles suddenly focused on the town banding together to fix homes damaged by the storm.

Cecily copied the pages she needed and put the microfiche back in place. Things seemed to work on the honor system. There was a tray for her to put the money for the copies into. After leaving the payment, she made her way downstairs.

The editor was talking on the phone to someone and motioned for her to wait. She studied the office while he finished his conversation.

"Find everything you need?" he asked.

"I did, thanks."

He nodded.

"Who do I call for a subscription for the tea shop?" Cecily asked.

"You're talking to him."

"Oh. Well, I'd like four copies delivered each week." She already had a subscription for one copy.

Cecily handed him a card with her address.

"We'll bill you for it," he said and Cecily left, making her way back to the shop while trying to consider what her next step would be.

It seemed that her mother's past wasn't her only worry. Glenda held some secret close to her heart. Cecily knew that Glenda cared for Emery. What she felt might not be love, but whatever put that special light on her face was worth exploring.

Cecily was hurt by Glenda's refusal to share her past with her. What could have happened that was so bad that Glenda couldn't share it with her? Did she think Cecily would think less of her? There was nothing Glenda could have done that Cecily wouldn't forgive. This was the woman who had taken in her mother and Cecily when the two desperately needed help and had nowhere to turn.

Cecily would explore on her own. She sighed. She couldn't betray Glenda that way. She was left with no option but to wait until Glenda was willing to share with her.

Granny Grant was waiting for Cecily when she returned.

"Now," Granny said once they were settled. "Where did we leave off?"

"Sissieretta had moved into the house as housekeeper."

"Oh, right." Granny nodded.

"Let's see. Hannibal's mom hung in there a good long while. You know some people just linger on. Eventually he hired my mom to help out too so Sissieretta's mom wouldn't have to work such long hours. One would get her up in the morning, the other would stay till about eleven.

"His mama lived on the second floor where most of the bedrooms were. Anyway they'd push her on the deck so she could catch the breeze now and then. Heard tell she did grow to love the island. Hannibal would spend time out there reading to her. She loved the classics.

"But the island was hopping with shipwrecks, too. They tried and tried to get the government to build a lighthouse but had no success. So Hannibal and the town got together about building one. Nobody had money but him. So he hired folks to build it on his land." Granny cocked her head toward the tall black-and-white stripped structure, "Out yonder. But said he needed people to help out with the manning of it. About that time the Government folks came up with a little money to pay the keepers.

"Well, he claimed Sissieretta didn't like having to walk the inside stairs every time she wanted to leave. She liked her privacy, so he built those stairs that led up to the second and third floor.

"Now my mama wasn't no fool. She saw the looks Hannibal and Sissieretta were giving each other.

"About a year later, Sissieretta left. They were high and dry with no cook. So Hannibal hired a couple of day folks to come in and take care of the cooking for both the lighthouse keepers and for his family. Now and then he'd hire somebody to spend the nights but she had to stay on the second floor. The third floor was closed off. And he'd take these little trips out of town for a few weeks at a time. Never told nobody where he was going.

"Finally his mama up and died. He didn't have a need for all them folks hanging around the big house. He just kept the cooks and a lady to clean up once or twice a week. And he spent more time away from the island."

"Where did Sissieretta go?" Cecily asked.

"They said up Washington, D.C. way. Wrote her folks that she fell in love with this boy a month after she got there. Love at first sight she told 'em and they up and married. Her mama's sister lived there."

"Did they have children?"

"We have to git to that. Hold your sail. Everything in due time."

"When did she return to the island?"

"Granny," someone called out. "It's time to go."

"Wait, Granny," Cecily said. "I want to hear the rest."

"I've got a doctor's appointment." She patted Cecily's hand and took a last drink of tea. "Don't you worry none. Granny's coming back. But you be careful, you hear? You and your aunt, I see some dark clouds circling round ya'll. There's some mighty jealous folks about. They don't like the fact that she up and snatched up Paul Emery. He hasn't dated anyone since his wife died. Not for more than one date anyway. Now he's going 'round prancing like a young stallion." Granny laughed and Cecily couldn't help herself but smile too.

"But love does that to a man, even an old fool."

"He's not that old, Granny," Cecily said.

"You right about that. He's still got a lot of frisky life in him."

With a chuckle still in her throat and with Cecily's help, Granny Grant heaved herself up from the couch and then she was gone.

Cecily was left wondering about Sissieretta and where she and Hannibal's son came into the picture. Unless . . .

The camp was less than a third full, but all of the cabins had been reserved.

Ryan thought that a few of the new cabins would be complete by spring break, but the foreman just informed him some of the lumber hadn't arrived.

"How long will it be?" he asked.

The man rubbed his bearded chin. "No more than a week or so," he said.

"Didn't you check the materials when they arrived?"

"We did, but deliveries are hard to get this time of year."

The man looked as if he'd been working construction for decades. Ryan would expect such an answer from a less skilled laborer, but not someone of this man's experience.

"How long will the project be delayed?"

"Only a couple of weeks at the most."

Ryan supposed he should be grateful for that, knowing construction jobs sometimes ran months over schedule.

"All right," he said. "We'll make adjustments in our reservations. I want you know this is costing me money."

"We're sorry about that."

Even though space for tents was what the camp capitalized on because the price was cheaper and more people brought their own tents, Ryan had thought the cabins were a bonus. Most of the winter was pretty mild. Most days hovered above fifty although evenings were cooler. But there was the rare year where temperatures dropped low. And since vacations were already planned, people wanted a warm place to spend the night. The cabins would more than pay for themselves quickly if business progressed at the rate it was going now.

He guessed he'd have to talk to Delcia and Carter. The two of them were so wrapped in Delcia's pregnancy, they spent less time thinking about the business lately. But any plan Ryan made seemed to go well with them.

As Ryan walked toward the camp store he began to think of that big house of his. After his parents moved out, he'd have the place to himself. Four empty bedrooms to wander in.

Before LaToya had moved in she'd wanted the house painted, and trying to please his wife, Ryan had painted all the rooms. They weren't even colors he liked. But he realized that women were particular about the way their homes were decorated. He'd wanted her to feel at home in what he considered to be their home.

The week after she moved out, he'd had every room in

the house repainted to the original neutral color—had the furniture he'd placed in storage replace hers. He'd used what was left of his first paycheck to install new blinds and gave the curtains she'd purchased to Goodwill.

And here he was again, falling for a city woman. Cecily was skittish, though. He wondered if what he felt for her was real or just his need for closeness. Whatever the magnet, it wouldn't let him stay away.

But Ryan couldn't help thinking, what if Cecily hated living here? Cecily had more barriers to cross than LaToya. Cecily had a past to live down. Some people were willing to forget, others weren't. He hoped she was strong enough to weather the storms of those who saw her mother in her. He knew Cecily was looking to place the blame someplace else. But the incident had happened years ago.

Ryan wondered if he should just help her. Then she could make her decision, to stay or leave, and neither of them would be living in this limbo. He wouldn't be constantly barraged by this whirlwind of emotions.

Mark came down the path. He was getting off work. "Man, we haven't been fishing in a long time. I think it's time we took off for a day. I need a break."

"What's going on?" Ryan asked his cousin.

"I don't know. My old lady's driving me crazy, is all. I finally get my degree and she still wants to wait to marry." Mark sat on a log with his elbows on his knees, his hands dangling. "She just got a promotion and she says she doesn't have the time to plan a big wedding like she wants to. Who can figure women?"

Ryan shook his head. "I'm certainly not the one to talk to."

"Who is? I need a break, man."

"Okay. Saturday, we'll do some fishing."

"You mean it?"

"Sure. I haven't gone this winter. You know how I love to fish."

"Hope it doesn't rain. With my luck lately, it probably will."

"Hey, don't be a pessimist."

"That Cecily sure is nice, for a city girl. Folks still talking about that Valentine's Day thing."

"She's okay. I didn't know you were moonlighting."

"Mia's working such long hours I need something to keep me out of trouble."

"I can understand that." Mia Samuels and Mark had dated for years.

"I'm supposed to be taking pictures at that grandmother, granddaughter tea. Ranetta coming?"

"Mom wouldn't miss it."

"You all spoil her. She's going to be a rotten something one day."

"Not my Rae, Rae." Ryan remembered he hadn't spent very much time with her lately. Perhaps he'd spend Sunday with her. Let her play on the beach or something after church. Get her a hot chocolate. She liked hot chocolate.

"Well, man. I've got to get going."

"Check you later."

Ryan stood there a few more minutes. What had hurt him most in his divorce was that after everything was done, LaToya had had an abortion without telling him. He would have kept their child and raised it alone and she knew that. She'd done it to hurt him because he couldn't change into the man she really wanted him to be. He'd never marry another woman who couldn't accept him as he was. He knew women were the ones with the maternal instincts, but he wanted children, too. The island was a wonderful place to raise them. He'd had the best of childhoods. He wanted to offer that to children of his own.

It would not be easy trusting another woman after the number LaToya played on him. The abortion had been her final revenge.


That afternoon, Cecily went to Pauline Anderson's home to talk to her about the three women. She'd called earlier asking if it was okay for her to visit.

"Cecily, come on in," Pauline said. "It's so nice to see you. I hope you don't mind Willow Mae. She was visiting."

"I don't mind. Hello, Mrs. Anderson."

Willow Mae grunted a reply.

Cecily sat at the table with the women. Willow Mae had baked some delicious cookies and Cecily feared she was making a pig of herself over them.

"I wanted to talk to you about the other three women who were in the room the day that money arrived."

"Who is she talking about?" Willow Mae asked.

"Taylor, Shelly, and Ruby," Pauline said.

"Oh, the three witches."

"Why are they called that?"

" 'Cause it's the way they act. Always were a tight, snooty little bunch."

Cecily pulled out her pad and pen and made a notation.

"You going to write everything down?" Willow Mae asked. "I don't know if I can go along with that."

"It's for my eyes only. I need to be able to go back and compare notes."

"Ought to let sleeping dogs lie, I say. But nobody's asking me."

"It's important that my mom is cleared of wrongdoing," Cecily said, and then added, "Did any of the women begin to spend more money than usual after the hurricane?"

"Not really. You already know Ruby's husband died in the same hurricane your father died in. That was two years before. You were only one at the time. Ruby came into a little insurance money, enough to pay the mortgage off, but not much else."

"I remember her complaining about him not getting enough insurance," Willow Mae said. "Women let men see to things back in those days. Not like today. Which is a good thing, to my way of thinking. But she's always had to scrimp, at least until her daughter got out of high school."

"I remember Ruby had put enough aside to send her to nursing school."

"She's a nurse? I didn't know she worked with Dr. Grant."

"She doesn't. She works at the hospital in Morehead City. Takes the ferry over."

"She hates that shift work, but it pays more money than she can make here."

"What about the other two women?" Cecily asked.

Willow Mae squinted through her glasses. "You know all three women worked at the bank back then."

"Taylor has always been a meticulous spender."

"Tightfisted with a dollar," Willow Mae said. "Holds on to a penny so tight it'll holler before she gives it up. Drives her car at least fifteen years before she trades it in. It turns into an antique right in her yard. Drives Wally nuts. Worries him to death about his prices. He's always got to cut them for her. Don't think that boy ever made a cent of profit off a' her."

"What about her house? When did she buy it?"

"It's her mama's place. She inherited it after her mama passed on. Stayed right there with her, too, till the end. Never moved out."

"What about the last woman?" Willow Mae seemed to do most of the talking even though she had warned Cecily to let sleeping dogs lie.

"That's Shelly. She's the only one of the bunch that's married. Got a nice husband. They do all right, just like the rest of us. Don't seem to live above their means. They aren't rich, but just live like regular island folks."

*Well, jeez.* That left her nowhere. Exactly where she was when she came to talk to Pauline.

"One of them stole that money. There has to be something weird or unusual about one of them."

"The whole bunch is unusual. But that doesn't make them thieves."

"I can't see Taylor stealing anything. What will she spend it on?"

"She'll hoard it, like she does with her paycheck now," Willow Mae said.

"Could the three of them have been in it together? Could they have tricked my mother into turning her head and made a switch?"

"Anything is possible."

"Ruby hated your mother," Willow Mae muttered.

"Why?"

"She clung to the hope that your daddy would return to her. But he met up with your mom at A and T. That nixed any chance for her right then and there. I remember them arguing during that first Christmas when he returned. She was hurt."

"Took her a long time to get over your dad."

"But, Willow Mae, they weren't serious. He thought of them as being friends more than anything else. He told her that in high school. If she put more into it, it was her doing, not his. He never misled her."

"But she put high hopes on him. That he would change his mind and marry her. You wouldn't know all this. You were away to college yourself when all this was going on."

"Back to the robbery. She left the room with me. She couldn't have done it," Pauline assured her.

"So that leaves the other two women."

"I could see Taylor knocking her in the head and taking it," Willow Mae said.

"Nobody hurt her."

"I know, but I could see that old bat doing it. Always running her mouth. Got something to say about everything. Makes me sick sometimes. Sometimes I want to knock her in the head myself."

"Willow Mae," Pauline sighed, shaking her head.

"I'm not the only one, either. I know she's gotten on your last nerve a few times."

"I can't dispute that," Pauline said as they heard a car careen into the yard. "Must be Ryan. Nobody drives as crazy as that boy."

"Men keep the wild in them for a long time," Willow Mae said. "Leave him alone. I remember Clay driving like that, especially when you weren't in the car with him. Had Delcia's and Ryan's heads jumping in the seats. They enjoyed every blame minute of it too."

Pauline looked horrified at her sister-in-law.

"Get real, Pauline. You're the only one who didn't know. Men are like that."

Cecily wasn't thinking about the kids and women any

longer. She took a quick sharp breath as Ryan entered wearing his beige Camp Coree jacket with neat blue stenciling stitching the name on the front and displayed in huge letters across the back. The jacket was open revealing a green camp shirt beneath and emphasizing the breadth of his strong shoulders.

"Good afternoon, ladies," he said. But Cecily swore that his eyes lingered on her longer than it should have, and she loved the sexy tilt of his mouth.

"Came home for food?" Willow Mae asked. "I don't know why you don't come by my place sometimes. I cook lunch every day. Not that Harry eats it half the time. He's always going to Wanda's place."

"I'll come by for lunch tomorrow. You going to have something good for me?"

"Don't I always, you rascal? I'll fix my clam and conch chowder."

Ryan smiled that sexy smile that made Cecily's toes curl.

"Git old and you young folks don't know how to visit anymore."

Ryan rounded the table and hugged his aunt. "You know that's not true, Aunt Willow Mae. I visit you all the time, now, don't I?"

"Maybe you do sometimes. But it's not often enough to suit me."

"I'll do better. Promise," he said, plucking two cookies from the dish.

"I'll forgive you if you bring Cecily by for one of my famous island meals. It's time she got some good island cooking. There's none better than mine."

"You're right there. I'll bring her by," he promised and made his way into the kitchen. "Anything here to eat?" he asked his mother.

Pauline sighed and started to get up. "I didn't cook today. I ate out. I thought you'd do the same."

"Don't get up," he said. "I'll fix myself a sandwich."

"You were near Cecily's place. Why didn't you get something from there?"

His answer was a shrug.

"I appreciate you ladies helping me with this. I think it's time I go." Cecily gathered her papers.

"Any time. If I remember something, I'll call you," Willow Mae said.

"Please visit sometime," Pauline said.

"I will."

"I think I blocked you in. I'll let you out." Ryan opened the door for her and they left together. But in the yard Cecily saw that his truck wasn't blocking her at all.

"You scoundrel," she said as they descended the back porch stairs and walked through the garden path to her car. The very air around her seemed electrified.

"The only reason I'm here is you." He gathered her in his arms. "I went to your shop for a late lunch and you weren't there." His lips brushed against hers as he spoke. It felt so good to be in his arms that Cecily didn't give it a second thought that his mother and Willow Mae might be pressing their noses against the window.

It seemed forever since she'd last seen him yet only a couple of days had passed. She inhaled the fresh scent of him as he held her close to him and rubbed her back. The gentle massage sent currents of desire through her.

"I feel better now," he finally said when he released her.

Cecily pursed her lips. "So do I," she said, rubbing her hands up his back. He smiled. Pleasure radiated outward. There was something totally wicked about his smile that sent her blood boiling through her veins.

"I want to kiss you again, but I'm afraid we have an audience."

"What?" Cecily asked and glanced toward the house. Willow Mae and Pauline were smiling at them. When the ladies noticed Cecily looking, Willow Mae waved. Ryan rolled his eyes heavenward. Cecily waved back.

"I'll be by tonight, okay?"

"Sure."

"Might be late. After I get off work."

"That's okay. Give me a chance to wind down after I close the shop."

She opened the car door and got in, tucking her purse on the floor under her legs.

Ryan watched her as she turned around and drove down the road. She could see him through her rearview mirror. She didn't take a complete breath until she had driven around a curve and he was out of sight. The taste of him still lingered in her mind as she drove the winding road to the shop. An inner voice warned her to move cautiously with Ryan. *Don't forget he's on the rebound.* Only half Cecily's mind listened to the warning. It was a long time before she thought of the three wicked women again.

With the information Willow Mae and Pauline had given her, it wouldn't be easy to isolate the one who had stolen the money. She knew two things—first that Ruby couldn't have done it. She had left the shop with Pauline. The two other women were left. Maybe it was the bigmouth Taylor who liked to run everybody's business. Her mother had been an outsider just as Cecily felt. They wouldn't have thought twice about setting her up especially after they probably blamed her for taking their friend's beau away from them, never mind that he never thought the relationship was serious.

Which woman could it be? Cecily wondered. And how on earth was she going to uncover the trail of the money?

When Cecily arrived at the shop, Emery's truck was in the yard. A couple of cars were there, too. Emery sat angrily looking at the food on his plate.

"Hi, Emery," Cecily said.

"Hey."

"I'll go relieve Glenda and she can eat lunch with you."

"Thank you." Some life finally returned to his face but it didn't take away the anger.

Cecily hung her coat in the back room and washed her hands. Then she went to the kitchen where Glenda was fixing a sandwich, her mouth pressed into a straight line.

"I'll take over, Glenda, so you can eat with Emery."

"I told him I wasn't going to talk to him. Go ahead out. I can handle this."

"What are you so angry about?"

"I told him I couldn't see him anymore. Stubborn man, won't take no for an answer. Wants to know why, like I have to have a convincing reason for turning him down."

She handed the sandwiches to Cecily and told her which table to take them to. Cecily delivered the food, asking the customers if she could get anything else for them. They were satisfied so Cecily escaped to the kitchen. Glenda was peering at Emery through a crack in the door.

"Why won't he just eat that sandwich and go?"

"Because he's fallen for you." During the last few weeks, even she could see how taken he was. "He deserves an explanation. I'd like to know too, but you don't owe it to me. He's a good man. Don't treat him like that."

Glenda's face crumbled. She shook her head in a tired manner. "If I told him the truth, he wouldn't go. I can't tell him."

"Ah, Glenda. You like him too."

"Too much to hold on to him," she added with a slight gesture of defiance.

A quick disturbing sensation knotted inside Cecily. "You're scaring me. What is it?"

"I'd like to know, too." Emery leaned into the doorjamb with his hands thrust in his pockets. The angry expression was still present on his face.

"You can't—"

"Glenda, I can handle the tables. You go talk with Emery."

"I—" Cecily noted the wave of apprehension sweeping through Glenda.

"Please, Glenda. You have to. You can't leave him like this. It isn't fair."

She blew out a long breath, then untied her apron. She went to the back room to get her coat and she and Emery headed for the beach.

Cecily had had such hopes for the two of them. And she still worried about Glenda. Cecily peered at them one last time. They were both stiff as they neared the water.

# Chapter 8

It was a pleasant day, but Glenda couldn't appreciate the calm water, the lack of a breeze, the hardy winter birds floating on the air. She had gone and done something stupid like falling for the guy walking angrily beside her. Another good man. Neither of them, Cecily or Emery, understood that she couldn't take the responsibility of something horrible happening to him. She wouldn't be responsible for his death.

They stopped near the water's edge. Usually the water relaxed her as she watched it from her balcony window. She loved watching the ebb and flow. But today it wasn't relaxing at all.

"Look at me," Glenda," Emery said.

Glenda closed her eyes. She didn't want to look at him for fear of seeing a mirror of her need in him. But she couldn't avoid his gaze. He cupped her chin and gently tugged her toward him.

"Did I move too fast for you, sweet cakes?"

How could she hold on to her determination when he called her by that name? Glenda closed her eyes again.

"Look at me, will you?" She felt the whisper of his breath on her.

She opened her eyes and gazed at the robin's-egg-blue sky. "No, Emery, you didn't."

"I did something you didn't like."

She inhaled deeply. "No, Emery. Can't you just—"

"You don't like the way I smell."

She laughed because he always smelled good when they were together. That man took more showers than anyone she knew. "That's not it. I already—"

"Okay, then. You don't like what I do for a living."

"You make a perfectly wonderful living doing exactly what you love to do. How can anyone disapprove with that?"

"Let's see now. If you say you don't like me I'm not going to believe you."

"Oh, so you can't accept that every woman isn't enthralled with you?"

"I know I don't knock every woman off her feet. I only want to knock you off yours."

"Damn it, Emery." His reasonable manner annoyed her.

He pulled her close. Lightly he brushed a loose braid from her cheek, "I want the truth. If you tell me that you don't want to see me again I want a reason, one that makes sense." He kissed her on the side of her mouth. She tightened her lips together. "Because you've absolutely knocked me off my feet. You've turned my boat on its head."

Then he covered her mouth with his and this time she couldn't resist the hunger of his kiss. She opened her mouth to him and their tongues mingled as one. She felt his hands on her, driving her insane with need. She had tried to keep things going at a slow pace. But her body wanted more. She couldn't give Emery more. She was out of her mind, letting him sweet-talk her into wanting him.

She tore her mouth away from him and stepped back from the circle of his arms, her anguish almost overcoming her control.

There was a calculating gleam in his eyes that broke her resistance. "You want me as much as I want you," he said.

"But I'm not going to have you. It's over. Believe me. I don't want to see you again, Emery. And if you don't leave me alone, I'll leave Coree Island." She turned and ran back to the cottage, but she bypassed the tea shop for her own second-floor apartment.

She fumbled the keys out of her pocket, slammed into the room and leaned against the door. She expected to hear Emery banging on the door. She wouldn't open it. She wouldn't be able to say no to him again. She waited and waited. But he didn't come. Tugging out of her coat, she dropped it on the chair and ran to her room. Cecily could handle the shop for a while. Her misery was so acute that it was a physical pain, as she gave in to her emotions and burst into tears.

Emery was the best thing that had happened to her in thirty-odd years and she couldn't act on her feelings for him because loving her could very well mean the end for him.


Cecily was looking forward to Ryan's visit that night. She hated to admit that she enjoyed his company, perhaps too much. Ryan was on the rebound and there was nothing stable about dating a man who'd just lost his love. She knew she was just his thrill for the interim. She couldn't afford to depend on him too much.

Who was she fooling? Obviously herself. She was so mixed up she didn't know which end was up. But she recognized that she was beginning to depend on him as the significant other in her life as she lit candles around the room. The temperature outside had warmed to a comfortable sixty-five degrees, but at night it would drop to the low forties. She envisioned herself wrapped in Ryan's arms and him taking the chill away.

A quick peek at the clock told her it was almost nine. She went to the kitchenette for snacks she prepared earlier and set the plate on the sofa table. She'd wait until he arrived before heating the quiche and scones. Ryan worked long hours. His mother had said he often ate on the run or skipped meals altogether.

She retrieved an ice bucket and filled it, then wedged a bottle of Chardonnay into the center and placed it on the table to cool, wondering what she was opting for tonight.

She realized that they couldn't go on as casual friends forever. They were on the edge of taking this thing to another level. She wondered if she was ready for that.

Then she heard the doorbell and her heart stopped beating. It rang a second time before she sprang into motion. She straightened her sweater, made sure it wasn't caught at her back the way sweaters tend to do; then she opened the door.

He wore a soft leather jacket, jeans, and a sweater that emphasized the breadth of his shoulders, the strength of his torso. Her breath caught and held. He came to her and kissed her, almost took her breath away. He smelled clean and fresh mixed with that male essence that was all his own with a touch of woodsy cologne. But she wasn't thinking about how clean he smelled. All she could think about was him and his strength, the male power that had tilted her on her axis. That sent her into tailspins every time she saw him. He lifted his head. Smiled. She breathed again. Barely.

"Hello," he said, the deep timbre of his voice rumbling through her body as if he'd caressed her with his powerful hands.

"Hi," she breathed as if she'd lost her senses and she'd be the first to admit that she had. Lost every bit of sense she had over him.

He shucked his jacket and she held it against her as she carried it to the closet. She took a moment to get her bearings as she hung it up. These emotions were for teenagers. Not for grown women acting like a fool. What kind of magic had he spun over her?

She turned. He sat on the couch nibbling on the hors d'oeuvres. She wondered what he thought when he kissed her. Did he wonder if she was as dishonest as he believed her mother to be? What would he do if he discovered she'd dated a married man, even though she hadn't known at the time that he'd been married? He didn't believe in her mother's innocence. Why would he believe the daughter was innocent?

She watched him pick up another hors d'oeuvre and pop it into his mouth. When he kissed her, when he touched her, she knew very well he wasn't thinking about anything more than making out. A man didn't have to believe in a woman to have sex with her. And if any creature exuded sex, it was definitely Ryan Anderson. And as difficult as she found it to resist him, she knew she was setting herself up for heartbreak and failure. Yet, she was compelled to see this through.

Ryan had connected with her more than any man had ever before. More so than that louse Trevor, and certainly more than the others before him. It would be easy enough for her to tell him about her past. But why should she? The past had nothing to do with today. She'd left all that behind her and begun with a clean slate. And he had no way of finding out the truth. There was nothing she could do about the past anyway.

Yes, she'd dated a married man after he'd lied to her and told her he was single. She couldn't make people believe otherwise, but the situation with her mother was different. Proof existed someplace. It was a matter of her finding where.

She glanced at Ryan again. He ate like a man who hadn't eaten in days.

"I'm going to heat up the other hors d'oeuvres," she said, pointing in that direction. "I'll just . . ." She cleared her throat. "I'll go get them."

"Okay. Don't be long, now."

She sailed out of the living room.

Ryan watched her leave and wondered if he stirred her nearly as much as she'd tumbled his world. As much as he didn't believe she would be here for the long haul, he couldn't stay away from her. He decided not to worry about the future. Wasn't a damn thing he could do about it anyway. Just wait for what life brought him.

Ryan picked up a finger sandwich and popped it into his mouth. Cecily returned and he watched her glide effortlessly across the floor. The sweater hugging her breasts captured his attention, almost stole his appetite until she passed the platter before him and he remembered he hadn't eaten since lunch.

"Looks delicious."

"I hope you're hungry," Cecily said, putting the platter on the table and sitting close beside him.

He was hungry, all right, and food wasn't his key desire. He smelled Cecily's sweet perfume. It wasn't cloying. The scent was just right. It made him want her more than he already did. More than he should have.

What was he going to do about this woman? He didn't know how he'd get her to fall for him as deeply as he was falling for her. He couldn't tell her a lie that he believed in her mother's innocence. He didn't lie. He laid out the truth and let what happened happen. He could only hope that the truth wouldn't stand between them.

Glenda had watched Ryan walk the steps to Cecily's apartment. She was still tapping her foot waiting for Emery. She didn't hear a peep from upstairs and could only wonder what was going on. She'd told Emery not to come by. But he wouldn't listen. Only said he was coming and hung up.

He was one bullheaded man.

An hour and a half later, after he'd said he was coming in fifteen minutes, Glenda heard Emery's truck pull into the drive. He was late and definitely not on her good side.

Glenda hastened to the couch and sat down, thinking she shouldn't let him in. But that scoundrel would stand there and knock on the door all night if she ignored him.

He might be making a pest of himself, but she didn't have to act as if the sight of him just thrilled her to pieces. She plucked up a magazine as if she'd been reading it all evening, instead of waiting for him. She straightened up her clothes and ran a hand over her braids.

Her heart was beating like a jackhammer. Glenda put a hand to her chest and willed her heart to slow down as if the deed would be done by sheer willpower. Then she picked up her magazine again and flipped to a page. Right then she didn't even know which magazine she was thumbing through.

Emery knocked on the door.

She tucked her pillow in back of her and settled more

# An important message from the ARABESQUE Editor

Dear Arabesque Reader,

Because you've chosen to read one of our Arabesque romance novels, we'd like to say "thank you"! And, as a special way to thank you, we've selected four more of the books you love so well to send you for FREE!

Please enjoy them with our compliments, and thank you for continuing to enjoy Arabesque...the soul of romance.

Karen Thomas
Senior Editor,
Arabesque Romance Novels

Check out our website at
www.arabesquebooks.com

SPECIAL OFFER!
4 FREE BOOKS

ARABESQUE®
A PRODUCT OF
★BET BOOKS™

# 3 QUICK STEPS
## TO RECEIVE YOUR "THANK YOU" GIFT
## FROM THE EDITOR

Send this card back and you'll receive 4 FREE Arabesque novels! The introductory shipment of 4 Arabesque novels – a $23.96 value – is yours absolutely FREE!

There's no catch. You're under no obligation to buy anything. You'll receive your introductory shipment of 4 Arabesque novels absolutely FREE (plus $1.99 to offset the costs of shipping & handling). And you don't have to make any minimum number of purchases—not even one!

We hope that after receiving your books you'll want to remain an Arabesque subscriber. But the choice is yours to continue or cancel, anytime at all! So why not take us up on our invitation to receive 4 Arabesque Romance Novels, with no risk of any kind. You'll be glad you did!

Call us
TOLL-FREE
at 1-800-770-1963

## THE EDITOR'S "THANK YOU" GIFT INCLUDES:

- 4 books absolutely FREE (plus $1.99 for shipping and handling)
- A FREE newsletter, *Arabesque Romance News*, filled with author interviews, book previews, special offers, and more!
- No risks or obligations. You're free to cancel whenever you wish... with no questions asked.

## BOOK CERTIFICATE

*Yes!* Please send me 4 FREE Arabesque novels (plus $1.99 for shipping & handling). I understand I am under no obligation to purchase any books, as explained on the back of this card.

Name _____

Address _____ Apt. _____

City _____ State _____ Zip _____

Telephone ( ) _____

Signature _____

Offer limited to one per household and not valid to current subscribers. All orders subject to approval. Terms, offer, & price subject to change. Offer valid only in the U.S.

AN023A

*Thank you!*

Accepting the four introductory books for FREE (plus $1.99 to offset the cost of shipping & handling) places you under no obligation to buy anything. You may keep the books and return the shipping statement marked "cancelled". If you do not cancel, about a month later we will send 4 additional Arabesque novels, and you will be billed the preferred subscriber's price of just $4.00 per title. That's $16.00 for all 4 books for a savings of 33% off the cover price (Plus $1.99 for shipping and handling). You may cancel at any time, but if you choose to continue, every month we'll send you 4 more books, which you may either purchase at the preferred discount price. . . or return to us and cancel your subscription.

THE ARABESQUE ROMANCE CLUB: HERE'S HOW IT WORKS

ARABESQUE ROMANCE BOOK CLUB
P.O. Box 5214
Clifton NJ 07015-5214

PLACE
STAMP
HERE

comfortably in the couch. She didn't even look up from the article that she didn't have a clue of what it was about.

He knocked again.

"Glenda," he said peeking through the glass door to which she'd left the curtains ajar. She sneaked enough of a peek over the top of the magazine to see that one of his hands was pressed against the doorjamb. He had a serious expression on his face. Her heart nearly melted. But she reminded herself that what she was doing was necessary. She never should have gotten mixed up with him in the first place. She had relaxed so much on this island that she'd forgotten her precautions.

"I can see you from here. You're not even subtle," he said. "Open up."

She flipped a page. "Go away. I'm busy."

He banged on the door again. "I'll stand here and knock all night if I have to. We're getting to the bottom of this once and for all."

"It's already settled." Glenda pressed her lips together and glared at him. He crossed his arms and glowered right back. This was turning into a staring match. Finally she got up, tossed the magazine aside and stomped to the door.

"You may as will come in," she called out, "since you don't know how to take a hint." She retraced her steps back to the couch and picked up her magazine.

The door opened slowly. Glenda turned a page in her magazine.

Emery cleared his throat. "I meant to come earlier."

"You didn't have to come at all." Glenda knew she was sounding like a witch but she couldn't help it.

Emery sighed and Glenda had to look away from the fatigue evident on his face. God, she hoped she hadn't put it there. But at least he'd get over that. There were some things a person could never get over.

"I got held up. One of the boats had a motor quit on him. Got in later than planned."

"Did they fix it?" Glenda asked, concerned.

"Yeah, they made it in safely."

He wore a flattering suede jacket. But she didn't offer to

take it from him. He sighed, shrugged out of it, and placed it on the back of a chair.

Glenda continued to flip through the pages in her magazine.

Emery hid one of his hands behind his back.

"Is it late?" she asked. "What time is it?" She made a show of glancing at her watch. "My goodness. I got so engrossed in this magazine, I didn't realize."

"Must be a good article."

"Oh, it is." She went back to staring at the lines. "I want to finish it."

She heard footsteps approach. She didn't look up.

"I hope these make up for my tardiness."

Glenda peered over the top of her magazine again and almost dropped it on her lap. Emery held a bunch of gorgeous lilies in his hands. It took everything in her not to come undone. But she had to be strong for both of them.

"I wouldn't lie to you, Glenda. I know lots of men lie about things. I'm not one of them. I really did have to wait for the boat to come in. I was worried. The water gets rocky sometimes around here and very unsafe. Storms come up out of nowhere. You must have heard about that. I couldn't come see you looking any kind of way. I had to shower first."

Glenda began to thaw. He looked earnest. He didn't have a clue.

She wasn't a witch and she couldn't pretend what she didn't feel. "The flowers are lovely. You know they're my favorite."

"I know. I knew I needed a lot to make up for my tardiness."

He was dressed in navy slacks, which cast his thighs in a heart-pounding light, and a sweater. His strong arms reached to long-fingered hands. He took her hand in his and brought it to his lips and kissed the back with a warm kiss.

Glenda was tired of having to be strong. She needed to be there for Cecily. Her brother was dead. Her best friend was dead. And she was treating the best thing that had happened to her in decades like trash. She couldn't do it.

But she couldn't hold on either. She was nearly sixty and she felt like a teenager without a clue of what path to take.

She'd done the right thing in letting Emery go. And everything would have worked out, too, if the stubborn goat would have just left her alone. But here he stood with the damn lilies after she'd treated him like dirt. He was still treating her tenderly. Not like a weak man, because she knew of the strength he possessed. But he was acting like a man whose shoulder a person could lean on in hard times. And she couldn't do it anymore. She couldn't act as if she didn't have a heart. Not in the face of his kindness.

The next thing she did was something she hadn't expected a nearly sixty-year-old fool to do. She burst into tears.

She felt the cushion dip as he slid into the seat beside her.

"Now, now. It can't be that bad."

She nodded her head up and down. "It is."

"Well, now. You aren't married, are you?"

She sniffed. "You know I'm not."

"You aren't dying, are you?"

"No. And will you stop the twenty questions?"

"Well, anything else we can work with."

"No, we can't. I've been trying to tell you. And you are just . . ."

"I know. Stubborn. I'll say it for you."

The strange surge of affection she felt frightened her. "So damn good, too. Too good."

"Oh, never that, sweet cakes. Never too good for my sweet cakes."

She laughed at being called the silly name. But she loved it when he said it. It was kind of sexy somehow.

"Now what is it that has you so upset? Old Emery here will fix it up for you."

He didn't look old at all. She never asked him how old he was. She frowned up at him. She knew she was an unsightly mess. She did not cry pretty.

He took a white handkerchief out of his pocket and wiped her eyes.

"How old are you?" she asked.

"You just getting around to that?"

"It's good to know."

"I'm fifty-three."

"What? You're too young for me."

"Age is just a number."

"It's more than that." She pulled herself away slightly. He tugged her close. "Now tell me the problem."

How was she going to let a younger man deal with this thing?

"I can't. You've got to go."

He threw up his hands. "How old are you, so we can get this thing settled? You're just throwing up more barriers and I'm not having it, Glenda. My patience is growing thin."

"I'm fifty-eight. Five years older than you."

"If you don't stop being silly ... The way you were talking you had me thinking you must have had four face-lifts and were pushing eighty."

Glenda hit him. "Don't be cute. You're still young."

"We aren't going to be silly about five years. You're using age as a delaying tactic. I want to know what's going on. Right now. It's worrying me. I can't sleep for thinking about it. You owe me that much."

Glenda sighed. She couldn't delay any longer. "Thirty-three years ago, I was a social worker."

He stroked her arm for encouragement.

"I worked on an abuse case where the husband did horrible, unspeakable things to his wife. I took over this new case. The old caseworker had tried for more than a year to get her to leave him. And then she died. Well, the wife finally decided to leave him and I put her in contact with people who could assist her. She needed a new identity. You know the authorities didn't take spousal abuse as seriously then as they do now.

"Anyway, she and the children left when he went on a trip to visit his family. When he returned he came looking for me. He blamed me for his wife's disappearance although she'd made the decision on her own. She didn't want to put up with his abuse any longer. And you know had she been my case from the very beginning I would have tried to convince her to leave. Women shouldn't put up with abuse.

"Anyway, he claimed since I'd taken something special from him, he was going to do the same to me, that he was going to be watching me. Every step I made. It frightened me. And for months I was on pins and needles expecting something to happen. I was alone so there wasn't anyone to hurt. But I didn't feel comfortable living there. So I started sending out résumés to other cities. I landed a job in Los Angeles. As time passed I started to relax. Then I met this guy. His name was Jimmy. We fell in love."

Emery must have sensed the change in her because he held her closer. "Go on."

"We planned to get married. One day . . ." Her voice cracked. After all this time it was still almost impossible to talk about.

"I'm here, honey."

Glenda nodded. "One day I went to his apartment. We were to marry in two days. We were celebrating our last night of freedom because he was having a bachelor's party the next night." Glenda squeezed her eyes tightly. And started again. "I'd planned to surprise him. I brought over a bag of groceries. We'd spent a lot of money for the wedding so we needed to save. I planned to fix dinner and have it ready by the time he arrived." Glenda cried out. "Oh, God."

Emery pulled her closer to him, stroked her arm. "Go on. You need to talk about it, sweetheart."

"I went in and—and he was—it was so awful."

Emery let her catch her breath.

"I don't know how another human being can do that to somebody and—he was sick in the worst kind of way. He'd sliced Jimmy to ribbons. He left a note saying 'I got you back. I'll always be watching you.' "

Then she turned to Emery with tears in her eyes. "Don't you see? He could already know. I can't live with being responsible for your death. I'm sorry. I never should have gotten involved with you. I was so irresponsible. It has to end right now. I can't see you again."

"Stop it right now. Calm down, sweetheart. Are you trying to tell me he got out of jail?"

"He never *went* to jail. He disappeared. They never found him. He could be here right now—on this island."

"We're going to deal with this. And I'm not leaving you. That was thirty-some years ago. He's started a new life. He's forgotten about you by now."

"He murdered Jimmy six years after his wife left him. If he carried his anger that long, he could still be after anyone I dated."

"Have you seen him since?"

"No. I took on a new identity. Changed my name, my Social Security number. But that doesn't mean he can't find me."

"I doubt he even knows where you are."

"Don't you understand, He's a sick man. I can't take the chance." Panic was rioting within her.

"You've got to calm down, honey. Because I'm not going anywhere. Do you have a picture of him?"

Glenda nodded.

"Then I'll give it to the sheriff and a few key people. If he shows up they'll get him."

"He won't look the same after all this time."

"He's not coming. If you made all those changes, he's not going to know where you are. Trust me, honey."

"But—"

His face was full of strength, shining with dazzling determination. "Trust me. He isn't a threat."

Glenda leaned her head against his chest, felt the reassuring rhythm of his heartbeat. "You are so bullheaded."

"And you like it."

Lifting her head, she held his face between her hands. "I couldn't bear for anything to happen to you."

"Nothing's going to happen. Trust me." He leaned down and kissed her softly. Because right now she needed gentleness. After the long kiss he tucked her head against his chest and held her.

"Thank you," she said.

"For what?"

"For being the wonderful scoundrel you are and for the lilies. They're absolutely lovely. Did you have dinner?"

He shook his head. "Couldn't eat. I was too worried about you."

"It just so happens, I have something warming on the stove waiting just for you."

"I'm mighty appreciative."

But Glenda didn't get up immediately. Emery took her in his arms and kissed her gently. He was some kind of man. Her kind of man, she thought as she gave herself up to his touch, his kiss. His hands roamed her body, sending her into a mass of sensations. She didn't know whether she was coming or going. All she knew was he was stealing her energy, her strength, her will to walk, to talk. All she wanted was as much as she could get of this strong, sensitive man. His kisses, his touch stole her will to stay away for safety's sake.

Glenda was a strong woman, but right now she was lost in Emery's strong arms, in his powerful kiss that stole her senses and turned her to mush.

"Let's forget about dinner. I'll dine on you."

"Ummmm. Music to my ears," Glenda said.

"Are you ready for me? For us?" he asked her.

She peered deeply into his eyes. "Oh, yes. I'm ready." She was more ready now than she'd been for decades. She felt as if every experience in the past had been leading to this one man, to this occasion.

He kissed her again, deeply, ran a hand over her. His fingers were warm and sure against her skin, playing her like a fine guitar, testing its strength against the notes of her skin, pulling deep sensations, eliciting earth-shattering reactions, drilling her to him.

"Which way?" he whispered against her neck.

Glenda stood on shaky legs. Led him to the bedroom where she'd installed the trusty king-size bed she'd had for twenty years. She'd purchased new mattresses, though. She didn't have time to think about that because he was nibbling on her neck.

"You're a fine-tasting treat, Glenda."

"Ummm. You're sure feeling fine, Emery. I love your lips." He lifted off her caftan and stood stock-still.

"I love a woman who's prepared." Glenda didn't have a stitch on beneath. He stretched her out on the middle of the bed. His mouth did wonders all over her, had Glenda singing a song that was too long in coming. It seemed like hours and her skin felt on fire when he finally made his way on top of her. First sliding on a prophylactic, he slid into her. She clutched on to him as if she'd never let him go. He felt so damn good, she cried out, unable to hold her emotions in. They rocked to a musical tune that was all their own. This man knew how to move. Knew how to give her every possible sensation. They moved until she sang out in release. His was close behind.

As Emery held Glenda in his arms, she wasn't prepared for, "Marry me, Glenda."

"What?" She propped herself up on her elbow. The lights shone in from the lighthouse. He tucked his hands underneath his head and looked at her with a serious expression on his face.

"Marry me."

"You don't even know me."

"I know all I need to know." He lifted a hand and smoothed back her braids.

"How can you say that?"

"I know when it's right. I knew with my second wife. I know as sure as I'm breathing that it's right now. I'm a for-keeps kind of man. I don't play games. I want to live with you the rest of my life."

"You're not doing a substitute game on me, are you? Pretending that I'm your first love."

"I'm hoping you're my last love. I know who you are. You're nothing like my first wife, or my second. I love you for you, for the joy you, Glenda Fayard, bring me."

Glenda shook her head and repeated herself, sounding like a broken record. "You don't even know me."

She sighed and lay back on his arm. He cuddled her against him. She hadn't felt this secure in a very long time.

But she wanted to be sure. And for an excuse she said, "Cecily needs me right now."

"Ryan's falling for her. She's got relatives. We'll all look out for her."

"I know. It's just . . ." She sighed. Ran her hands up his arm—strong, hairy arm—smoothed her face against it.

"Be honest with me."

"I've been single all my life. I'm . . ."

"What?"

"Damn it, I'm scared."

He laughed. One of those big, belly laughs. Glenda punched at him. But the effort was weak at best. She wouldn't hurt him for the world. He was one of the gentlest men she'd ever met. Strong too.

"Scared is okay. Marriage is a big step."

"Ruby isn't going to like this. She'll be even a worst enemy to Cecily."

"Who gives a damn what she likes? I don't like her. I love you, you crazy woman. I must be out of my mind."

"You're taking your proposal back?"

"Hell no. I want to marry you, and you're bringing up all these crazy reasons. But we'll work on that. As long as you say yes."

"Ohhhh."

"Say yes, Glenda."

"Yes, Glenda," she parroted facetiously.

"Come on, woman." He tickled her in the sides. Glenda was very ticklish and fell in a fit of laughter and squirming. This man brought more joy to her. She'd better not let this get away.

"All right. I'll marry you."

"When?"

"We have to decide everything tonight?"

"Yeah, we do."

"Let's not rush into anything. Give me a little time, all right?"

"Tell me you don't love me."

Glenda looked into the depths of his eyes. All jokes aside. "I love you, Emery Cleveland. I truly do."

"Then marry me soon."

"Trust me enough on this to wait. Okay?"

He sighed. "Okay. But not too long."

"Let's keep this to ourselves for a while. I want to tell Cecily about your proposal but after the grandmother, grand-daughter tea. It's so important to her."

"You treat Cecily as if she were your daughter."

"In a sense, I feel that way. She's been a part of my life since her mother left here with her."

"I'm glad my cousin's daughter and wife had a friend like you, Glenda. Sometimes I think things happen for a reason. If Marva hadn't left, you wouldn't have come here and I wouldn't have this joy with you right now."

"A lot of people were hurt, Emery. I can't see any joy in that."

"Yeah, I know. It wasn't a picnic."

"Times were tough before we met up."

"But you did. And you saved her in a sense."

"She saved me too. And my brother. He was so in love with Marva and Cecily. He couldn't have children of his own. Like me."

"That's okay. We have each other. That's enough for me. I hope I'm enough for you."

She reached up and touched his cheek. "You're more than I've ever dreamed of."

# Chapter 9

The grandmother, granddaughter tea was tomorrow. Cecily should have been at the tea shop being anxious over preparations, but she found herself at the courthouse going through old records. Part of each day had been spent there researching the wicked ladies, Taylor and Shelly in particular. Just because Taylor had said she'd used the retirement money to open her shop didn't mean that she had.

For additions to homes, a permit was needed. Cecily had discovered Taylor had made additions to her house two years after the theft. She had also paid for the taxes five years in advance. Why would a penny-pinching woman pay taxes years in advance when she could make interest off it by buying a CD, stocks, or bonds? Taylor berated Ruby about not saving enough money, yet she paid taxes in advance. Not a prudent move. But advance taxes and additions to her house weren't enough to convict her. Screening in her porch didn't take close to two hundred thousand dollars. Neither did the taxes.

Cecily had also researched the other ladies. She hadn't been able to find much on them, except for the new house Ruby had built five years later. That in itself wasn't very much since her husband had died years before. She worked. It was conceivable that she could afford another home, especially if she used the insurance money her husband left. That was probably why she was always broke.

Cecily had finally completed her search through the old files and started her journey back to the shop. A couple of customers were eating at tables in front of the window. March had finally arrived and the days were balmy and beautiful. It was time for her to put out her porch furniture. She'd do it right after the tea or on Monday, her day off.

As she entered the shop, she glanced at Glenda. The older woman had relaxed a lot since talking to Emery the other night, but worry still furrowed her brows at times. Cecily knew Glenda couldn't completely abate the worry.

Glenda had finally told Cecily about her past the day after she'd spoken to Emery. Cecily had asked her if her mother had known. She had, Glenda had said. She'd told her immediately, not wanting to put her or Cecily in danger. But her mother had accepted her help anyway.

Cecily felt left out, that everyone was keeping secrets— her mother, now Glenda. She wondered why neither of them had thought to share that information with her. She didn't need to be protected to that extent. Secrets were far worse than the truth.

Look at what Glenda had put poor Emery through before she'd confessed to him. And look at how happy that man was now. He was practically walking on air these days. Stopped by every day after work.

"Ryan's here," Glenda said.

Cecily glanced around but didn't see him.

"In the other room."

Cecily got rid of her jacket. Ryan was sitting at the table enjoying a sandwich and soup. He glanced up as soon as he saw her and a welcoming smile spread on his face.

"Can you join me for a few minutes?"

"Sure," Cecily said. He pulled out a chair for her and sank into the cushions. Seeing him had a way of brightening her day.

"I didn't know how long I was going to be able to make this food last. I've eaten slower than a turtle moves."

Glenda brought a sandwich and soup for Cecily.

"Thanks," she said. Even though she hadn't asked for it.

"If I didn't remind you, you'd forget to eat sometimes."

"The tea will go fine tomorrow," Ryan assured her.

"That's not what's bothering me," Cecily said.

"What is it, honey?"

He'd never addressed her by that endearment before.

"You don't want to know."

"Yes, I do."

"I can't find anything to prove my mother was innocent."

"Cecily, a person can't always find proof, not when that much time has passed."

"It has to be there. I'm just overlooking something." Cecily rubbed her forehead. "It has to be there."

Ryan regarded her for a long moment.

"You don't have to tell me you don't believe me. I already know that." She turned away from him and focused on the door.

"I'll help you," he finally said.

She chuckled. It wasn't a humorous chuckle. "I'm not asking for your help. Besides, how much help would you be when you don't believe in my mother's innocence?"

"I know these people. I'm not promising anything. What we find might not be what you expected. And we may find nothing at all. But at least your conscience would be clear."

He ate a spoonful of soup in the silence. "Then you can get on with your life."

"Whatever that may be."

Ryan remained silent as he regarded her. But he continued to watch her for a full minute as he bit into his sandwich. It wasn't long before he finished and asked her to walk him to the truck. She rarely saw him with his SUV. He usually drove the truck. She saw his thermos on the seat took it inside and she filled it with coffee, then handed it to him. They stood by the truck's door.

"I won't see you tonight," he said, tugging her close. "But I'll see you tomorrow."

Cecily nodded just before he lowered his head and kissed her.

She was so wrapped up in the kiss that she didn't notice a car approaching until Ryan let her go. The car came to a halt near them. She noticed Granny Grant sitting in the passenger seat.

Though only weeks had passed, it seemed as if months had gone by by the time Granny Grant came into the tea shop again and settled on the couch. Although the day was sunny outside, she wore a fierce frown on her face.

This time, Cecily produced a full tea for Granny with finger sandwiches and cookies along with the pot of tea. She was in a tea mood today, but she was concerned about Granny's disposition.

"What's wrong, Granny?"

Fear, stark and vivid, glittered in Granny's eyes. "I see a storm coming, child."

Cecily had heard stories that Granny was forever predicting, foreboding. She saw dark clouds and storms all the time. Cecily was a bit skeptical of these old sayings.

"I'm worried about you and Glenda, child. It don't look good."

"We'll be okay, Granny."

"I don't know."

Cecily handed her a plate with the sandwiches. She sighed and took one. "I know you don't believe in this old woman on account of the way you were brought up. That'll change." She grabbed Cecily's arm in a firm grip. "You be careful just the same, you hear?"

"I will," Cecily assured her.

"Don't disobey me on this, Sissieretta."

Maybe Granny was looking back in time and was thinking about the first Sissieretta.

Still, Cecily acquiesced. "Don't worry. I'll be careful."

"Things aren't always as they seem."

"Are you going to talk about Sissieretta?" Cecily asked her, wanting to steer her away from the macabre topic.

Granny blew out a long breath and finally ate the sandwich she'd taken off the plate. After she'd swallowed the food, she started on the story.

"Sissieretta was in D.C. and Hannibal's mother had died." Cecily reminded her.

"Now I remember. Well, a year later, Sissieretta's mom got a letter saying her husband had died and they had a son together."

"She came home after that?" Cecily asked, anxious for Granny to get on with the story.

Granny shook her head, her gray and white hair swaying. "She stayed on in DC for another year. Then she came home with the baby. She said he came a couple of months early. Liked to not have made it. She was dressed all pretty. Wore the new fashions from DC. Two whole trunk loads just for her. And her son had his own stash of clothes.

"Well, she didn't have a job, so Hannibal offered her her old job and the top floor of the house for her and the baby. She accepted. He had the nursery done up all fine for that boy. Wasn't a better done-up child's room on the island. Boy had more toys than he could ever play with. Pretty little ship sets. As he grew older, he and Hannibal would build those little toy ships together. Some of 'em are in the lighthouse right now. You shoulda found some in here when you moved in. You did get a look in there, didn't you?"

"Yes. I've been in there once." Actually one ship was on the shelf above them.

Granny nodded. "That boy was way too light skinned to fool anybody. Although Sissieretta said the boy's daddy was a real light-skinned man, everybody knew that boy was Hannibal's. But what they didn't know was that Hannibal and Sissieretta had gone and gotten married in DC on his first trip there. She kept a little diary of the goings-on. My sister found it when she died. Unfortunately it got lost way back when.

"Anyway, her job at the house was to supervise everything. And she spent a lot of time with the boy. Hannibal did too. Treated him just like he was his son. Took him places. White folks didn't like that too much. But they were a minority on the island. So they kept their feelings amongst themselves, I guess.

"The older that boy got, the more he started looking like Hannibal. So you know nobody was fooled."

Cecily knew that, emotionally, that situation had to have been tough for Sissieretta and her son. People still look unfavorably on mixed marriages. It was worse for African-American women than the men. Back then Sissieretta must have had to put up with enormous harassment.

Granny glanced toward the door. "You ready, Doc?" she asked.

By now Cecily knew better than to offer to take Granny home. The older woman only liked to talk for a little while.

"Your tea tomorrow will be a fine affair," Granny said. "You're going to do very well here," she added before she left the chair and walked with them to the car.

Cecily stared after them wondering about Sissieretta and the trials she went through for love. She must have loved Hannibal to even take the chance of having a child by him. Without love it wouldn't have been worth the trouble. She wondered if their love resembled the love her mother had had for her father, and she felt sadness that she couldn't talk to her mother about it right now. She felt sad that what her mother and father had shared had been for such a short time.

In an hour, the children would arrive for their reading hour. Cecily arranged the library with extra floor pillows. She moved a chair in front for Pauline. Even now, she smelled the aroma from the cookies Glenda was baking for them.

An hour later, Cecily stood at the door glancing about the room and listened to Pauline as she read the story, then stopped to show the children pictures.

Eighteen children were scattered about the pillows on the floor and couch, all giving their attention to Pauline and the book.

* * *

Cecily had dressed in an elegant gown for the grandmother granddaughter tea. The night before, she, Glenda, and two helpers they'd hired had worked for hours setting the tea shop up.

In each little girl's seat was a bag filled with treats and an elegant card with the menu so that she could put it in her memory book.

"Good afternoon, Ms. Ranetta. You are very beautiful today."

"Thank you," the little girl said. She unbuttoned her wool Rothschild's coat to reveal a pretty dress. She also wore a smart hat with the outfit and carried delicate gloves. Many of the other girls had also been dressed similarly for the occasion.

Cecily had hired Mark to take pictures again. He'd done such a fantastic job on the Valentine's affair. Right now he snapped an extra picture of Ranetta with her grandmother, and Cecily led them to their seats. Cecily had asked for an extra one so she could surprise Ryan with a framed gift.

"This is truly a special occasion, Sissieretta," Pauline said.

"I hope you and Ranetta enjoy your tea."

Next Cecily seated Shelly and her granddaughter. The woman had dressed the little girl to the nines, not to be outdone by Pauline Anderson, of course. But Cecily readily admitted to herself that she was prejudiced. There was something special about Ranetta. Then too, all little girls seemed special today.

Waiters began serving, and Cecily worked with the photographer, getting the pictures into frames. She had found bargain porcelain frames matching the teacups. So even with the giveaways, she would still make a profit today.

The event was halfway over when she caught Ryan sneaking in. Instead of the usual jeans, he wore dress slacks and a shirt. She approached him in the foyer and whispered in his ear.

"Uncles aren't allowed."

"Sexism," he whispered and kissed her quickly. "That whispering is turning me on," he said, and Cecily blushed. He carried a camera in his hand. "I want pictures of Ranetta and Mom."

"I've already taken pictures of them."

"I want one, too," he said.

"Men. I have one for you. It was supposed to be a surprise."

"May I snap a few anyway?"

Cecily rolled her eyes. He hugged her. "All right," she said and he strolled through tables to reach them.

"Uncle Ryan!" Ranetta called out with a smile when she saw him.

He moved toward the little girl, stooped next to her chair, and kissed her on the cheek, giving her a generous hug. "I can't believe you're my ragamuffin niece. What happened to her?"

"Am I pretty?" she asked.

"So pretty, I'm going to take pictures of you."

"Uncle Mark took pictures already."

"I want my own. Is that all right with you?"

"Okay." The little girl straightened in her seat, clearly accustomed to posing for him.

Ryan snapped off several shots, but he took pictures of other tables as well, as did her photographer. Cecily wanted pictures to put on her wall in the tea shop.

There was something so touching and tender about seeing him in her shop, especially with the children.

"I'll see you later, okay?" he said before he left, but didn't forget to kiss her—in the empty foyer.

Cecily's spirits had climbed even higher. Near the end of the festivities, she began to pass out the bags with the teacups and saucers. In the bags were the framed photos. She gave each grandmother a matching framed photo.

Everyone promised to return to her shop. Cecily hoped this was a turning point for her tea shop.

Suddenly she remembered Granny's Grant prediction.

And wondered if there was any truth to those old wives' tales.

 

This had been the second busiest day in the tea shop since the doors had opened for business. After Cecily showered she was too invigorated to sleep. She was downstairs in Glenda's apartment. Her feet were on the ottoman. Glenda had stretched out on the sofa, her feet in the chair.

"It's been a long time since I worked this hard," Glenda said.

"I'm going to have to hire more help."

"I had help. We don't need any more yet."

"I hope we will."

"How are things between you and Ryan?" Glenda asked.

Something had been on Glenda's mind. Cecily could tell by her manner. One of the reasons she'd come by was to lend an ear if Glenda needed it. Funny the way one could know someone that long and read her so well.

"Things are fine with Ryan."

"Think you could settle down here with him?"

Cecily choked. "We certainly haven't gotten that far yet. He's still on the rebound, remember?"

"That doesn't mean that what he feels for you isn't true. Besides, who says he's on the rebound?"

"He hasn't had a chance to get over his wife yet."

"From what I've heard, he's had plenty of time. The marriage went bad from the day they said 'I Do.' "

"We'll see," Cecily said.

Glenda looked out the window, which lent her a great view of the lighthouse and the flickering light on top.

"This island is wearing on me. I like it here. I think I'd like to settle down here."

"Really?"

"How do you feel about that?"

"I don't know. I like it here. I'm thinking I like the tea shop more than I thought I would. If business picks up, I don't want to leave."

"How are things coming with your research on your mother?" Glenda asked.

"That's another story. Very slowly." Cecily updated her on her progress.

"With Delilah coming tomorrow, things always get worse. That girl is bad news."

"I can't exactly stop her from coming."

"I've got some news of my own." Glenda seemed to be weighing something on her mind.

"Yeah? What?"

"Emery proposed to me."

"What?" Cecily straightened in her chair and dropped her feet to the floor. "That man moves fast. What did you say?"

"I said yes. But I wanted to wait awhile."

"Tell me you love him."

"I do."

"Oh, Glenda." Cecily went to the woman she thought of as an aunt. "I'm so happy for you. You deserve each other."

"But you're so unsettled."

"What does that have to do with your marriage? Life goes on, Glenda. I can't do anything about the past except to right a wrong. I can do that with you married."

"I always told your mama you were a smart one."

"And don't you forget it." Cecily returned to her chair and got comfortable. "Why are you making him wait? That is, if you're sure about your feelings."

"You're going to think I'm crazy."

"You better not elope."

"I wouldn't do that."

"What is it, then?"

"I'm . . . I'm scared. I couldn't bear for anything to happen to Emery. I'm scared out of my mind that I'll find him dead . . . just like . . ."

Cecily was out of her chair and clutched Glenda around the shoulders.

"Glenda, you've changed your identity. You moved across the country from that maniac. He doesn't have a clue

of where you are. If he did he would have done something
to Mom or me years ago."

"I don't know. And Emery is impatient."

"What spell did you put on my cousin?"

Glenda finally smiled, and Cecily returned to her seat.
"Nothing but good loving, girlfriend."

"Uh-oh. He's toast."

"And don't you know it."

"About time, I say. For the both of you."


The next day, Cousin Delilah showed up like a bad omen.
She carried one suitcase this time instead of the four she
usually traveled with. Cecily took the lack of luggage as a
good sign. Delilah wouldn't be staying long this trip.

"This place is absolutely fabulous," Delilah said, dropping the luggage at Cecily's feet and starting to climb the
stairs. "The ocean. Summertime must be out of this world.
I'll have to come back then. Spend a week or two."

It wasn't as if Cecily had invited her. But Delilah didn't
feel she needed an invitation. Family was there for her to
mooch off of.

Did she really expect Cecily to carry her suitcase up
three flights of steps? "You forgot your luggage," Cecily
reminded her.

"Be a dear and get it for me, will you? My back has been
acting up lately."

Cecily sighed, picked up the suitcase like a bellman, and
staggered to the stairs. Sooner or later Delilah would get to
the reason for her visit.

She wouldn't let the woman put a damper on Glenda's
upcoming nuptials. But before she could climb the stairs,
Ryan's pickup roared into the yard. He parked beside Delilah's rental car.

At the sight of a handsome male, Delilah came charging
down the stairs, bad back and all. She patted her hair into
place just as she reached Cecily.

"Hi," Ryan said to Cecily and kissed her.

Delilah cleared her throat.

Ryan smiled toward her. "Hello," he said. Cecily rolled her eyes. What red-blooded male could resist Delilah's beauty? She was cheerleader thin, with the perfect face and carrying the simpering southern manner to a fault.

Delilah extended a perfectly manicured hand. "A pleasure to meet you. I'm Cecily's cousin."

Ryan captured her tiny hand in his and they shook hands briefly.

"Delilah, this is my . . ." She couldn't introduce him as her boyfriend or anything. They hadn't formally gotten that far yet. "My friend Ryan," she amended.

"I consider any friend of Cecily to be my friend, too."

Ryan nodded and took the suitcase from Cecily. "Will you be in town long?" he asked.

"Depends," Delilah said.

"Oh." The three of them fell into step and made their way up the three floors. Cecily took the lead and Delilah hung behind with Ryan, trying her wiles on him. Cecily didn't look but she could imagine Delilah sidling up close to Ryan, inadvertently rubbing against him, stroking his hand as she talked, as that was her style. She didn't care whom the man belonged to, even if he was married, if she wanted him.

"Why don't you go ahead of me?" Ryan said. "The steps are a little narrow," he continued.

Cecily smiled. From the sound of things, Delilah's wiles didn't appear to be working. So far. But Delilah was a hard woman to resist. Hadn't Cecily heard that before?

The average woman would hustle Delilah ahead of her and, cousin or not, wouldn't let her within a hundred feet of her man. But if Cecily couldn't trust Ryan, she might as well find out right now, instead of months, years down the road. Some kind of temptation was bound to come within their path. She wasn't going to run interference every time it happened. Either he wanted to be with her or he didn't.

They made it to her door, which she unlocked.

"Where do you want me to put this?" he asked Cecily.

Cecily pointed toward the second bedroom. "In there," she said.

Delilah started to follow him. "I can take care of it," he pointedly said to her.

Delilah and Cecily stood in the entrance, Delilah's gaze following Ryan's progress as he carried the suitcase to the room.

"Did you have a good trip?" Cecily asked her, trying to divert her attention. She would be the last to admit that the green-eyed jealousy monster was showing itself.

"Very good."

Ryan came back. Kissed Cecily on the lips right in front of Delilah. "I'll talk to you later, okay, sweetheart?"

"Sure," she said, wondering why he'd come in the first place.

He delivered a curt nod to Delilah and left. Cecily watched him descend the stairs and slowly closed the door.

Delilah walked to the couch and laid her jacket and scarf on it. "That your new beau?"

"Yes."

"He's cute."

"Why are you here, Delilah?"

"Just came for a little visit, cousin dear."

"Delilah, you never come for a little visit. But let's get something straight." Cecily wasn't taking the high road any longer. "Ryan is my friend. Don't try your wiles on him again okay?"

"Well, if it's so good, he won't respond, will he?"

"Don't even play that game."

"Okay, okay. I didn't come to steal your boyfriend," she said sulkily.

"As if you could." Cecily spoke with more assurance than she actually felt. Ryan hadn't made any promises to her.

"I've done it before," Delilah said as if she had the power to do so to anyone she wanted.

"They were losers. You're welcome to them."

"But not Ryan?"

"Not Ryan. If you try, you'll find yourself sleeping in your car. You got that?" Cecily wasn't going to be anybody's doormat any longer. In the past, she'd let things slide with Delilah. Enough was enough. And she wasn't keeping him away for fear of Delilah either.

"Ryan will be around during your stay. You won't be making snide touches, or these come-hither looks. You act like any normal person would act around a friend's boyfriend. Are we clear on that?"

"Cousin, do you think you can unsheathe claws sharper than mine?"

"Yes, I can."

"I never knew you to fight over a man."

"I'm not fighting now. I'm laying down the ground rules. Do you understand them?"

Delilah gave her a long, measured look. Then she sighed and nodded.

"Now that we understand each other, why don't you unpack? I have a phone call to make."

When Delilah left the room, Cecily picked up the phone and dialed Ryan's cell phone number. He picked up on the second ring.

"Hi," she said.

He greeted her.

"You never got around to telling me why you came by."

"I was working nearby and wanted to see you."

"You should have stayed."

"With your cousin about to eat me alive?"

"We've come to an understanding. She won't be a problem."

"Good, because I've been too long without you."

"So come over tonight. We'll have dinner."

"Sounds like a winner to me, but I'm going to be late again. I'm spending a lot of time at the new site during the day which leaves me catching up on work at the campground later. Nine okay?"

"That works for me."

# Chapter 10

Cecily served high tea for the reading group that Saturday afternoon. The ladies raved over the finger sandwiches, scones, and deserts. She'd pulled a couple of comfortable love seats and cushioned armchairs into the library. The bookshelves gave the area a cozy feel.

She set out four teapots labeled with the different blends of tea so that the ladies could pour whenever they chose without being disturbed.

Many campers visited the tea shop. She had conversations with some who had formed clubs and met a couple of times a year. They liked her shop, even bought special blends to take home, and asked to be on her mailing list.

And although the shop closed early this time of year, she kept it open later for the book club and straggling campers who were thrilled at having access to food that normally wasn't available.

At seven, Ryan arrived and the ladies were still deep into their discussion. Cecily refilled the teapots and left a plate of cookies for them. She would have loved to join the book discussion. She'd read the book and the conversation was interesting, but she didn't intrude. So she and Ryan sat at a table in another room. Even from there she glimpsed a couple of people from the reading group. One woman in particular paid very little attention to the book discussion. She was about Cecily's age and she wasn't participating. But she eyed Cecily and Ryan sharply. As a matter of fact, she'd watched Cecily closely all afternoon.

It was impossible for Cecily to miss the keen dislike in the woman's eyes. Cecily guessed the woman might have been one of Ryan's old girlfriends. She'd ask him later.

Another hour passed before the group left.

Someone said, "It's nice not having to clean up afterward."

"Or worry about what to bring for snacks," another member said.

"Or worry about cooking."

"Or worry about children and husbands underfoot."

"You can say that again," another woman agreed.

They'd voted to hold their meeting at the tea shop every month. And they left a hefty tip.

With Glenda's help, Cecily rearranged the room to its normal position. Then she washed the teapots and other dishes, swiped down the tables, swept, and did a thousand other chores before they finally turned the lights out, leaving only one small night-light burning.

Ryan had invited her to the bonfire that evening. She'd have to take Delilah with her.

"By the way, don't worry about Delilah. She's going out with Emery and me tonight," Glenda said. "And she's spending the night with me. You'll have the apartment to yourself."

"Be for real. I'm not letting her impose on you. Besides, it's not fair to her to put her out of her bed the second night she's here."

"Better you than me, young lady. You go out and have fun. There's no way you can have fun with that alley cat around. Besides, you need time with Ryan."

"So she'll ruin your evening instead? I don't think so."

"I'm your aunt. Just do as I say for once, will you? She's

already prepared to go with me. And that's the end of the discussion."

"Don't say I didn't try."

"I won't. Have fun."


Delilah was sulking on the living room couch when Cecily entered her apartment.

"This is the most boring place I've ever been to," Delilah complained.

"I'm sorry I couldn't entertain you, but I have a business to run. Besides, you'll have fun tonight."

"Oh, please. Running around with old folks?"

"At least you were invited. Delilah, don't embarrass me with your bad behavior. Emery and Glenda didn't have to invite you out."

Cecily headed to her room. "I have to take a shower."

"Where are you going?"

"To the bonfire at the campground."

Delilah instantly perked up. "Will Ryan be there?"

"He'll be there, but he didn't invite you and you aren't going to impose. You already have plans."

Delilah returned to sulking on the couch and flipping through television channels. Cecily couldn't remember the last time she'd turned on the tube. She preferred the sound of the surf. The tube now sounded eerie in the normally quiet apartment.

Cecily showered quickly, dressed in jeans and an aqua sweater that blended nicely with her features, and drove to the campground.

Glenda had come for Delilah by the time Cecily made it out.

"Don't you look pretty," Glenda said to Cecily.

"You think it's okay?"

Delilah, who was three sizes smaller than Cecily's size twelve, rolled her eyes.

"You'll knock his socks off. Have fun," Glenda said. She started to the door. "Come along, Delilah. We've got a fine evening planned ahead."

Cecily left soon after. She was in a fine frame of mind as she drove to the campground. Darkness was closing in but the campground was brightly lit.

When she arrived, she parked near the reservations office. The temperature had dropped and she pulled her jacket tightly against her after she exited the car.

A huge fire roared in a clearing a hundred feet away and a circle of people stood and sat around it. Some of the kids held very long water soaked sticks with hot dogs on them toward the blaze, under adult instructions, mostly admonitions like "turn the hot dogs so they won't burn." She could easily decipher the campground employees by the Coree Island sweatshirts and jackets they wore. But even those were deceptive since some of the campers had also bought the insignia sweatshirts from the gift shop.

Mark grilled hamburgers and Cecily started to speak to him, but a woman approached him and they began to argue in very low voices. Cecily passed a table topped with potato salad, rolls, chips, baked beans, corn on the cob, big juicy tomatoes, lettuce, and condiments for the hot dogs and burgers as she searched for Ryan.

She saw his father first, soothing Ranetta. Her hot dog had fallen on the ground.

"There now. We'll get you another one, sweetie pie. Don't you cry now. Grandpa will fix it."

Pauline handed him a hot dog and he guided it onto the stick. He held on to Ranetta's little hand as she extended the stick toward the fire.

"Cecily, I'm glad you could come."

Cecily turned to address Delcia. She didn't wear the Coree Campground shirts like the others, but rather a maternity sweatshirt that was loose on the bottom. She was a tall, striking woman with the gait of someone who was due any minute.

"I take it you're due soon?" she asked.

"Another month. The baby has dropped. I can't wait until she or he is born."

"You didn't want to know the sex?"

"We want it to be a surprise. We painted the nursery

green. So it will fit either one. My brother is around here somewhere, but in the meantime, join us."

Cecily ended up in a chair beside Pauline.

"I'm happy you're here," the woman said.

Clay and Ranetta finally finished their hot dogs. Clay turned and spoke. "Hi there, Cecily."

"Ranetta and I are the cooks today. We'll have a hot dog done up in two shakes. Is that one for Grandma, Rae, Rae?"

"Oh, I hate that name."

The little girl shook her head. "It's mine."

"I thought we were going to feed everybody else first, pumpkin."

"It's mine," she said and put it into the bun on her grandmother's lap.

"That's okay, sweetheart. You eat your hot dog," Pauline said, holding on to the bun so it wouldn't fall.

"Come on, Ranetta. Let's go to the table for some ketchup."

Delcia and Ranetta left.

"Well, I guess I'm the cook," Clay said.

"I'll help you," Cecily offered.

"That's mighty fine of you," he said and stuck a hot dog on a stick and handed it to her.

Cecily remembered what she'd seen the others do. She'd never been to a bonfire cookout before, and she watched the enraptured expressions on the campers' faces as some talked while the others cooked. There were bricks surrounding the fire, forming a line that no one passed.

Clay took a hot dog of his own and extended it.

"Gotta say, I enjoy this. Being around all these people. You're going to have to make this a regular occurrence when you can get away," he said.

"How often do they have bonfires?" Cecily asked.

"At least one night on the weekends during spring. Some weeks when it's not too hot in the summer." He looked at the campers milling about. "They enjoy it."

"I can see that."

"You settling in all right?"

"I am. I'm considering opening the lighthouse this summer."

"Want me to go through it with you? It'll be good to have it opened. We made enough repairs to keep it going through the years but a lighthouse is history. Needs to be a living history for people to explore—see how things used to be," Clay said.

"I can't agree with you more."

"Well, if you want to go through it Monday, just let me know."

"I wi—" Someone circled her waist from behind, cutting off her response.

Ryan kissed her neck. "Hi, beautiful."

Wrapped in the warmth of his arms she smiled. "Hi, handsome." She'd only just seen him a couple of hours ago, but her heart started a staccato beat just the same. It seemed always to be this way when he was near. With his arms circling her, she hoped he couldn't feel the accelerated rhythm of her heart.

"Enjoying yourself?" he asked against her neck.

"Very much."

His father chuckled. "Ready for a hot dog, son?"

"Not yet," Ryan said, releasing her. "Got too much to do."

"We'll take care of Cecily. Don't you worry about her."

"I won't," he said before he left.

Clay smiled as he watched his son disappear and then he glanced at Cecily. She didn't want to read too much in that smile.

After Cecily ate her hot dog, she went to get drinks for Pauline and herself, and brought them back. Clay and Ranetta had disappeared. But Delcia had cried fatigue and gone home. Clay and Pauline offered to keep Ranetta for the night.

"This is really a nice campground," Cecily said to Pauline. "You must be a very proud parent."

"I am."

"How did it all get started?"

"You wouldn't believe it but it's something Delcia always wanted to do. Clay and his brother, Spike, owned the land the camp is on. They both had separate pieces," Pauline said, thrilled to tell the story to Cecily.

"Spike would bring his fishing buddies here. After a few years of inconvenience, he threw up a rickety shower and an outhouse. Then the wives and kids started to come with his buddies. Before he knew it, the summers were full of his camping friends spending a week or two at a time out here. Didn't cost anything and it was a nice summer vacation to go fishing, hiking, and spending time on the beach. The summers really are nice here. There are only a few really hot days because the wind usually blows and keeps the heat manageable. Really, one could do without an air conditioner. Coree is perfectly situated that way."

"Did Clay and Spike start the campground?"

"Actually no. It was an informal place all through Delcia's childhood. But she always told Spike that she wanted to turn it into a campground. And Ryan was always under Spike's feet during the summer. He went fishing with him. Stayed in the tent with him until he put up a little shack for the two of them. Wasn't much of anything, but it suited them.

"Delcia talked so much about that campground that Spike told her he'd deed the land to her and Ryan. So when he died he did exactly that. But they needed part of Clay's land too. Clay wouldn't give it to them until Delcia finished college and Ryan promised to go. He realized he couldn't keep Delcia waiting that long.

"So Delcia finished high school a year early, she was so eager to start. She went to summer school every summer and took a really full load at college so that she graduated a year early. So she was about twenty and Ryan seventeen when they started. I was surprised at the work that Ryan put into it. But he stuck right along with her. Delcia married shortly after that to a construction worker—her high school sweetheart. She talked him into leaving his construction job and working with Ryan and her. And he did. As you will learn, my daughter, Delcia, can talk just about anyone into just about anything. This campground has been successful from the day they started it. Some of the people who used to stay for free were a little miffed at having to pay, but Delcia treated it like a business from the first day.''

"And Ryan?" Cecily asked.

"Ryan. He loved the campground but he wanted a life too. He played football in high school but he worked after school, weekends, and all summer. He did his share. He wouldn't put the responsibility on Delcia since he owned half. He felt he had to do his share of the work. That's one of the things I like about my kids. They have a keen sense of responsibility.''

Which explained why he was willing to give up all his money to a wife who didn't deserve it, Cecily thought.

Cecily saw the sadness cross Pauline's face; then the woman looked at her and smiled. Cecily couldn't help but smile back. Pauline was hoping that this time Ryan had found the love of his life. Cecily didn't have the heart to tell her that rebound situations rarely worked out. Ryan was just recovering from his divorce. Even with his sense of right and wrong, he didn't know what he wanted just yet.

But Cecily saw him from across the fire. The blaze was half the size it had been earlier and half the campers had left for their campsites.

Cecily knew she wanted Ryan more than she'd wanted any other man. He had touched facets of her no one had been able to touch before. Whether good or bad, rebound or not, she was taking a risk. She was playing this out to the end and she'd see what it would bring. What was life without risks? If she didn't take a chance with him, she'd be too closed off to find the kind of love that Sissieretta risked all to experience—that her mother had carried in her heart her entire adult life. It was the love she had reflected on fondly on her deathbed. Love of that magnitude didn't come without risks.

Love? Was she crazy? She couldn't possibly love Ryan, could she? She wasn't willing to admit anything further than a strong attraction.

* * *

Ryan followed Cecily up the curving staircase to the top floor. He wanted her like the very air he breathed, but he held back. LaToya may have done a job on him but she hadn't killed all his sense of decency. He knew that what he shared with Cecily could go no further than lovers. He wanted sex with her. An invisible web of attraction built between them. But desire wasn't enough. She deserved more—much more than he could give her right now. She deserved trips to New York, nights at the theater. She deserved cruises to the Bahamas. She deserved jewels he couldn't afford.

The sense of urgency dissipated. He couldn't give her those things. And he wouldn't leave her with the impression that what they shared right now would ever lead to more. Sure he liked her. More than he wanted to. The attraction was strong and spellbinding.

Walking behind her as they climbed the stairs, Ryan watched the sway of her tight backside clearly visible beneath the short jacket. Her sweatshirt had ridden up, giving him a clear view. Blood was roaring in his ears and every place else. Even though the temperature had dropped, his internal temperature had soared twenty degrees. He'd better get himself under control or else he'd be in an embarrassing situation by the time they reached her apartment. He unbuttoned his coat and let the cold wind rush in.

Cecily's womanly curves enticed him like nothing else as the March wind roared. His conscience nudged at him again. Cecily was a little innocent in a way. Still fighting for her mother. He knew some women could be a treacherous lot. She didn't see it. She was setting herself up for disappointment in the end when she discovered there was nothing to uncover.

A stab of regret touched him. He didn't want her to experience that treachery. But there was nothing for it. He'd soothe her in the end—or at least try to. That was as much as he could do. But right now, his mind was filled with having her. He debated with himself about whether this was right.

After the two-flight climb, she was a bit winded. She laughed when she dropped the keys. He wondered if she was as keyed up as he was.

She faced him. The light that flashed from the lighthouse cast her in an enticing manner. She finally got the key and pushed it in, opening the door to the warmth inside.

Cecily dropped the keys on a table near the door, then pulled off her coat. Ryan was steaming hot and shucked his leather jacket. She hung them in the closet and came closer.

Her breath was still fast from the climb. There was something very sexy about a woman's chest quickly expanding and contracting when she was winded. Her eyes were brighter pools of enticement. She approached him, saying something he didn't hear.

Ryan caught her in his arms, kissed her urgently—he had wanted to hold her all evening. She tasted sweet and welcoming.

"When's your cousin coming back?" he asked.

"Tomorrow," she whispered.

Too much temptation, he thought as he lowered his head to hers. There was nothing to stop them from doing what was driving him out of control.

He pressed her body tightly to his. Felt the tips of her breasts against his chest. The sensation served to arouse him even more. He left her mouth, swirled his tongue around her earlobe. She moaned, almost sank into him.

"You like that?" he whispered.

"Yes," she whispered against his neck her warm breath making his breath quicken. He strung kisses along her neck, her chest, before he returned to her mouth. Her arms closed tight around his back. He caught her hips in his hands and held her against him. She felt so damn good against him. He was thankful she didn't starve herself the way many women did. He liked holding on to something more than bones when he held a woman in his arms. He enjoyed her soft curves.

He slid his hands under her sweater, stroking the silken

texture of her brown skin. Then he felt her hands on him and he almost lost control.

He tore his mouth from hers. They were breathing as if they'd run a marathon.

"I want you so bad I hurt," he said, peering into the depths of her eyes. "I can't make any promises for tomorrow."

She kissed his chin. "I'm not asking for any." She stepped away from him. Her breasts strained against an aqua bra that reminded him of the waters of the Bahamas. His breath caught at the magnificence of her.

He'd roamed this house since he was a kid, so knew his way around as he grasped her hand and led her to the bedroom. He barely noticed the beautiful eyelet bedspread or the zillion pillows stacked against the headboard. He shoved the pillows aside, pulled the feminine spread back. She gazed shyly at him. He kissed her lightly on the lips and then he unhooked her bra and closed his eyes a brief second trying to gain some control so that he could love her the way she deserved to be loved.

Keeping his eyes on hers he shucked his shirt and shoes and then he climbed in beside her. He gathered her face between his rough hands. Then he kissed her lightly before he bent lower and swiped his tongue over the tips of her breasts and suckled them.

Her low moan drove his desire to a fever pitch. Blindly he reached lower, caressed her stomach and thighs through the jeans, and he unbuckled the pants, sat up, and tugged them down her hips. Amid her moans of joy he kissed her thighs, kissed his way up to her soft stomach. He felt her fingers on his arms, his shoulders, any part of his body she could reach. Then he found himself pushed onto his back.

Cecily straddled his thighs and feasted her eyes on his powerful, muscled chest. She ran her hands through the curling chest hairs. Loving the mixture of crisp hair and soft skin beneath. He had her body on fire for him, but she didn't want it to be one-sided. She wanted the pleasure of feeling him all over. She leaned over him, kissed his chin, chest, neck, and then she kissed his mouth. He held her hips tight against him, pressed her back to him. And they stayed that way for what seemed forever, tasting each other. Then she sat up, slid down his body, unbuckled his pants, and pulled them down.

Her breath caught. She got the first view of the impressive body the jeans had concealed.

"You are one magnificent man," she said.

And found herself on her back.

"Wait, the top drawer," she said. He fumbled with the drawer, finding the prophylactic that she slid on. He nearly exploded as he eased himself inside her. She was tighter than he expected.

"Am I hurting you?" His whispered question was full of emotion.

"Not much," she said.

He slowed his pace even more trying to be easy, as he filled her completely.

"You feel wonderful," he said.

"I love the feel of you," she responded and then he was moving against her in a rhythmic motion that rocked his soul. They moved until the stars shattered in a cataclysmic eruption.

Then he tugged her gently into his arms as he caressed her face. They talked sweet nothings for at least a half hour before she left the bed, bringing a wet washcloth to him. She'd refreshed herself and pulled on a long robe. He could tell there was nothing underneath.

"Would you like some tea?" she asked.

Sensing her need to be alone a few moments, he said yes. While she was gone, he pulled on his jeans but nothing more and went to the living room.

She brought a tray filled with little sandwiches that seemed always to be handy and a floral china pot with tea and two delicate cups.

She poured the tea for both of them. Handing a cup to him she leaned back in the couch and he placed his arm around her shoulder.

He wouldn't spend the night, but he wanted to enjoy her company awhile longer. He couldn't yet express what he'd experienced with her. It was special, beyond what he'd ever encountered before. Actually something otherworldly.

Later that evening, or at least earlier that morning since it was close to three A.M., Ryan evaluated what had happened. Lovemaking with Cecily hadn't been hot, frenzied, lust-filled sex. Certainly it had been hot, but also deep, and a soul-wrenching coming together of spirits. Even now as Ryan drove into his driveway and parked his truck, he felt as if he'd left part of himself behind with her. Some part that would never be quite the same again.

A light shone in the kitchen. Ryan unlocked the door and headed there to get a bottle of water. When he entered the room, his father was sitting at the table. Clearly he'd been waiting for him.

Ryan almost chuckled as he shucked his coat and hung it on the peg, watching his father as the older man sipped on his coffee and carefully placed it on the table. His dad had sat in that very same spot many nights during Ryan's teenage years, especially if he had a lecture to deliver. At thirty-four, Ryan was too old for father-son lectures, but that wouldn't stop his father from saying his piece.

"Couldn't sleep?" Ryan asked.

"I can sleep just fine."

"Rae Rae's asleep?"

"Just like a baby."

Ryan pulled his bottled water from the fridge, being careful not to get too close to his dad, hoping the aroma from the coffee would cover the scent of sex clinging to him.

He sat at the other end of the table.

His father watched him closely and Ryan regarded his drink.

"Son."

Ryan sighed. "Yeah, Dad? I know what you're going to say."

"I'm going to say it anyway whether you want to hear it or not. It needs to be said." Regarding his son with keen eyes, he set his cup on the table and leaned back in his chair.

"Don't think I don't know what's going on when you leave work to slip home to shower before you go back to work and don't make it back home until . . ." He glanced at the wall clock. ". . . three in the morning."

Ryan leaned back in his chair. When did a man get too old for lectures from parents? he wondered. Probably never.

"I know at your age men have certain urges."

"Well, I don't think it's just at my age. You and Mom fairly keep that back bedroom hopping."

"Don't be disrespectful now. What's between a *married* man and woman is a private thing."

"Sorry, Dad." He had stepped over the line there. Sons weren't supposed to know what their parents were doing behind closed doors.

"But you *aren't* married, son, and neither is Cecily. I won't take kindly to your playing fast and loose with her. She's a nice young lady and I expect you to respect that and her."

"I respect her, Dad."

"Enough to keep yourself to yourself until the 'I do's'?"

Ryan remained silent. He wasn't about to talk about his sex life with his father. His parents came from the old school. They were like most North Carolina parents of their generation, with very strict moral codes. *Go to bed with a nice girl, marry her.* He wondered why he never got this lecture about LaToya.

"Dad, I'm not going to discuss Cecily with you."

"Then stay out of her bed. You get me? She was my best friend's daughter. I'm not going to have her name sullied by my son."

"Dad—"

"That's my final word on the matter. I've said my piece. I'm still your father. I don't care how old you are." His dad stood, went to the sink, and rinsed out his cup before placing it into the drainer. Then he started out of the room. With his back to Ryan, he said, "Let your head rule, not your body. You remember that, son—and the Bible."

Ryan listened to his father's footsteps as he made his way down the long hallway.

He read the veiled message beneath his father's word. And they were *Marry Cecily*.

He would not marry for sex again, damn it. Even if he had to do without.


On Monday Ryan and Carter looked over the property. It was almost ready for occupancy. Plumbers and carpenters were completing the last of the work in the showers.

Ryan had tried to use what was already there so as not to destroy the property. The land was relatively flat. Campers preferred a little grass.

They had started with cutting tall grass in various areas. Some of the land had to be leveled out and reseeded and he was grateful that the temperature had climbed to the sixties during the day. Sprouts had started to come in. Just a few trees had needed thinning out, underbrush mostly, and new volunteer trees. To keep expenses down, they'd used campground maintenance employees to do a lot of the work. Ryan had pitched in quite a bit himself. It reminded him of the old days when he, Delcia, and her first husband had worked together to start the first campground. He'd never been a stranger to hard work.

Ryan was rather pleased at how things were progressing.

He heard a truck drive into the yard long before he actually saw it. He had hoped it might be Cecily coming to pay him a visit as she did occasionally. He hated to admit that he was waiting for her. The truck pulled to a stop. It was a campground truck. Ryan's dad exited the truck.

"Coming along well," his dad said.

Ryan glanced at his watch and looked toward the tea shop. Usually if Cecily was coming, she'd be here by now. "Yeah. Just about finished," he said.

A crew was stringing up cable hookups. Electrical hookups had been strung the other day. People might like nature and the out-of-doors but they still appreciated creature comforts.

"Think we'll get much use for this space this year?" Carter asked. "With the economy being down?"

"According to Barbara, many are coming here in place of their usual trips. Cheaper at campgrounds than springing for hotels. The main campground is already full for most of the summer."

"There is that."

"Well, in another couple of weeks, you'll have your place to yourself," Clay Anderson said.

"Your house is ready?"

"Just about. Your mama's calling the furniture store making sure they deliver on time. Said she's too old to be sleeping on a pallet."

"You don't have to worry about that. You can camp out at my place for as long as you want."

"We know that. We appreciate it, too."

"Are the signs ready to go?" Carter asked.

"Yeah." He went to the beginning of the first path. Today they were putting up signs.

They worked for a couple of hours. Clay took a water break. "Some lemonade would hit the spot about now," he said. "Even tea the ladies are so stuck on."

Ryan grunted.

"You didn't let Cecily know you'd be hanging out here today so she could sneak out for a visit and a drink?" Carter said.

Ryan grunted again. "She's got her own work to do."

Carter shrugged.

Ryan caught his father watching him with an odd expression on his face. Ryan tried not to let his emotions show. He felt confused. He'd let himself believe sex was love.

Even around Cecily he couldn't seem to get his stupid body under control. This relationship had no prospects for the future. And Cecily was the future kind of woman. She'd lost so much. No mother and no father. When his relationship ended, he had family who cared about him. Mother, father, sister, and even an in-law. Cecily only had Cecily. And Glenda. Her island family still felt strange and she wouldn't confide in them.

She clung to that stupid hope of pinning the blame for that robbery on somebody else. She was a dreamer. Probably read too many of those romances. He used to shrug when Delcia read them under the tree. Thought of it as a little harmless fun to spin their dreams around. But when unrealistic dreams crushed the spirit, they weren't harmless any longer.

Cecily finally arrived. She'd walked as usual. "I'm ready to tour the lighthouse any time you are," Clay said.

"It can wait until you finish here."

Ryan eased his way over to Cecily and they walked a distance away from the other men.

"Ryan, who was that woman staring at us Saturday? The one with the reading group?"

"I don't remember anyone staring at us."

"We could see her from our table. She was so intent on us that she didn't pay any attention to the discussion."

Ryan thought back to that night. His focus had been on Cecily and wanting to take her to bed so badly he hurt. Then he remembered. "Hazeline, Ruby's daughter."

"Oh. She looked like she really hated me. I guess I know why."

"Hmmm." The real reason was that Hazeline was coming on to Ryan but he wouldn't mention that. "Don't worry about her."

"How much longer will you be here?"

Ryan swiped his brow. "Quite a while. We have to get this finished up. Dad won't work much longer though." He took a long drink from the tea she brought him.

"Why don't I bring something for them to drink and maybe a snack?"

"You don't have to, honey."

"It's no problem."

Ryan reached into his pocket for his keys and handed them to her. "Drive my truck, then."

They talked for a few more moments before Cecily left for their drinks. Ryan stared after her so long that his father said, "What's up, son?"

"Nothing, Dad."

# Chapter 11

Cecily perused the deceptively gentle Atlantic shore. In the absence of lofty cliffs dropping precipitously into the sea or rock-strewn inlets, one would think the flat featureless area was a safe place for mariners. But this area was extremely dangerous for anyone caught in the grip of a storm or piloting in the dark. Over time, the shoals and shallows had earned the name the Graveyard of the Atlantic. Thousands of ships and lives had been swallowed up. Entire crews lost their lives on these shores, often leaving their loved ones to wonder at their tragic end.

By the time Cecily had climbed the many steps to the top of the lighthouse, her legs were leaden and weak, but the window beckoned to her. There she glimpsed the expansive view of the beach and burial ground for ships. When she thought that probably some ships and sailors were more than likely buried under the sand of her tea shop and lighthouse due to the changing shore, an eerie feeling moved through her.

Clay finally made his way to the top. The window didn't hold the same appeal for him that it did for her. He found a dusty chair and willingly sank into it. ''Used to climb these stairs like nothing with your daddy way back," he said, taking a huge white handkerchief out of his back pocket and dabbing his face with it.

"You did?" Cecily asked, watching Harry as he finally stumbled up the last step and sat right where he was.

"Your daddy almost bit his tongue clean off one year when he fell down on these steps," Harry said. "Clay and your daddy wouldn't climb those stairs for a week. That's the longest they could keep them away from those stairs." Harry shook his head. "But you know boys. They were right back into mischief quick enough."

Cecily guessed this place would be a nifty temptation for growing energetic boys.

"Used to be a path from our place to this one."

"It's long gone now," Clay said.

Cecily wondered why they hadn't taken the beach the way Ryan often did on his jogs.

"We gonna have to get a teen to do the touring on the stairs," Harry said.

"You're right about that. I don't think I'll be climbing them anymore."

"Somebody's got to spruce the place up a bit and get rid of the cobwebs," Harry lamented, swiping at one dangling near his head.

"I'll do that," Cecily said.

"It'll take some climbing and more than one person," Clay said. "We'll get Ryan to do that."

"I can wield a mean mop and bucket," Cecily declared. "He doesn't have to do all the work."

"We'll get a group of men to take care of the cleaning. It's enough that you're letting us use the money for charity," Clay murmured, but was clearly satisfied that she'd offered.

"Don't you worry about a thing," Harry assured her. His breathing had finally slowed to a normal rhythm and he stood and began to look around the circular area. His eyes sparkled with anticipation. Since he and Clay were in charge of the lighthouse project, it gave him something more to look forward to than his front porch rocker and daily trips to the local restaurant.

Cecily glanced up at the light that by nightfall would be flickering above the ceiling. She was getting as excited as any kid would be about the opening, the prospect of new business, and the recounting of the tale of the lighthouse's history—her family's history would be remembered forever on this island.

As Clay, Harry, and Cecily left the lighthouse, they were dusty. Clay and Harry headed toward Clay's truck. She walked toward the back of the Victorian building and saw Granny at the back of the cottage.

"I was hoping you were home," Granny said, leaning against a post. "I know you're closed today, but I took a chance on coming anyway."

"I'm glad to see you. Take a seat on the porch while I go to my apartment for the keys to the tea shop."

"No need," Granny said, shading her eyes against the bright sunlight. "It's nice out here. I'd like to sit on the porch a spell and watch the water while we talk."

"At least let me get you something to drink." Cecily put her foot on the bottom stair.

"No need," Granny repeated. "Can't expect to be wined and dined every time I come."

"Now, where were we?" she asked as she settled into the cushions of her favorite couch. Many of Cecily's customers loved that chair. They ate there, sipped tea and enjoyed conversations with friends.

"You were talking about Sissieretta's son."

"Oh, right. Caton grew up and went away to college at A and T University. Course it was a college back then. But he graduated from there. Sissieretta was a proud mama when that boy graduated. He was the first in that family to get a college degree. Sissieretta's mama was still living then. You shoulda seen the pride on her face, even though she didn't like what everybody knew was going on in keeper's cottage.

"Well, soon after that, Hannibal passed on and left that house to Sissieretta and Caton. Now you know that caused the tongues to wag. But the place was hers and she moved

from the top floor to the main floor, although it's been said
she really stayed with Hannibal at nights anyway. After
Caton left, the top floor was more for show than anything
else."

"Did Caton return to the island after he graduated?"

"No. Liked to broke Sissieretta's heart when he moved
up North to Washington, D.C. Hannibal paid for him to get
his medical degree at Howard University. But he didn't
move back here after he finished. Didn't want to settle in
North Carolina."

"Did the island have a physician?" Cecily asked.

"No. Like I said, Sissierett's mama was the closest thing
we had to a doctor on this island. People didn't think so,
but those old remedies she used worked. Healed a lot of
folks. It was Sissiereta's mama that passed the gift of healing
on to Caton."

Cecily had read someplace that the medical community
was beginning to study some of the old remedies and incor-
porate them into modern medicine.

"When Caton was in his thirties, Sissieretta got real sick.
That was when he moved back here so he could look after
her. He came back with a slicked up car when most folks
were still driving horse and buggy. Most islanders couldn't
afford cars.

"Caton and his wife moved into this house and your
daddy Walter was born right upstairs in the big bedroom.
They used a couple of the rooms down here for Caton's
offices. His wife didn't like having folks coming in her
house every day, but what could they do? Sissieretta's boy
had to see to the lighthouse, too, although he hired on folks
to help. And let me tell you, your daddy loved this island.
He and Clay ran through this place like a bunch of wild
boys." Granny cackled. "Mischievous as they could be.
But they were good boys. Always visited Granny. They
liked my blackberry pie. Said nobody could bake them like
Granny."

"I'd love to try your pie," Cecily said.

"Well, now, I'll bake you one."

"Walter's mama wasn't used to island life though she

did find a way to fit in just like you're gonna have to find your way. She was an outsider. You were born here. Your roots are right here in this house.

"With the boys taking off on the boat whenever the mood struck 'em, and the rough waters, it turned her hair gray overnight. Clay's brother's liked to fish and sail too, and he'd made sure they didn't drown. Got so after a time, Walter didn't tell his mama where he was going so she wouldn't fuss over him so. Made him feel hemmed in. Just showed up with a bucket of fish or crabs for her to fix. She had to have known, but he was home safe and sound then. Too late for her to worry. Walter's dad had grown up on the island, and although he knew the dangers, he wasn't as fearful. You get used to your way of life. You be careful, but life can be hard. Know what I mean?"

Cecily nodded, then frowned remembering Granny had said Clay Anderson was wild. "Clay Anderson wild?" she asked. Wild didn't fit the image he presented.

"Boys will be boys," Granny said. "He gave his mama a few scares. She made them older boys keep an eye on him and Walter. It wasn't until later when they were older that Emery started hanging out with them, since he was a few years younger than the other two and wasn't quite as wild."

"Tell me more about my father," Cecily asked.

Granny squinted her eyes. "I would but it's time for my nap," she said around a huge yawn. "I'm plum tuckered out."

Cecily stifled a cry of distress. She craved more information on her daddy, and Granny was taking her sweet time in telling the story. Cecily imagined the woman wanted an excuse to return to eat cakes and sandwiches, and drink tea, and perhaps the attention Cecily lavished upon her. Whatever the reason, Cecily would have to wait another week or so before she returned out of the blue.

When Cecily returned to the cottage, Delilah was flipping through a tabloid.

"Enjoy your day?" Cecily asked. "I wish you had taken that walk with me or toured the lighthouse." Delilah might get on her last nerve but she was family and Cecily was going to treat her as such. Given time, she might come around.

But that was too much to expect. Delilah threw down the paper and sighed heavily. "I didn't want to take a boring walk outside. The wind's blowing and kicking up dust and pollen. It bothers my sinuses." She hopped off the sofa and pranced to the window. "I'm leaving tomorrow."

"So soon?" Cecily asked, but she couldn't help but be glad and felt guilty for it. Guilty or not, she wasn't about to discourage Delilah.

"I've got to get on with my life. A friend is waiting for me in Raleigh. There's more to do there. But I might bring some friends here for the summer."

Cecily remembered that Delilah could throw some wild parties. "I only have two bedrooms, Delilah. And I'm not giving up mine."

"We'll probably rent a cabin or something. Anyway, I came here to talk to you about something."

She hesitated and Cecily's internal alarm turned on. They were finally getting to the purpose of Delilah's visit. "What is it?" Cecily steeled herself for some disaster.

"While I was subleasing your place I started chatting with this guy on the Internet. I got bored. Thought it'd be a pretty cool thing to do. It's not like I do it often." Delilah left the back window and walked to the French doors that led to the balcony. "Anyway, we talked about a month; then I met someone and that was the end of that. But you know how my life is kinda boring. And I didn't want to sound boring to this guy over the Internet. So I . . ."

Cecily knew she wasn't going to like what she heard next. "You did what, Delilah?" she said softly.

"I took on your identity."

"You what!"

"It's not like I gave him your name or anything. I just told him that I owned a tea shop on Coree Island and . . ." She shrugged at a loss of words.

"There's only one tea shop on this island. It won't take a genius to figure out who I am," Cecily snapped.

"I'm sorry, already."

"You're always sorry, Delilah. How could you do something so stupid? I've got this fool e-mailing me already. Now I know what's going on."

"I tried to cut it off, but he kept e-mailing me so I got it disconnected."

"Well, it didn't work. Now he's hassling me. Why did you have to use my name in the first place?"

"There's no reason to get nasty. I didn't mean to cause you harm. He just started e-mailing me. There's nothing I can do about it now."

"Just don't use my name for anything in the future. I'm tired of the messes you get me into. And the only time you come to visit is when you want something. I've had it with you, Delilah. You didn't have to give him that information about me. You could have made up anything."

"I don't need a lecture from you. I came here out of the goodness of my heart. I didn't have to come, you know." Delilah now had a stubborn look on her face.

Cecily walked to the back window. Delilah never did a thing out of the goodness of her heart. Cecily was so angry she was shaking. All kinds of weirdos frequent the Internet. Delilah didn't know what she got her mixed up in or with whom.

"Delilah, don't force me to sever our relationship. It isn't something I want to do."

She heard Delilah's shocked expression. "I didn't mean to hurt you. I'm family."

"I don't care anymore. Family is as family does. I'm just . . . tired of the mess you get me into. If you're in trouble or need help, call, and I'll help you, but otherwise, stay out of my life. Eventually you're going to get me hurt or killed."

Cecily grabbed her coat and went outside. She found herself walking toward the water. She'd been deluding herself for years. She'd given Delilah many chances. She remembered the night she almost got raped by two men when Delilah had left her at the fast food place without telling her. After Cecily purchased the food and had gone outside, she couldn't find Delilah. Cecily wouldn't believe that her own cousin would just up and leave her stranded so she'd walked around the parking lot trying to find her. Two men suddenly stopped in front of her and tried to pull her into their car. If a dear old man hadn't hollered and started running toward her, she didn't know what would have happened. Cecily had called Glenda for a ride home. Glenda had made Cecily promise never to go out with Delilah again.

Cecily jogged along the water's edge. High tides were coming in and the sun was beginning to set, presenting a fantastic tableau.

Cecily didn't understand it. Delilah was her blood cousin, yet she only used Cecily. Yet Glenda, who had no blood connection to her at all, treated her with care.

Up ahead she saw a jogger approach.

Cecily wasn't jogging any longer, but was walking at a fast pace. A minute later she recognized that it was Ryan who was approaching her.

He slowed to a fast walk, too. He was winded. They met near a log.

"Want to sit down?" Ryan asked between breaths. He walked to cooled down.

Cecily was still winded herself. "Sure," she said, catching her breath.

After a couple of minutes, they both sat on a weathered log that looked as if it had been there for years, but probably hadn't. Water did strange things to wood.

It was minutes before their breaths slowed to a near normal pace. Ryan leaned his elbows on his thighs.

"How did the lighthouse tour go with Dad and Uncle Harry?"

"Wonderful. We really don't have to do much to start giving tours. Your father offered to help me get it into shape and with the paperwork—and he offered your help."

"You know that you can count on me."

"Thanks."

He leaned close to her and kissed her. Her heart, which

had just slowed to normal, picked up its pace again and she shivered. She didn't know if it was from the dwindling heat or from his nearness.

"Cold?" he asked and put his arm around her and pulled her close against his strong body.

"Not anymore." He nuzzled her neck and then he kissed her again. "I know I smell like hell."

"No more than me." She was sweaty, too.

"You always smell good," he said as he nuzzled her neck again. "I miss you, honey."

She touched a hand to his face. "No more than I miss you." She tilted her chin and kissed him. He gathered her close.

Seagulls squawked overhead, drawing them apart. In the distance a swarm of birds was flying north. Ryan relaxed and they watched the birds fly off in a V formation. It was a beautiful sight. Then it was quiet. She knew that Emery's boats were out there somewhere.

This was what she loved about this place. The peace. It wasn't the hectic pace she lived in New York. There, she'd had a packed schedule. She wouldn't know what she'd do with herself if she hadn't planned something specific for a day off, but today she'd just meandered. She'd let come what came.

She hated to break the peace but she thought she should tell Ryan about what Delilah had done.

"We have to tell the police. But later. I like holding you right here for now."

"Don't worry, I'm not moving."

Suddenly he stiffened beside her and blew out a long breath. He took his arm from around her and leaned forward, his arms folded at his stomach.

"Ryan?" Cecily rubbed his back. "What's wrong?"

"I don't know. Suddenly, I've got this awful cramp."

Cecily felt helpless but she continued to rub his back. "Do you think you ran too far?"

"I run farther than this all the time."

"Oh," he moaned and then he fell off the log.

"Ryan!" She knelt down beside him. He didn't respond.

"I'm going to get help."

He nodded.

She didn't want to leave him. She knelt beside him but he was doubling over. "Oh, Ryan, I don't want to leave you."

"Something's wrong. Go . . ." he said weakly.

Reluctantly Cecily stood and she ran along the beach at full speed. She was soon coming up on the house. Emery and Glenda were exiting Emery's truck.

"Ryan's sick! Down the beach!" she hollered out.

"Call nine-one-one," she told Glenda.

"Hop in the truck," Emery said. "Things work a lot slower here than in the city."

He backed the truck and drove along the beach. In less than a minute they came upon Ryan, who lay motionless in the sand.

"Oh, my God!" Cecily cried out.

All three of them flew out of the truck. Cecily barely noticed that Emery had left the motor running. They stooped beside Ryan.

"Ryan," he called out.

Ryan only moaned and the sound was extremely weak.

Emery frowned down on him. "I'm going to pull the truck close and we'll put him in the truck bed." He sprinted to the truck.

Tears Cecily could no longer hold slipped out of her eyes as she tried unsuccessfully to comfort him.

She heard Emery say, "Glenda, spread out the blankets. They're behind my seat."

It seemed forever, although she knew it took no longer than a minute before she heard the truck stop beside them. She and Glenda lifted Ryan's feet and Emery handled his upper body as they struggled to move his solid form and lay him out in the truck bed. They used all the blankets for him to lie on because the back of the truck was hard. Cecily peeled off her coat and placed it over him. She sat near his head and placed his head on her lap. But soon she felt Glenda shoving Cecily's arms into her own coat.

"Come on, Glenda, get in the truck," Emery snapped impatiently.

And then the truck was moving and they were speeding along the dirt-packed area bordering the water until they sped up the lane and were on the blacktop road. The cold wind nearly whipped her breath away as Emery increased to breath-stealing speed en route to the clinic. Ryan didn't even stir in her lap. She kept trying to talk to him, tried to get him to talk to her, but he was balled up on his side, motionless.

Emery must have called the clinic from his cell phone because a gurney and orderlys were waiting for them when they arrived. Dr. Grant, crawled into the truck bed to examine him before he was moved.

"Get him inside, stat!" she called out.

Cecily wanted to ask what was wrong, but the doctor was working at a frantic pace and Cecily didn't want to impede her progress. In seconds they had him inside the clinic through the double doors. Cecily tried to go with them but she was stopped by a staff member.

A nurse came out of a back room with a clipboard and began to ask Cecily questions. "Do you know what he ate last?"

The antiseptic smell of a hospital brought back memories of her last moments with her mother. Cecily tried to get around the past that was quickly throwing her into a panic. Ryan wasn't going to die!

"Cecily." Glenda prodded her gently. "The nurse asked you a question."

How did they expect people to remember anything at a time like this? "No," she finally said. Then she remembered lunch. "Around ten I took tea and sandwiches to him. I don't know what he ate after that."

"What was he doing before he collapsed?"

"He had jogged from his house to the tea shop, but we'd been sitting on a log for at least twenty minutes before the cramps started."

Just then the outside doors opened and the Andersons

and the Matthews came rushing toward her with painfully anxious expressions on their faces.

The nurse tried to calm them down, but she had no response that could alleviate their worries. She began asking them the questions Cecily hadn't been able to answer.

Cecily held her arms tightly across her stomach and paced the confines of the room.

"Couldn't have been the sandwiches," she heard Clay say, scratching his mustache. "Carter and I ate them, too. I feel fine."

"So do I," Carter said.

The nurse continued to question them about what Ryan ate later that day. They really didn't know. Most days he ate on the fly.

Cecily couldn't stand pacing any longer. She sank into the chair holding her elbows tightly. Her heart raced. He'd come to mean so much to her in the last two months. She looked up toward the heavens but stared at the sterile white ceiling, and closed her eyes. She imagined a place whose height couldn't be measured. *Please . . . please let him be all right,* she prayed.

She felt the seat give beside her and realized her eyes were shut tight. Glenda gathered her in her arms.

"They're taking very good care of him back there," she said in a soothing voice.

"I just don't understand. One minute he was fine. Then suddenly he was bowled over with pain."

Emery stooped on his hunches beside her. "Dr. Ellen is very good," he assured her.

But Cecily knew that even the best of doctors couldn't cure everything. Then the nurse left and she was surrounded by Ryan's family just as if she were a member—as if she were one of them. She felt some connection to him through them.

They all sat in the waiting room and waited . . . and waited and waited.

It was an hour before the doctor returned.

"He's ingested some kind of poison," she announced to the startled audience. "I've sent samples to the hospital in

Morehead City for analysis. In the meantime he's stable. But I'd prefer if he didn't have visitors.''

Pauline and Clay returned home the next morning. It was almost four o'clock. The results of the poisoning had come back. It was made from an exotic flower that grew in the tropics. Just a touch of the essence of that flower could render him helpless and induce intense pain. Two drops would kill. It couldn't thrive in North Carolina climate.

"How could he have come in contact with such a plant?" Pauline wondered aloud but didn't expect an answer. Ryan had been given the antidote and was resting peacefully. They had left Cecily with him. She refused to leave his side.

"Poor Cecily. The poor child was beside herself."

"I think she loves him, Pauline," Clay said.

"I do too. It's about time he found someone special. This time it's right. I can feel it in my heart, just the way I felt about Carter and Delcia," Pauline said.

"I'm really worried about him." Clay sat wearily on the side of the bed.

Pauline rubbed his back. "I am too."

"We're going to have to keep a close eye on things."

"Just the other night I was lecturing him about being fast and loose with Cecily. Told him to rule with his head. If anything had happened . . ."

"But it didn't. Don't think that way, Clay."

"But somebody tried to kill our son." He looked at her unbelievingly. But yet the truth was there. Ryan was in the hospital recovering from being near death.

"If they hadn't just happened to run into each other . . . He always runs alone."

"Fate was on our side, honey. Don't think about the worst."

"Somebody's going to have to be with him from now on. He can't go around running alone until we find out what's going on."

Her husband could be a little overbearing at times, so

Pauline tried to warn him gently. "He's not going to let us treat him like a child, Clay."

"Well, we've got to look out for his safety, don't we?"

"He has to be careful. And we'll do what we can."

"Uh-huh. Well, it's near time he starts thinking about marriage."

"You're going to have a battle on your hands there."

"I don't see why. Anybody can see Cecily is perfect for him."

"Honey, he has to see it, though. Things will happen in their own time."

"I don't like the fact that they're taking the marriage privileges without the marriage."

"Honey, this is the twenty-first century."

"Still doesn't make it right."

Pauline raised her eyebrows. "You weren't exactly a virgin when we married."

Clay glanced away from Pauline. "My parents didn't talk to me the way I talk to him."

Pauline shook her head. "He's a healthy male, Clay. He isn't going to stay celibate with an enticing woman like Cecily around. And she isn't going to turn him down, because she loves him."

"We're going to have to work on this marriage thing."

"Don't start a rift between you and Ryan the way you did with Delcia." Pauline glanced worriedly at the man she loved. She felt stress coming on just from the thought of the battle ahead. Clay was so stubborn. When he got that look on his face, he didn't listen to a word anyone said. "I can't take a repeat of that."

He patted her hand. "Don't worry, honey, I won't."

"Clay?"

Clay yawned, wrapped his arm around her waist. "What, sweetheart?"

"I worry when you tell me not to."

# Chapter 12

Ryan rubbed Cecily's hair. She'd fallen asleep and her head was resting near his chest. It was really comforting watching the even flow of her breathing—having her beside him on the bed. He smoothed a hand down her back and remembered how she'd stuck by him yesterday. She'd been frantic with worry.

The police had come in late last night and interrogated him as soon as Doc would allow. But he wasn't much help. He didn't know how he came in contact with the poison. That worried him—a lot.

He shifted positions. He hated this feeling. He felt as weak as a kitten.

Doc Ellen came into the room, wearing her lab coat and stethoscope around her neck.

"How are you feeling, Ryan?" she asked as she checked his vital signs.

"As if a truck ran over me."

She listened to his heartbeat—took his pulse before she spoke.

"Well, I'm going to release you. You'll be a little weak for a couple of days, but other than that, you'll survive."

"Thanks for saving me, Doc."

"Any time. But, Ryan. Be careful."

Cecily stirred and set up.

"Are you going to take him home, Cecily?" Doc asked.

She blinked rapidly and rubbed her eyes. "He can go? Already?"

"Yes. I want to go over a few things with you. You can tell Pauline to call me if she has any questions. I want him to take it easy for the next couple of days. He should be okay after that. The nurse will come in and go over things with you and give you his prescriptions."

"Talk about me as if I'm not here, okay?" Ryan cut in but the ladies ignored him.

"Is there anything he shouldn't eat?" Cecily asked.

"He can resume a normal diet. Food didn't do this. He was poisoned through skin contact. It takes anywhere from one to two hours for a reaction. So think very hard about what you did within that time frame before you became ill. I'll see you before you leave."

Two hours later they pulled into Ryan's driveway.

His mother and father met them in the yard.

"Let me help you there, son."

"I can make it, Dad."

"Don't want you falling now."

"I won't."

Ryan made his way inside, with everyone following him. The only thing he wanted was to lie down. And he wasn't a sleeping-in person. He liked to be on the go. There was so much to do at the new campsite yet that he couldn't afford to be sleeping the day away.

"Thanks for bringing him home, Cecily. Come on in for a while," Clay said.

"I'll be back later. I want to see my cousin off to the mainland."

"Well, you come back soon then."

Cecily kissed Ryan, thinking to make it discreet in front of his parents, but he had other ideas. He held on to her tightly and pulled her against him for a long kiss before he released her.

"My hero," he said.

"Heroine." She touched his cheek with the back of her hand.

"Come by after work?" he asked.

Cecily nodded and cleared her throat. Both his parents were watching closely. She stepped back from him.

"Pauline, I have instructions from the doctor." She went over everything and handed over the prescription she'd had filled on her way to his house.

Pauline hugged Cecily. "Thank you, dear. If it wasn't for you . . ." She was so agitated she had to inhale a couple of breaths before she could go on.

"You're more than welcome," Cecily murmured. "I'll see you later, okay?"

Cecily kissed the woman on the cheek and went to her car. Once there, she leaned on the steering wheel a moment before she put the car in drive and left.


Delilah was waiting for Cecily when she arrived.

"How is Ryan?" she asked.

"He's okay. It was a close call though."

"I'm sorry about that, Cecily."

"Thanks, Delilah. Do you need help with your luggage?"

"The trunk's already packed."

"Where are you going next?"

"To Raleigh." She thrust a piece of paper at Cecily. "Here's my address and phone number . . . just in case."

"Thanks. I hope you enjoy your time there, Delilah. I hope . . ."

Try as she might, she couldn't just break all connections with Delilah. "Send me a card, will you? Let me know how you're doing." She wouldn't go as far as to say visit. Cecily wasn't ready for any more of Delilah just yet. Maybe one day. Not yet, though. Cecily hugged her cousin and walked her to the car.

Delilah swept her gaze toward the water. "This is a beautiful place. You must love it here."

"I do."

"Be happy, Cecily." And then she was in her car and was driving down the driveway until she disappeared from sight.

Cecily watched the space where the car had disappeared for a moment before she went inside and showered. She was so exhausted she could drop. But several cars were parked in the tea shop parking lot. She quickly dressed and entered the shop.

Glenda was harried as she worked between serving and her regular chef's duties. She breathed a sigh of relief when Cecily walked in.


The next day Ryan went in to the office for a few hours. He still felt weak but not as weak as before. He wanted to take a jog as he did daily, but his mom and dad would pitch a fit. And they certainly weren't going walking with him. He worked the cash register in the store. Delcia was working with the reservations for the new campground and put him out of his office. Carter was doing the last-minute preparations for the new area. Ryan's dad had gone over to work on the lighthouse so they could do a few tours by next week when an onslaught of college kids would arrive. He even talked Cecily into working up a flyer for the campground to hand out.

But Ryan wasn't accustomed to sitting around idle. His mother had put up a fuss when she realized he was going to work. But he was feeling weak again, damn it. Maybe he'd go over to Cecily's. His mom and dad had disappeared last night to give them privacy when she visited. His dad made sure they were in the living room—not the bedroom. He needn't have worried. Ryan didn't have the strength to do anything except stretch out with his head in Cecily's lap. Her sweet perfume and scent soothed him some how. But the thought of it today was having the opposite effect.

A grandfatherly-like camper who wore a beard and mustache approached the cash register. He was a newcomer.

"Enjoying your stay here?" Ryan asked.

"I am. But I forgot a few things."

"That's what we're here for. Will you be with us long?"

"Until some time next week. I was lucky there was a cancellation. The first time I called, you didn't have a room available. This is a pretty neat setup. I'm not much for camping but I like the cabins."

"We just added more cabins. Some people like the conveniences."

"I'm one of them."

Ryan rang the items up and stashed them into a plastic bag. The man paid him and picked up the flyer on the tea shop from the stack on the countertop. "This tea shop," he asked, "is the food any good?"

"Very. It's new. Just opened up last month. You should try it."

"I think I will. Is it far from here?"

"Not at all." Ryan pulled out a map and drew directions for the man.

"Take just a few minutes to get there," he said.

The man thanked him and left.

Ryan smothered a curse when he noticed Hazeline coming toward him.

"Hey, Ryan. Didn't know you'd be here. Heard you were under the weather."

"I'm better now."

"Well, I came by to get the package for Mama."

"Sorry, you wasted a trip. She picked it up yesterday."

"She didn't tell me. Is there anything I can do for you? Get your medicine or anything?"

"Thanks, Hazeline, but that's all taken care of."

She leaned a narrow hip against the countertop. "Heard you were poisoned. You don't think the tea shop owner did it, do you? What's her name? Something strange. Cecily. I don't think I'm going back there."

"It wasn't a food poison."

"How did you catch it then?"

"I don't know. Must have touched something."

"Whoo. That's scary." She backed up a few paces as if to keep from being contaminated. "Well, I've got to get going. Hope you're doing better."

"Thanks, Hazeline."

Delcia entered the room looking like a cheerful beached whale. "Time to go, Ryan. You've worked long enough today."

"Don't start it, Delcia. A couple of hours is not a full day."

"You look like you're about to fall out. Let's go."

Mark came around the back. "I'm manning the cash register. I could use the extra hours. I need the money. You go on home. Maybe we'll take in a little fishing soon as you're up to it. Was that Hazeline I saw walking out?"

"Yeah."

"You know me and Mia took in a movie in Morehead City the other night. Afterward we went to Wendy's and we saw a buddy of mine I took classes with at the community college. He works at the hospital with Hazeline. Said he took a cruise to the Bahamas in February."

"Mark," Delcia called out, "he's supposed to go home to bed. You can tell him your long-winded stories some other time."

"Delcia, forget it. He isn't going to bed. Anyway, he said he saw Hazeline and her mama on the cruise with her uncle and his wife and kids."

"She told everybody she went to Charlotte."

"She may have but she went to the Bahamas too."

"Hmmm."

"Ryan, it's time for you to go," Delcia cut in.

"Yeah, yeah, yeah" Ryan said, giving up the fight. The heck with them all. He was going to see Cecily. At least she didn't treat him like an invalid.

Delcia stopped him and kissed him on the cheek, enveloping him in as much of a hug as she could manage over her round stomach. "Take it easy, okay?"

He sighed. What could you do with a caring family? "Okay."

He got in his truck and directed it toward the tea shop. It was only two and already his day was over. He'd only gotten in at noon after his mother had fussed over him all morning.

Across the path in the opposite direction Carter was direct-ing the crew. Ryan started to pull in, but knew he'd get the same treatment he got from everybody else. He turned right into the path to Cecily.

She was pleased to see him. The lunch crowd had died down and she and Glenda were sitting at a table sipping tea and working on the supply list for next week.

"What are you doing out and about?" Glenda asked. "Shouldn't you be in bed? You took a few years off me the other day."

"Trying to find something to do." He leaned over and kissed Cecily, then pulled a chair close to hers and sank into it, putting his arm around the back of her chair. She smelled sweet.

"I'll call the order in. You go with him. Else he's going to work himself into a lather. All that excess energy."

"Have you had lunch?" Cecily had.

"Mom all but spoon-fed me."

Cecily laughed. "She's worried, is all. Come on, big boy. Let's go." It was so nice outside that she didn't bother with a jacket as she led him to her apartment. As soon as the door closed he took her in his arms and leaned back against the wall so she pressed against him. "I've wanted this all day."

"Me too." She maneuvered him over to the couch. And she pressed him back and leaned on him. She felt so good he could scream. "Let me . . ." She snaked a hand up his chest beneath his camp sweater, followed with stringing kisses. It damn near took his breath away. ". . . take care of you." She brushed a kiss on his nipple. He went halfway crazy. Then she pulled the sweater over his head, tossing it on the table, and had her way with him.

"I knew there was a reason I came here." His moan was deep and throaty.

"Ummm." Cecily rubbed his penis through his jeans. It felt so good he couldn't stand not touching her a minute longer and he brushed his hand under her top to feel the silky softness of her skin. She was driving him insane with need.

She slithered up his body and kissed his cheek; then she flicked a tantalizing tongue along his lower lip before she dipped inside. He crushed her to him as they tasted each other. She reached down, unzipped his pants, and stroked the hard length of him.

"Oh, baby," he whispered against her lips. He heard a knocking and knew his chest was beating double time against hers. He slicked his tongue against hers, his heartbeat accelerating by the second.

Suddenly she stopped and looked toward the door.

"Cecily." Knock, knock, knock.

"Shit." Ryan didn't even try to smother his curse.

Cecily bolted up. "I look like hell."

"You look like a million bucks."

"I've got to run in back and straighten up. You answer the door."

"Like this?"

"Be there in a minute!" Cecily sprinted to the bathroom and tore her fingers through her hair. She straightened her clothing and tried to decrease her heartbeat; then she ran to the door and opened it. Ryan was standing at the sink drinking a glass of water. He'd managed to pull his shirt and straighten his clothes but he looked so angry he could eat raw meat.

"Hi. All finished," she said to Clay.

Clay craned his neck, looking around the room. "Thought I saw Ryan's truck out there."

"Come on in," she said. "He's in the kitchen."

Clay tucked his hands in his pockets ambled into the room and caught sight of Ryan. The breakfast bar concealed the lower part of his body. "Thought I saw your truck out there."

"No doubt."

"Since you're feeling better I could use a little help."

"I'm feeling tired."

"I'll take you home."

"Dad . . ."

"Ryan, go on with your father."

Ryan threw an angry glare at his meddling father. He was so frustrated he could barely stand it.

"You go on," he finally said. "I'll be out in a little bit."

His dad looked from Cecily to him. "I'll wait for you. On the top step. See you later, Cecily."

"I'll bring over a drink."

"I'll be mighty grateful." He opened the door and left.

"Damn it," Ryan cursed. "I could—"

Cecily pressed a finger to his mouth. "He's kind of sweet, really."

"Sweet, my—"

"Don't say it."

"He's a meddlesome, bothersome troublemaker."

"I'll see you tonight?"

"He'll find a way to mess that up too." Ryan grabbed his jacket off the coat tree and stormed out the door, all signs of weakness long forgotten.

Ryan jerked the lighthouse door open and went inside. He paced back and forth in the small space. A moment later his father followed him in.

"Why can't you leave it alone, Dad? I've been on my own for years."

"Now, son. I know you're feeling put out right now."

"Doggone right."

"And you're feeling right randy, and Cecily will feel really good especially with you being cooped up most of the time like you are, but it's not the time to take advantage of her."

"I'm not taking advantage."

"Yes, you are, unless you plan to marry her?"

"How do I know who I'm going to marry? Or if?"

"Well, then, take it slow until you decide."

"Look, you told me it's none of my business what's between you and Mom. The same goes for me and Cecily."

"That's where you're wrong, son."

"Most fathers stay out of that part of their sons' lives.

Why do you have to interfere? Why do you have to be spinning guilt on me?''

"Because I have to do what's right.''

"I'm thirty-four years old. I don't need my dad talking to me about sex. I don't need you spying on me.'' In sheer frustration, Ryan raked his hand over his head. "I'm going home—to take a *nap*.'' He tore out of the building but suddenly fatigue stole his energy. He'd felt energized lying on that couch with Cecily.

He stomped across the yard and climbed into his truck. In seconds he roared out of the yard, seashells spinning under his wheels. He wished his father would mind his own business.

# Chapter 13

Ryan's strength had returned by spring break when hundreds of college kids from various locations in the country descended on the campground.

Cecily barely saw him at all that week. Her tea shop was teeming with people from the moment she opened it at 6 A.M. to closing time at 11:00 that evening. With the crowd that arrived on Friday night, her supplies trickled down to almost nothing. First thing Monday morning she tripled her delivery order and she hired enough people to handle the extra traffic. Glenda saw to that.

This island was slowly growing on her. It had come as a shock when she realized she loved Ryan and she was never leaving this island. Glenda wanted to settle here, and she'd grown to love it just as much as Glenda had.

"Morning."

Cecily heard a rattling of the doors.

"Anybody in there?"

At 5:45, Cecily was running late. The first batch of tea hadn't been completed, athough the smell of blueberry and apple scones was wafting in the air. Right now Harry Anderson's voice wasn't the one she wanted to hear.

She put the teapot on the countertop and went to open the door. She saw a couple of college kids toting backpacks trotting along the beach.

"I hope you got coffee ready. Willow Mae's sleeping in. My coffee isn't fit for the hogs to drink."

"Have a seat anywhere, Harry. Coffee's coming right up." Cecily hurried around the counter. Coffee had started to drip into the first pot. Harry stood on the other side of the counter.

"You're here early," Cecily said.

"Yep. Got the tours to do this morning. Thought I'd get an early start," he said all-importantly.

"But they don't start until nine."

Harry nodded. "Yep. I know. I'm going on over there after breakfast and set things up."

Cecily didn't know what he had to set up.

"What time does the kitchen open? I'm gonna order some breakfast."

Just then the door opened again. This time it was Emery.

"Your lunch boxes are ready. I'll go get them," Cecily told him.

"Keep doing what you're doing. I know the way." With a whistling tune on his lips, Emery disappeared in the kitchen. Cecily knew he wouldn't be out for a while.

Cecily turned to Harry. "What can I get you, Harry?"

"I'll take some eggs and bacon with a couple of them scones. Don't forget the butter."

"All right." Cecily poured him a cup of coffee and handed it to him; then she passed his order through the window. Glenda had a helper in the kitchen today.

The door opened. The woman she hired to man the cappuccino machine hustled in the door. "Sorry I'm late. Car trouble." She ran to the back.

On her heels, Ryan came barreling in and frowned when he saw Harry standing at the bar. He looked far too sexy this early in the morning.

"No need to look ugly at me," Harry said. "I'm not meddling in your business."

"I thought I'd get here before the crowd."

"You a little slow on the uptake for that," Harry said around a chuckle.

"I'm a little slow for a lot of things," he said, accepting a cup of coffee from Cecily. After his sip he smiled. "Perfect." He rounded the counter and put his coffee down. Then he caught her in a hug and kissed her. "Good morning." His voice was low and husky as if the sleep hadn't completely cleared away.

"Good morning," Cecily responded.

"I'm coming by after closing tonight. This is going to be a hell of a week."

"It's been one already."


Ryan's brother-in-law, Carter, was a retired SEAL and he had contacts in the security business. Ryan asked him to check out financial information and bank accounts on the three witches, which he promised to do.

The week had passed at warp speed and the following Monday morning found Ryan and Cecily driving to Charlotte.

"If Carter is from Baltimore and was a SEAL, how did he and Delcia meet?"

"It's a long story," Ryan said.

"We've got a long drive."

Ryan explained that Carter had gone through various foster homes, but it wasn't until he turned 14 and moved in with the Roberts' that he had truly found a loving environment.

What had happened was much more tragic than those simple words. Cecily thought about her mother a lot lately. If her mother had been convicted, she would have ended up in the foster care system.

For the first time Cecily began to look at her mother's situation in a new light. What if she had stayed on Coree Island and fought? What if she'd been convicted? Cecily hadn't been able to find anything to clear her so far. Who would have taken care of Cecily? Who would have assured her mother that her daughter would be raised and loved in the way she'd done?

Cecily never doubted for a moment that she was loved. She'd lived a charmed live with her mother and stepfather. It was hard thinking of Otis as her stepfather. He had been a man like Carter. He'd loved her unconditionally. Maybe instead of resenting her mother for keeping secrets, she should thank her for her sacrifice.

In another fifteen minutes, Cecily fell asleep and Ryan glanced at her with a mixture of warmth and longing.

He didn't know how he felt about her. Only that she was special somehow. But marriage? A chill spread through Ryan at the thought and he shook his head. He wasn't ready for that step. Didn't know if he'd ever be. He did know that life would be miserable without her. He'd come to depend on her. He drove in the silence of the truck and turned on the radio to an oldies station that serenaded him for most of the trip to Charlotte.

He was still worried about the poisoning. What if Delcia or Carter were poisoned? Who would want him dead? He thought about the poisoning while Cecily slept.

Cecily didn't waken until they were an hour away. They talked until they arrived around noon.

It was tedious work going through city records in the dingy room in the basement. Ryan glanced at Cecily. Her brows were furrowed in concentration as she read pages of information. Marriage. He'd been thinking about it a lot lately—thanks to his meddlesome dad. Then he started to wonder. Why shouldn't he marry her? The differences between Cecily and LaToya were like night and day. She seemed to like living on the island now. And goodness knew he didn't have any money left. She had as much to lose as he did. Right now, they were pretty much even financially. But more importantly, she wasn't concerned about changing him. She seemed to be pretty much satisfied with who he was. He didn't have to be on guard around her. He could be himself.

Before he knew it, he found himself saying, "Marry me, Cecily."

Her head jerked to the side. Her brown eyes seemed to light up in the dim lighting. "What!"

Ryan paused a moment, thinking he'd lost his mind. But he repeated himself. "Marry me."

Cecily was off the seat and threw herself into his arms with such power he rocked back in his seat. She strung kisses along his face and he immediately got a gigantic hard-on.

"I love you, I love you, I love you," she said.

He laughed under her onslaught and held her tight against him. He closed his eyes. Felt the pleasure of her breasts pressed against his chest.

And then they heard an "Ahem."

A couple of people were smiling and looking at them from the other side of the room. It was a moment before Cecily returned to her seat. He scooted his chair closer to hers.

"When?" she asked.

"Sunday."

"Which Sunday? A Sunday three months away?"

Ryan smothered a smile and shook his head slowly. "This Sunday."

The smile froze on Cecily's face. "I'm not going to point out to you anything about wedding planning because you have to already know since your sister has married twice."

"Yep." He nuzzled her neck.

"I'm not going to elope."

"My parents would kill me, and Glenda would kill you," he said. She smelled delicious.

"So, let's be a little more reasonable about this. I'm not pregnant. There's no emergency here."

"Except me needing to have you . . ." He tugged her closer. ". . . in my arms every single night." He kissed her lightly. The light dancing in her eyes stole his breath. She appeared so beautiful looking down on him, he almost lost his cool.

"Oh, you're a scoundrel," she murmured.

"I'm not one for long engagements. You can look for a gown wedding dress before we leave Charlotte. Something long, even though we'll only have a few people. It's still a special day. That okay with you?"

"Have you heard of fittings?"

"I'll tip her."

"I thought you were broke."

All humor was lost. "Does that bother you?" He steeled himself for her answer.

Cecily lost her smile and caressed the side of his face with a gentle touch. "No. Not for a second. We'll build our lives together." She sealed her pledge with a kiss.

Ryan couldn't fathom how he'd lucked out to find a woman like her. "Sunday?" he whispered against her cheek.

"Sunday."

It took another two hours before they found the information they needed. Ruby's brother had paid for his house six months after the theft. The trouble was, how were they going to prove he had paid for it with the money stolen from the relief fund?

"You know," Ryan said, "I saw Ruby just before I went on that jog."

"Do you think she poisoned you?"

"I don't see how."

"I would think she'd try to hurt me, not you."

"Her daughter came on to me. Wanted me to take her to the Valentine's dinner."

"And you'd invited me."

Ryan wasn't about to say he invited her because of the invitation.

"Be careful, Ryan. I couldn't bear it if anything happened to you."

Her caring warmed his heart. He reached for her hand, brought it to her lips and kissed the back. "Nothing's going to happen to me."

But the worry didn't leave her face.

Cecily didn't know whether it was right or not to destroy this woman—if she indeed had stolen the money—after all this time. Perhaps she should take the high road. Her mother couldn't be hurt any longer. She closed her eyes tightly. Her mother was dead. Her mother wouldn't see her walk down the aisle to Ryan—or see her grandchildren if they were so blessed. But more was at at stake.

If Ruby had tried to kill Ryan, it was unforgivable.

All that was left of her mother was her name, and Cecily wouldn't have her name desecrated through the rest of time. People had long memories. If Cecily didn't clear this up, her children would have to deal with hateful comments about their grandmother.

Children. *Take it easy girl, you're getting ahead of yourself. You're not even married yet.* But six days! She'd be a married woman in six days.

Once they were on their drive back home, Cecily called Glenda, who screamed with cheer over the phone.

"Have you set the date yet?"

"You don't want to know," Cecily warned.

"Not next year, I hope. Don't wait too long."

"Well, then, you'll be pleased that it's Sunday." Cecily held the phone away from her ear.

"Are you crazy! Put Ryan on the phone."

"He set the date, Glenda."

"Traitor," she heard Ryan say.

"Let me speak to him, right now."

"He's adamant. You're not going to get him to change his mind. So you better start thinking about the reception."

"Put him on the phone right now!"

Cecily handed the phone to Ryan. "You're a big boy."

He raised his eyes to the ceiling as he maneuvered the car onto the main highway.

"Hi, Aunt Glenda."

"Oh, you devil," Cecily said. She could almost see Glenda melting into a soft puddle. So instead of trying to get him to change the date, they started talking about where the wedding would be held, times, and other details.

"You need to talk to Cecily about that. But if she agrees, I'd like to have the ceremony in my church." They spoke a few minutes more before he handed the phone back to Cecily.

# Chapter 14

The next few days passed in a whirlwind. Glenda and Cecily had sat up for hours the night before deciding on the wedding dinner. Cecily and Ryan agreed to marry after the shop closed and they'd have the dinner after.

As Cecily put through the order for the food she needed for their wedding dinner, and with the millions of things on her checklist still to be done, the last person she expected to see walk through her tea shop door was Granny Grant.

"Well, well, dear," Granny said as she ambled across the wooden floor. "You're really settling in as our island girl. I was worried for a spell that you might decide to go back to New York. But your home is here. Granny's mighty happy for you."

"Thank you, Granny. I'm tickled myself."

Cecily had visited her the week before. Granny baked a blackberry pie while she visited. Cecily helped her, although she wasn't a baker. Glenda was the expert baker at the tea shop. Granny tried to teach Cecily the fine points of creating the perfect flaky crust.

This time they settled on the porch where the wind blew constantly, keeping the area comfortable.

"Your daddy was a good man, Cecily. He was fun loving." Granny's rummy eyes regarded her seriously. Her
chair rocked, the joints squeaking. "You know, Cecily, some
people go through life just getting by. I think your daddy
enjoyed every day of his life. You rarely saw him moody
or sour or displeased. He brought energy into a room. Now,
everybody has bad days, but he rose above the gloom. He
could be serious when he needed to be.

"He played football in high school and in college. I don't
think he found anybody that touched him, you know. Any
woman he could really be serious about. It takes longer for
some boys. I know you've heard that he dated Ruby a
couple of times. I knew that wasn't going to work. Their
personalities were too different. Ruby was sour. She looked
for the worst in life instead of the best. Living with her
would have stolen his spirit. He was sensible enough to
know that, even if she wasn't.''

"Mama was serious," Cecily said. "She wasn't easy
going."

"It's true she was serious. Probably kept him grounded.
But she was a goodhearted woman, not coldhearted like
Ruby. Watching Walter and Marva, it was clear they made
a good match." Granny nodded. "They truly did. She fit
right in with island life. And they loved you, darling. You
completed their joy."

Granny patted Cecily's hand. "You and Ryan will have
a long, wonderful life together. It's only fitting with Walter
and Clay being best friends."


Butterflies were dancing in Ryan's stomach the night
before the wedding. He'd been so busy all week, he hadn't
given himself time to think about what he'd gotten himself
into. He had no second thoughts. And he'd done the right
thing in pushing Cecily to marry immediately. And his haste
wasn't due to sex. It nagged him that she'd told him so
many times that she loved him and although he wanted her
more than anything, he couldn't feel that kind of love again.

He knew he'd give Cecily everything she ever craved for that he could provide. He'd make certain that she was happy.

"We can't sit at the bar," Mark said, urging Ryan to a back room. The room was filled with guys, all with eager smiles on their faces.

What was Mark up to now? Ryan wondered. A lone chair sat in the middle of the floor. The other chairs circled it but far enough away to give him space. Mark led Ryan to it and he sank into the hard chair feeling he was on display. He hoped they hadn't gone out and gotten a lap dancer. That was so tacky, but definitely something Mark would do.

Everyone had either beer or shot glasses in their hands. This could get rowdy quickly, Ryan thought as someone shoved a glass in his hand. Then he heard scintillating music and the room grew quiet except for the music. Everyone looked toward a back door as the music continued to play. Then the door opened and seconds ticked by. Suddenly a beautiful deep brown sister emerged. The dance was graceful. The sister moved sinuously to the beat of the music. A path was made for her as she danced across the floor and stopped in front of Ryan. All grew quiet and then she began to dance again, capturing everyone's eyes with the sway of her hips, her arms, her breasts. As the music grew faster, guys began to clap, stomp, and roar.

Obviously she was accustomed to the attention she was getting. But the men stayed back and enjoyed the view.

They had given Ryan a bachelor's party for his first marriage. That time they'd had a woman emerge from a cake. He had to acknowledge that this was more tasteful. He was certain that this would be his last bachelor's party and settled in to enjoy.

The morning of the wedding, Ryan's house was so shiny he was almost afraid to do anything in it. After his parents moved, his mom had hired a cleaning crew to do the house from top to bottom. Yesterday she'd made his bed up with new sheets, a pretty, woman's kind of spread for his king-size bed, put new curtains on his windows. He had to sleep in the guest room last night for what little time he'd had.

He was attaching the cummerbund on his tux when his father peeked a head in his room before widening the door and stalking in.

"Still not speaking to me?" he said around a pleased smile.

"Nope."

"I'm giving the bride away. You've got to talk to me some time today."

Ryan frowned at his father. "Says who?"

"You know I'm supposed to give you sage advice today."

"You've given enough advice."

"Tell me you're marrying her because it's what you want—not because of sex."

"If I didn't want to marry her, I wouldn't have proposed."

"That's something at least." He clapped Ryan on the shoulder. The men stood shoulder to shoulder. His father got a serious expression on his face. "Be happy, son, okay? That's all I want for you."

Ryan gave up all pretense of anger. "I will."

His dad clasped his shoulder again.


Cecily was a vision as she and Clay walked down the aisle of the church between rows and rows of islanders. Carter stood beside Ryan watching them as they made their way toward him. A lump formed in Ryan's throat. At Cecily's beauty and this massive step he was taking at this time in his life.

Boyd Thompson snapped pictures. Mark operated the video camera.

After the ceremony, and goodness knew how much longer to pose for pictures, they made their way to the tea shop where dinner was served. The three witches were in attendance. They sat at a table for five. Ruby, Hazeline, Taylor, and Shelly and her husband all huddled together with deep frowns and twisted mouths. Cecily would have liked it much better if they'd stayed away. But she was sure that they came out of respect for Ryan's parents. Cecily refused to let them put a damper on her day.

"No frowns on your wedding day," Ryan said and she smiled at him.

She wasn't given long to reflect on the women because soon, Ryan escorted her onto the floor for the first dance. Being encased in his arms was a lovely feeling, and as the romantic melody weaved around them, she was lost in him until his father tapped him on the shoulder.

Clay Anderson began to whirl her around the floor as Ryan danced with his mother.

"Welcome into the family, daughter."

Tears come to Cecily's eyes. "Thank you," she murmured, touched by this man's ready acceptance of her.

"If you ever need anything, you can always come to me and my wife. I want you to remember that."

Cecily's throat was too clogged to answer so, glassy eyed, she nodded. Clay smiled and continued to dance as he talked to her. He was a wonderful dancer. Cecily imagined he had been quite dashing in his day. She'd learned that he and her dad had been quite the ladies' men. But she wasn't given long to contemplate on the thought because soon she was in Emery's arms and Ryan was dancing with Glenda.


"Well," Pauline said as she slid out of her pumps and began to unzip her dress.

Clay brushed her hands aside and took over the job. He kissed her on the neck.

"Well, what?" he asked after another nibble.

"You got your wish. Ryan and Sissieretta are married. Are you happy?"

"Very. She'll make an excellent wife for him."

"I have no doubt of that."

He stilled himself in the process of sliding the dress off Pauline's shoulder. "Do I hear a but in there?"

"I don't know if *he* knows he's in love with her yet. And that can be quite painful for her."

"Pauline, you worry about nothing. If he didn't love her, he wouldn't have asked her to marry him."

"Men have done worse things for sex."

Angrily, Clay paced to the window. "It's their wedding day. Don't try to burst my bubble on this."

"Far be it from me."

"He loves her."

"I know he does. He just doesn't know it yet. I think they'll weather it through, but a storm is coming, Clay. And Sissieretta is going to get hurt."

Clay rounded on her. "Why didn't you say something before if you felt that way?"

"Because I knew you weren't going to give them any peace. And truly I believe they'll work it out. It was going to happen whether they married or not."

"You're wrong this time, Pauline. You should have seen them the other week when I went to her house and he was there."

"Clay—"

"I didn't want him taking advantage of her. It wasn't right for him to take liberties without any kind of commitment."

"Honey, when are you coming into the twenty-first century?"

"Everyone doesn't have to be alike, Pauline. Just because we see things differently doesn't mean either of us is wrong."

Pauline couldn't help the worry. Sometimes she just wanted to shake some sense into her family. Clay was all gung ho in getting Ryan settled and married. While she thought Sissieretta would make a wonderful wife, they needed time to develop their relationship. Clay couldn't see that. At least now they'd have the distance from him to discover each other without his interference. She unclipped her earring and put it into her jewelry box, wanting things to be perfect for her children.

"This time, my darling Clay, I hope you're right."

*  *  *

Ryan nudged Cecily gently. Her head rested comfortably on his shoulder. He kissed her on the top of her head. "Wake up, Mrs. Anderson. The plane's landing soon."

"What?"

"The plane's landing soon. Take a look out the window." It was night and the bright lights shone clear and dazzling in Los Angeles.

"Did you sleep at all?"

"I don't sleep well on planes."

"You must be exhausted."

"Not too exhausted. You did the planning."

"Men. You have a one-track mind. You're never too worn out for that."

Ryan chuckled and hooked his seat belt. Cecily's was already hooked. It had been a trying ordeal checking into the airport. He'd never gone through so intense a security check. Made him feel like going back to his peaceful island. He felt as if he were in another country almost.

After picking up their luggage and rental car, they drove to the hotel and checked in.

The bellman opened the door for them. Ryan lifted Cecily into his arms and carried her across the threshold. The bellman smiled over.

"Newlyweds?" he asked.

"Yes," Cecily said around her laughing.

"Congratulations."

Ryan put her down once they were in the room.

Then she took her bearings.

The bellman went about setting their suitcases in the room.

"Ryan, you shouldn't have."

"You only get one first honeymoon. I wanted it to be perfect."

"It is. But all I needed was you."

The bellman started to tell them about the room, but Ryan quickly hustled him out with a generous tip.

Ryan turned to Cecily. "You're all mine now," he said and captured her in his arms.

"I'm so dirty I can't stand myself. Just a quick shower, okay, sweetheart?"

He moaned. "Promise it'll be quick?"

"Very."

Gently sliding out of his arms, she opened her suitcase, pulled out the things she needed, and dashed into the bathroom.

Ryan pulled off his jacket and unbuttoned his shirt. Then he stood in front of the window. He'd made the right decision this time. He and Cecily got along well—very well.

Moments later he heard the shower stop. He imagined her doing the things women do as they prepared for bed, but he was getting impatient. He could take a shower while he waited for her to dress. It'd be another half hour at least before she'd be ready and he didn't know if he could wait that long.

# Chapter 15

Ryan and Cecily had a honeymoon of dreams. Reality was a million miles away.

The next morning after a quick stop in Ventura where Ryan and Cecily purchased the freshest and most delicious strawberries they'd ever eaten, they drove the picturesque Highway 1, hugging the California coastline. Viewing the mountains on the right side and the panoramic Pacific on the left was a breathtaking experience.

"Do you want me to drive, Ryan?"

"I'm fine."

"It's almost noon. Want a sandwich?"

"Sounds good. There's an overlook coming up. Want to stop there?"

"Yes."

Ryan drove around a narrow curve and turned left into the overlook.

They climbed out of the car, glad for an opportunity to stretch their legs. Ryan stretched his lean body that captured Cecily's attention even more than before. She climbed into the backseat and gathered sandwich fixings from the cooler.

"Smoked turkey okay?"

"Sure."

Cecily quickly fixed the two sandwiches and grabbed two bags of baked chips. Ryan gathered two bottled waters and led the way to a rock, where they sat.

As they ate, they watched the seals lie on rock croppings several yards out in the ocean. Several cars stopped for a minute or so, other travelers engaged them in short conversations, and then drove on until a recently retired couple made a stop.

"Where are you from?" the woman asked.

"New York," Cecily said at the same time Ryan said, "Coree Island."

"We're actually from Coree Island, North Carolina. We're newlyweds."

"You're on your honeymoon. Congratulations."

"Thank you."

"We're from Connecticut."

"We spent the winter in the South and then went West. Now that spring has come we'll travel north."

"Sounds like the ideal vacation."

"It's something we've wanted to do for a very long time."

Cecily was a little surprised when Ryan said, "We own a campground in Coree. If you ever get out that way, stop by."

The woman's husband asked for a business card. Ryan handed one over and gave them a card on the tea shop as well. Cecily hadn't realized that he had cards of the shop.

She told how the old mansion had been turned into a tea shop and the old lighthouse they also owned. The couple were intrigued and promised they would stop by.

Ryan and Cecily soon left and continued their drive up the coast. They passed Big Sur, which seemed much larger on television. They made a quick stop at Santa Barbara.

They spent the night near Hearst Castle and ate at a local restaurant recommended by the hotel. They hadn't expected the elite fare in such an out-of-the-way place.

That night after their lovemaking, Ryan felt the difference between what he'd shared with LaToya and what was so evident with Cecily. What he and Cecily shared wasn't just hot sex, but it was truly a matched lovemaking experience and a blending of souls.

Progress was slow along the coast road because of the spiraling curves. The next day they arrived at Monterey. They toured the city, passed the golf course where Tiger Woods played. And they spent the night. The next day they drove east past garlic fields and fruit orchards and saw Mexican workers in the fields. They made it to the Sierras and drove to Yosemite National Park where they viewed Bridal Veil Falls, saw the El Capitan rock cropping and Mirror Lake. Then they descended the mountain and climbed another group of the Sierras to the Sierra National Park to view the mighty redwood trees.

At first the trees seemed large but not gigantic until she noticed a stump that was wider than a cabin. Since all the trees were huge, they seemed smaller than they were.

Ryan and she arrived back in Los Angeles the next morning. They planned to leave for North Carolina the next day. They had thought they might tour Universal Studios but decided to spend the next day in quiet. The trip had been invigorating and tiresome.

They rode the elevator alone to their room after lunch at a nearby restaurant. Ryan placed his arms around her and tugged her close.

"What are you thinking about, sweetheart?" Ryan asked.

"About Ruby, the poisoning. I want answers."

Ryan sighed. "So do I. I worry about someone else getting poisoned."

"You don't just pick this stuff up from the island. You have to know where to get it. Do you know anyone who have gone there lately?" Cecily asked.

"Both Ruby and Taylor, but at different times."

"I knew it had to be someone in that group. You have to talk to the sheriff when we get back."

"I already have, honey. Let's not think about them right now, okay?"

Cecily smiled. "Okay."

"Did you enjoy your honeymoon, sweetheart?"

Cecily placed her arms around his waist and rubbed his back. "It was the best, but it's not over yet. I wish it could last forever."

He chuckled, kissed her on the top of her head. "It will."

"We'll have to bring the kids one day."

"Kids." Ryan smiled. "How many will we bring?"

Cecily looked up at him. "Hmmm. Three?"

"Three's a good number."


On Monday afternoon, Ryan and Cecily returned home. As they rode the ferry to the island, they stood at the railing, Ryan with his arms wrapped around Cecily's waist. He'd enjoyed the honeymoon but he was ready for home.

Before he knew it they were leaving the ferry. When they made it there, a banner with WELCOME HOME, NEWLYWEDS swayed in the wind on the porch. Ryan opened the door, then lifted Cecily in his arms and swung her around.

"You're going to drop me."

He pretended to slip and she screamed and clung to his shoulders.

"You hardly weigh a thing."

Cecily thought of how tight her size-twelve clothes were fitting her and knew he was lying. But it was nice to hear. They had eaten well on the trip.

"I'm going on a diet."

"You're a nice armful."

"A man who doesn't complain about weight. I think I'll keep you forever."

"You better believe it," he said as he lowered her to the floor but not before he kissed her.

"Somebody's been cleaning," Cecily said.

The house had been cleaned from top to bottom and was left with a slight orange scent. The wood glowed. The floor sparkled.

On the table between two candles were a beautiful fruit basket, a bottle of wine, and a note telling them dinner was in the fridge.

Ryan's parents had moved out.

Ryan decided to stop at the campground and Cecily visited Glenda.

---

"I heard from my friend while you were gone," Carter said. "It seems Ruby and her daughter went on a cruise to the Bahamas. She has a hefty bank account. The money she earned from her job and from her husband's insurance was enough to cover her assets if she invested wisely. But then Shelly and Taylor both have some unexplainable money. Taylor took a cruise to Panama last month."

"I thought Ruby was the thief."

"She may be, but you can't tell by her bank balance," Carter said.

"I don't understand why Ruby lied about her trip. Why lie about going to the Bahamas? A trip like that isn't unreasonable. Lots of people vacation there." Ryan slit a letter with a letter opener.

Carter shrugged. "Those women might be friends, but there's some jealousy there, too."

"All the more reason to be truthful. She could brag about it. Taylor's always bragging about the things and money she has." He glanced at his letter. Junk. He dumped it into the trash.

"Yeah, well, I don't know what's going through those crazy women's minds. Well, now that you're a happily married man, do you think we can get some work out of you?"

"Hey, I'm not here until tomorrow. I'm still on my honeymoon."

"From the looks of you, things went well."

Ryan nodded. But he couldn't get his mind off the witches.

"Glad you're back. We need to talk about those construction workers. At the rate they're going we'll be next year before we rent those cabins."

"Not again. I'm going to talk to the foreman."

*　*　*

Cecily let the last customers out of the restaurant and locked the door. The phone rang as soon as she reached the counter.

She always loved hearing Ryan's voice.

"Hi, sweetheart."

"Hi yourself."

"We're having a problem at the campground. I'll be home in a couple of hours."

"Okay. We're just closing. We should be out of here in another hour. I'll keep dinner warm."

"What would I do without you?"

"Danged if I know."

He chuckled and hung up.

"Was that lover boy?"

"He'll be late."

"Hmmm."

"Glenda when were you going to marry Emery and put him out of his misery?"

"I don't know."

Cecily knew why Glenda was delaying. She and Emery were loving one minute and the next Glenda was picking a fight with him.

"You've put your life on hold for too long for that man. It just isn't right."

"A lot of things aren't, but what can we do about it? I'm happy for you, but it's not right for everyone."

"I don't believe you. Not for a moment. Everyone wants happiness—someone to love them. You don't want to be on the outside looking in for the rest of your life." Cecily started to the window to close it. She'd left it open to catch the warm breeze.

"I can live this way," Glenda said. "I couldn't stand it if something happened to Emery. I still feel responsible for my fiancé even though I didn't kill him. Once was enough."

"I—"

Cecily heard a faint yell.

"Did you hear that?" Cecily moved toward the door.

"Barely," Glenda said, frowning and following her. "Sounds like it came from the direction of the ocean."

They hurried outside and ran toward the ocean. A woman was flailing in the water.

"Oh, my stars!" Glenda said.

"Let's get the boat. Hold on!" she called out. "We're coming." She knew the woman couldn't hear her from the rushing of the tides and her own screaming. She was too far out to identify.

They ran around back and pulled the little canoe from beneath the porch and dragged it to the water, praying all the time that the woman could hold on. She could imagine what the light keepers had had to endure as they guarded these shores. Cecily and Glenda hopped in the canoe and paddled out, continuing to call out to the woman. She knew that there was a strong undertow. She was surprised the woman held on this long.

After paddling and paddling, they finally reached her. The boat had tipped over. She was clinging to the side. Cecily recognized Ruby. The woman was drenched and looked as if she were at the end of her wits. "Hold on, Ruby." Cecily maneuvered the boat beside her. The boats touched in a V shape with the woman between the two.

Cecily reached out to haul Ruby into their boat, but the woman was dead weight and Cecily got pulled into the cold water. Water was dragging at her feet. Cecily was a weak swimmer and the shoes and clothing she wore were a heavy burden that worked against her.

The boats separated and Ruby pushed Cecily underneath the water. Her grip was strong. Cecily didn't grow up around water, never before felt how helpless one could be in the churning waves.

This can't be the end, Cecily thought as she caught Ruby's arm and tried to move away from her hold. Suddenly she was free but Cecily felt a hand on her again. This time she was being dragged up. As soon as she cleared the surface her burning lungs inhaled huge gulps of air. She reached for the side of the boat but felt arms dragging her away. All her strength had gone, but she tried to fight Ruby off. Her movements seemed to go in slow motion and in the struggle she swallowed salty water. She kicked, she hit Ruby and finally freed herself and reached for the boat.

Glenda reached for Cecily, and Cecily tried to cling to the side of their canoe with one arm. Glenda started pulling her into the boat, but Ruby grabbed her around the waist and tugged. Cecily kicked out, heard Ruby grunt. Then Cecily felt a sharp pain in her shoulder and she could no longer cling to the boat. She saw blood in the water. Glenda was screaming and so was Ruby. Cecily wondered if a shark had attacked her. Something was hitting her and she was disorientated. It was evening and feeding time for sharks. But wasn't the water still too cold for sharks in this area?

Then she heard Glenda scream again and she felt herself sinking.

Then Ruby was talking about stealing and men.

"Cecily!" she heard Glenda shout. "Hold on. Don't go!" Cecily was sinking, sinking, and losing consciousness . . . and suddenly something strong grabbed her like a manacle. She struggled thinking the shark had finally gotten her and was going to eat her. She had forgotten to tell Ryan she loved him before she hung up. She was jarred by her body's contact with a hard surface. The shark hadn't gotten her yet. As if from afar she heard the sound of Glenda's voice but couldn't make out what she was saying. She was hurting and shivering and then she didn't feel anything.

# Chapter 16

When Cecily awakened, she heard Ryan's voice as he screamed at somebody. In place of the smell of the ocean, she smelled an antiseptic. She opened her eyes to a bright light shining on her. And she saw Dr. Ellen leaning over her.

"Welcome back. Your husband is about to tear the place down." But the doctor continued her examination and ignored Ryan's bellowing.

Cecily cleared her throat. She felt she'd gone a round with Muhammed Ali. Her cloudy memory was slowly returning.

"What happened?" She asked.

"I'll let Glenda tell you. Right now I want to patch you up."

"Is Glenda okay?"

"She's fine."

"Did a shark get me?"

"A human shark. Ruby tried to kill you."

"What?"

Ellen stuck a needle in Cecily's arm.

Cecily heard Ryan's shout.

Dr. Grant sighed. "He's disturbing the patients. You better let him in," she said to the nurse. "Go get him, please."

The woman smiled and left. In seconds Ryan charged into the room. "You okay?" he asked, making for the examining table. He looked her over anxiously and his mouth tightened when he saw her arm. "Just wait until—"

"I'm okay." She smiled to reassure him.

He kissed her tenderly. Cecily noticed his hands shook.

"Now that you see she's going to live, can you calm down so I can clean her wound and stitch her up?"

Ryan gave a curt nod, but Cecily saw the muscle working in his jaw. She'd never seen him that angry before. She still wondered why Ruby tried to stab her.

Ryan stood on the opposite side from the doctor and rubbed her good arm. The nurse shoved a chair by him and he sank onto the surface, keeping a hold on Cecily's free arm.

"Make sure you don't hurt her," he told Ellen.

"If you don't stop telling me what to do you're going out of here. Do you understand?"

He tightened his lips again but nodded.

"The area is numb. I can't feel a thing," Cecily reassured him.

He seemed to relax a little.

Ellen cleaned the wound and used nine stitches on her.

"You're lucky the knife didn't touch muscle."

"Why did she stab me?"

"It's a long story," Ryan told her. "I'll tell you once you're settled."

"Since she passed out, I'm going to keep her overnight," Ellen told Ryan. "We'll put a cot in her room for you." Obviously she already knew Ryan wasn't going to leave her side.

The doctor fixed up her other bruises and soon Cecily was in her room with visitors beginning to pour in. Ryan still hadn't told her the full story.

Glenda, Emery, Pauline, Clay, Delcia, Carter, and even Harry and Willow Mae had been waiting for more than an hour to see her. It was unusual to let so many people in one room, but this was a small town and Ellen allowed them to stay for a little while.

"I don't want you to tire her out," she said. They waited for Ellen to leave before they began talking.

"Who would have thought?" Pauline said.

"I still don't know what happened." Everything was just a cloudy jumble in Cecily's mind.

"Ruby tried to kill you and me," Glenda said.

"Why?"

"She wanted Hazeline to marry Ryan and she hated that Emery dated me."

"Wait a minute. She was married to Emery."

"She wanted your daddy," Pauline said.

"That woman was a crazy fool," Willow Mae said.

Emery nodded. "I knew something wasn't right with her when we were married. She hated your daddy for marrying your mother. She married me just because she couldn't get him. I couldn't stay with her. She was vindictive and evil."

"She was going to kill us over men?"

"She tried to poison Ryan. She'd given him something the day you all had to rush him to the hospital," Willow Mae said. "Something she picked up from the islands."

"Oh, my . . . How could she do such a thing?"

"He didn't love that witch Hazeline." Pauline was in high dudgeon. Ruby tried to kill her baby. Never mind that he was six-one and in his thirties. She had a mother's protective instinct.

"The girl's got the disposition of her mama," Willow Mae said.

"She stole the money, too," Harry offered.

Cecily straightened in the bed. "Ruby?"

"Lie back," Ryan said and urged her back with a gentle hand. He sat on a chair near the head of her bed.

"The relief fund?" she asked.

"Yes," Pauline declared. "She revealed that information when she was arrested. She switched the pouches when your mama wasn't looking."

Clay shook his head. "I think something finally broke in her. She was filled with hatred and evil."

"Hatred does mean things to people," Willow Mae muttered, shaking her head. "Been living up right fine with that stolen money. And blaming your mother for it all these years. How could she do that?" she asked.

"You know, when I think of all those years ago, I remembered the town really coming together," Pauline mused.

"Yep, it did," Harry agreed.

"How so?" Cecily wanted to know.

"Didn't have enough money to fix everything up so people started pitching in. We recorded what everybody needed and the repairs the insurances wouldn't cover. You remember that, Pauline? We helped record that."

"I remember."

"Then everybody pitched in. Repaired roofs. Cut trees. Replaced broken windows. Cleaned debris."

"I recollect it wasn't all bad either," Harry said, scratching his whiskers. "Folks got right friendly. Took us a few months. We worked on weekends mostly, but everything got done."

"They were some pretty good times," Clay said. "But I missed your daddy. We would have worked together like we always have. We were as tight as twins. He'd barely been gone two years."

Dr. Grant came charging back into the room. "Time for everybody to leave," she commanded.

Pauline was the first to stand. "We'll visit you later."

"See her when she gets home," the doctor said. After they hugged Cecily one by one, everyone piled out. The room seemed unusually quiet.

Doc Ellen checked her vital signs again. "Grandma wanted to come by, but I wouldn't let her," she said, taking Cecily's pulse. "She'll see you in the morning before you leave."

"I'm here right now." Granny came huffing in the door. She was out of breath as if she'd walked a couple of miles.

"Grandma," Ellen scolded, "I thought I asked you not to come tonight."

"You did. But I had to see my girl. Make sure she was okay."

"I told you she was all right."

"Had to see for my own eyes." She waved Ellen on. "Just go on. I know it's late. I won't keep her long."

Ellen narrowed her eyes at her grandmother. "How did you get here?"

Granny tilted her chin. "I walked. It's a good evening outside."

"You live a mile from here. You know better. It's late and dangerous at night."

"A good walk never hurt nobody. And this is Coree, remember? Not the big city."

Ryan left Cecily and guided Granny Grant into a seat. "I'll take you home when you're ready," he told her.

"Thank you, young man. Go on, Ellen. We're gonna visit for a spell."

"Don't bother, Ryan. I'm leaving in ten minutes and *she's* going with me." Hanging on to her temper by a thread, Ellen sailed out of the room. With her aggravated departure, they heard her mutter, "Stubborn woman" as she disappeared down the hall.

"There, there now," Granny said, patting Cecily's hand. "You had a close call there."

"Too close."

"It wasn't in the cards for you to go yet. But I still feel uneasy. So you take care of her, Ryan. Keep a close eye on her. Our girl isn't out of the woods yet."

"I will, Mrs. Grant."

"You're married to kinfolks. Call me Granny like everybody else."

Ryan chuckled. "Granny it is."

She regarded Cecily closely. "Heard you got sliced up. Let me take a look at that." She leaned over to inspect Cecily's shoulder wound, but it was covered with a bandage. "I should have brought some of my herbs to tuck in there. Heal real quick."

"I heard that," Doc Ellen said.

Granny sent a scowl in Ellen's direction. Then she said, "She doesn't think much of my remedies, but they work all the same."

"Not in here they won't," Ellen stipulated.

Cecily and Ryan chuckled. They visited a few more minutes with Granny before Ellen dragged the older woman out. "I'll be by to see you tomorrow," Granny said.

"Okay," Cecily said, stifling a yawn. "Thank you for coming," she added as Granny left with Ellen. But she felt good, too, that so many people cared about her. It left her with a warm and comforting feeling—like being tucked in tightly with a soft and warm blanket.

Cecily was so sleepy she could barely hold her eyes open. It was late. She turned to Ryan. He looked drained and her heart poured over with love for him.

"Why don't you go home, sweetheart? It's been a long day for you."

"Wild horses couldn't drag me from you." He nodded to the cot. "I've got my own bed. But I'll wait for you to fall asleep."

"You won't have to wait long." She had to almost pry her eyes open to stay awake. "Have you had dinner?" she remembered to ask.

"The nurse put my plate in the fridge. I'll nuke it in the microwave and eat later."

She covered a yawn. "I don't think I can stay awake any longer."

He kissed her, then smoothed a hand over her hair with a gentle touch. "Go to sleep, darling."

He didn't have to repeat himself, because the next thing Cecily knew, it was morning.


Cecily's left arm was in a sling and maneuvering with one hand was difficult. She found herself wanting to use her left arm. Still, by eleven she was ready to check out. Glenda had told her not to come to work today, but Cecily didn't see why not. Ryan, however, insisted that she stay home, which wasn't a bad thing since he stayed there with her.

Ryan put her bag on the dressing table. "Are you in pain?" he asked her.

"No. They gave me medication this morning after breakfast."

"Let me know when you need some."

Cecily smiled at him. "You're so sweet but, honey, I'm not helpless. I don't want to take more of your time from work. You go in. We've been away for a week."

"As soon as I leave here, you'll go to the tea shop. I'm not having that. Besides, I could use another day with my new wife."

As Cecily began one-handedly to unpack the bag, she watched her husband. She didn't know how she had lucked out to get such a wonderful man. Nobody was perfect, but this was about as perfect as she could get. She wondered how LaToya could have let him go.


A week later, Cecily was feeling much better. There was still soreness in her arm, but she could at least use it.

The days were longer now. April had come in with showers and warmth. Blooms burst in a rainbow of colors on springtime flowers and trees. A multitude of birds were flapping their wings overhead on their journey north for the summer.

"Glenda, let's move the tables to the front porch."

Glenda gave her the eye as she had often this last week. "I'll get someone to help me move the tables. You will supervise."

"My arm is much better."

"Not that much better. Besides, we're not doing it until tonight at closing." She glanced at her watch. "We close in an hour."

"I guess. But the students have school tomorrow. I can't keep them late. The tables are light. I promise to use only one arm. Will that suit you?"

"No, it will not. Those tables aren't light. You wanted to make sure they could withstand strong winds so you purchased heavy tables, remember? I should know. I cleaned them up yesterday."

"Maybe you're right."

"What's wrong, baby?"

*Baby.* "You're going to want to kill me. But I need to see Ruby."

Although the theft of years ago had been cleared Cecily still needed to see Ruby. She wanted to face the woman who tried to murder Glenda and her. Everything happened so quickly she could barely fathom the details. Right now Ruby was housed in the island jail, which wasn't very large.

"That hateful woman? Why?"

"I need to know why."

"She's sick. You already know that. She wanted Ryan free to marry Hazeline."

"She didn't try to kill LaToya."

"Maybe she knew they had problems from the beginning. Who knows. Any fool can see that Ryan's really in love with you."

That'd been bothering her, too. Goodness knew Ryan had been the best of husbands. She couldn't ask for any better. The best lover. He was solicitous. Their relationship was just about perfect. So what bothered her about them?

She loved him with all her heart. Suddenly she was dumbstruck. Ryan never said he loved her. Cecily felt weak.

And she felt as if her heart were missing. She told him often that she loved him. Lord knows she was madly in love with him. But he'd never—not once—uttered the words to her. She felt stupid. As if she were making waves where none lay. On the surface everything seemed fine, but it wasn't, not quite.

Although she didn't want to muddy the waters, she couldn't stand not knowing. Cecily had always plunged in whether for good or bad.

"I'm going to see Ruby," she said, a stubborn tilt to her head.

"Cecily."

"I have to, Glenda."

"Well, I'm going with you."

"You don't need to. Her beef wasn't with you. She hated me."

"And me. Remember Emery?"

"I don't even want to talk about Emery and how you're treating him."

Glenda stubbornly pressed her lips tight. She'd picked another fight with Emery. But more customers arrived and they went back to work. More and more locals had come to the restaurant since her mishap. More seemed to accept her.

Emery and Ryan arrived at closing time. Glenda glared at Emery. When the last guest left, Cecily fixed them plates.

"Are you going to join us or sulk?" she asked Glenda.

Glenda fixed her own plate and sat with them. Emery had the patience of Job. He still came by practically every day after work.

"If he's here he already knows about me. You may as well give in," he said to Glenda and kissed her lips when she came to the table.

"You are by far the most stubborn man I've ever encountered in my entire life, Emery Cleveland."

"And don't you forget it."

She shook her head and smiled. "I give up."

He threw up his hand. "It's about time, woman. See what persistence does for you?"

"You're way past persistent. You're mule-headed."

"If that's what it takes."

After they ate, the men moved the tables from storage to the porch.

"I don't know if I like the porch filled with tables," Cecily said. "We need some rockers out here, too." She stood in the sand, looking onto the porch.

"I saw plenty of them in the storage shed," Glenda said.

"Are you telling us we've got to lug these heavy tables back to storage?" Ryan said, frowning at her.

"Maybe one or two. The ones on either side of the door, I think. Four rockers will do, won't they, Glenda?"

"I think so."

They all trudged back to the shed. Cecily and Glenda looked the rockers over and selected the four best ones.

"Come to think of it, I could use a couple of them on my balcony. I love sitting out here at night."

"I don't like your being out here all by yourself at night," said Emery.

"I haven't had a minute's trouble since I moved here," Glenda told him.

"I still don't like it," Emery reiterated. "How about going on a boat ride with me Monday?"

"I've got the day off. I thought you had to work."

"I'm the boss. I can take a day off if I want to."

"Sounds good," Glenda said.

# Chapter 17

Later that evening, Emery followed Glenda up the stairs to her apartment. Emery was more than a little peeved at what she'd put them through.

"I'm too old to be putting up with anybody's 'tude," Glenda said when she saw his face.

"I'm too old to put up with the foolishness you've put me through. And for what?"

Glenda sniffed. "I had a good reason—that you wouldn't listen to."

"Don't put me through that again," he said and slowly guided his hand through her thick braids.

They glared at each other for several clock ticks. Finally Emery said, "Come here, woman." He tugged her to him and kissed her the way he'd really wanted to do for so long he'd built up a huge ache that just wouldn't relent.

"Emery, I'm so frightened," Glenda finally said. "I care so much for you and if . . ."

"Don't say it. I've told you before you're worried about nothing. Be reasonable, Glenda. That man isn't still looking for you after nearly thirty years. He's moved on with his life by now. Probably mistreating some unfortunate woman."

Glenda shook her head. "I hope not."

"Unfortunately, that's the way it usually happens, sweetheart." He gathered her hand in his. "Cecily's married and settled. That leaves you and me sweet cakes."

All of Glenda's loneliness and confusion welded together in one surge of devouring yearning.

"You and me. I like the sound of that."

The emotions roiling in Emery's eyes made her catch her breath.

He gathered her close and Glenda gave in to her needs. For the first time in a very long time she let nature take its course. She wouldn't second guess the future or try to control a course over which she had no control.


Cecily unscrewed her bottle of perfume, applied some to the back of her neck, between her cleavage, behind her knees, and on the pulse beat of her arms. Sitting at her dressing table getting ready for bed, Cecily wore a sky-blue short nightgown Glenda had given her as a gift.

She watched her handsome husband who never failed to increase her heartbeat when she saw him in this near naked form. He only wore a towel around his waist. His hair was damp from the shower and the breadth of his shoulders never failed to fascinate her. Dropping the towel, he went to the dresser, gathered black briefs, and tugged them on. Then he watched her from the corner of his eye. With the look he gave her, she needn't have been a psychic to discern what was on his mind. Then the slow smile, the one that melted her to her bones, appeared on his freshly shaven face.

Her heartbeat accelerated and she wet her lips. He closed the distance between them and kissed her. Stooping between her thighs he rubbed the short gown all the way up to expose the matching thong. His fingers stroked her. His mouth nuzzled her neck and the tops of her breasts. She moaned at the pleasure spreading through her body. And her fingers dug into his broad shoulders, caressing the soft skin that shielded rock-hard muscles. She loved his touch—loved to touch him.

His hands spanned her rounded hips. And she rose just a little, letting him ease the slip of fabric off her. He kissed her thighs, beginning at her knees—little darting kisses mixed with the hot stroke of his tongue. And then he kissed her intimately and she was gasping for breath. She just about hopped out of the seat, the pleasure was so exquisite. He stroked her with his tongue, building up the pleasure, and increasing the pressure until she exploded.

He stroked her tenderly until she came back to earth; then he placed her on the bed, and she curled her hand along his hard sex, stroking him in long, smooth strokes. They touched each other, built up the pleasure until finally he rolled her beneath him. His big body settled above her and the long dark length of him entered her and her softness stretched to accommodate him. She cried his name in pleasure.

"Do you like that, sweetheart?"

"I love it."

They moved in a rhythmic cadence, danced to a metrical beat. She stroked his broad back, pulling him closer. He kissed her cheek and settled his mouth over hers. The kiss was frantic. The kiss was sweet. He moved to settle her legs over his shoulders, letting her feel even more the exquisite length of him. They moved, they danced, until they exploded in a world of stars and comets.

Fifteen minutes later, Cecily's head rested comfortably on Ryan's shoulders. She was sated in the aftermath of their lovemaking. Once again she'd told him that she loved him, and he'd failed to respond likewise.

"Ryan?" she asked, drawing a fingertip along his hand that rested across her stomach.

"Hmmm?" He stroked her arm tenderly.

"Do you love me?"

He stiffened beside her. His arm tensed.

"I absolutely adore you," he said.

She squeezed his hand. "But do you love me?"

He was quiet so long, the silence alarmed Cecily.

She couldn't see his face in the dark, but she turned to

face him anyway. "It's not a trick question. A simple yes or no will do."

"It's not so simple."

Cecily closed her eyes against the pain of his rejection. "If you can't say you love me, why did you ask me to marry you?"

His arm tightened around her as if to keep her from fleeing. "I feel a special connection with you... With you I feel complete."

Cecily tried to stymie the disappointment and hurt that impaled her motionless. "That's not enough to build a marriage on. Why weren't you truthful with me before now?"

He blew out a long breath, covered his eyes with his other arm. "I was truthful. I want to be married to you. Otherwise I wouldn't have asked you to marry me."

"It's a lie of omission." She moved from his arm but suddenly she was too weak to move any farther.

He moved his arm from his eyes and leaned over her, supporting himself on one elbow. "Tell me you haven't been happy."

"My happiness is built on grains of sand, nothing solid. It can scatter with the first good wind or high tides."

"Our marriage is more solid than that. I'll always be here for you."

"You loved LaToya and that marriage didn't last a year." Cecily hopped out of bed and cut the light on.

Ryan sat against the headboard and shook his head. "What I felt for LaToya wasn't love." He drew his knees to his chest, the sheet dangling half on, half off.

"I never wanted to be in a one-sided relationship. It just doesn't work."

"We work. I've already promised you everything I have."

"Except your love."

"What about enjoying the same things? What about companionship? There's a lot that women claim they want that doesn't include the word love."

Cecily started to the closet.

"What are you doing?" he asked, coming off the bed.

"I'm—"

The phone rang, shattering the mood.

Ryan grabbed the receiver, barking a "Hello."

"Right now?" he asked, breaking the frown with a weary smile. He talked a few seconds more, then hung up.

"What is it?" Cecily asked.

"Delcia's in labor."

"Is she at the hospital?"

He nodded.

Cecily tried to styme the hurt, tried to force a calm she was far from feeling. "All right. Let's shower and go there."

"What were you doing before the phone rang?" he asked.

"We'll deal with us later," she said and headed to the shower.


Cecily had heard horror stories of women who were in labor for hours and hours, but at 4:10 that morning, little baby Matthews arrived. A squirming tiny boy.

Carter and Delcia were in seventh heaven. Clay and Pauline were beside themselves with having their second grandchild. But Cecily noticed Clay watching her from time to time.

"Are you all right?" he asked at one point.

Cecily smiled. "I'm fine." Then she looked through the window at the tiny wrinkled baby with the blue cap and felt this scene would not happen with Ryan and her and sadness stole her breath.

Ryan and Cecily didn't make it home until almost six. Cecily fixed breakfast. Although she and Ryan ate together, the meal was a tense affair. The more time passed, the more edgy Cecily became. Neither she nor Ryan was very hungry.

"Breakfast was delicious," Ryan said.

"Thank you." She couldn't tell by his plate. It was still half full!

He left the table and disappeared down the hall.

Cecily went to the bedroom and pulled off her housecoat and dressed. As Ryan pulled his Camp Coree sweatshirt over his head he watched her closely.

"I think we both need time to think about last night," he said.

Cecily nodded. "So do I."

He cupped her chin. "I'm where I want to be. I'm happy with you. Remember, I wanted to marry you."

Cecily nodded again, a sudden sadness shredding her insides. Just by the look in his eyes, she could tell he wanted to love her. He just couldn't. She couldn't blame him for not loving her. Love came naturally like it did with her parents. And it was like she had said to him the night before. Either he did or he didn't.

He kissed her as he always did but this time he seemed a bit desperate. He gathered her tightly in his arms and held her as if he didn't want to let her go. Then he plopped his hat on his head and left.

Cecily knew that for now the marriage would be okay. But one day the woman whom he really loved would come along. And where would she be? Either he'd have to stay with her out of a sense of duty or he'd leave her for his true love. She knew he had a keen sense of right and wrong. He felt strongly about responsibility. He might just stay with her because it was the right thing to do.

Cecily didn't want that kind of marriage. She pulled her suitcase out of the closet. She hadn't yet brought all of her things over. All her furniture was still in her apartment. Her bedroom was still decorated just as it had been when she'd lived there. Maybe she sensed in the back of her mind that something wasn't quite right. Perhaps that was why she hadn't moved completely.

Cecily couldn't keep the tears at bay as she packed. She left a note for Ryan on the table. By eight when she drove to the shop, she had stored her things in her own closet. Glenda was opening this morning. But she needed to be there soon.

Cecily walked through the doors leading to the balcony. The morning breeze was still cool. The wind blew steadily and dried the wetness on her face. It was better to sever the ties now than to live with him for years and become totally attached and then have to part. She could never have him stay with her out of pity.

Ryan usually arrived around one for lunch. At twelve-fifty, Cecily gathered her purse and went to the kitchen. To avoid a confrontation, she wouldn't be around when he arrived.

"Glenda, I have to run an errand. I'll be back in an hour or so."

Glenda looked up from grilling the chicken breast. "Isn't Ryan coming?"

"I'm not sure. We haven't talked."

"Is everything okay?"

Cecily shrugged. "I'll be back soon." Then she left without telling Glenda her destination. Glenda wouldn't approve. Neither would Ryan. But this was something she needed to do.

She tried not to look at the campground as she passed it on her way to the sheriff's office. It was funny how a person could be so happy one day and the next sink into the depths of depression and misery. A broken heart was really a euphemism. But when love hurt, the heart really did feel broken—its pain stabbed as powerfully as a physical blow.

In a few minutes Cecily arrived at the police station and asked to see Ruby.

The officer tried to talk her out of seeing the woman, but Cecily needed this.

Ruby didn't look like the well-dressed woman Cecily usually encountered around town. Gone was the makeup, fine clothes, and manicured nails. Even though the county jail was small, a plexiglass partition separated them from chest level up.

Ruby sat in her utilitarian gray chair. She looked older somehow. And she stared at Cecily as if she hated her. She picked up the phone. Cecily did likewise.

"What are you doing here?" Ruby asked Cecily.

"I have some questions I wanted answered."

"Ask away," she said with a bored expression. "I'm not going anywhere."

Coming over, Cecily had thought of a thousand questions she wanted to ask. Suddenly nothing came to mind.

"Why did you try to kill me and not LaToya?" Cecily asked.

Ruby laughed. "I knew that tramp wasn't going to last. It was just a matter of time before she left. She hated the island. And Ryan wasn't leaving. But you're different. You were staying. Your mama had no business here and neither did you."

"You and my dad broke up long before he married my mother."

"He would have come back to me if she hadn't married him. She stood in the way of my happiness just like you are responsible for my daughter's unhappiness."

"But you didn't try to kill my mother."

"Humph. I had already taken care of your daddy."

Cecily hesitated, blinking with bafflement. "What are you talking about?"

"I killed Walter along with that worthless husband of mine who tried to stop me."

Cecily shook her head. Ruby must really be sick. If she did such a thing she'd never admit it, would she?

"I'm not going to tell a soul. You'll never be able to prove it." Cecily listened with bewilderment. "My confession will be my word against yours."

"My father died in the hurricane."

There was an evil gleam in Ruby's eyes. "I killed him. If I couldn't have him, I wasn't going to let him live with that woman."

And Cecily suddenly believed her. She did kill her father.

"Why did you kill your husband?"

"He tried to stop me. I didn't love him and I didn't love Emery. And I tried my best to ruin your mama too. But she left before they could send her to jail where she belonged."

"Well," Cecily said with an ironic smile, "you're in jail now. Exactly where you belong."

Ruby suddenly banged her hand against the Plexiglas.

"You should be dead. When I get out I'm not going to miss next time. You can count your days."

Cecily backed away from the woman.

Ruby banged the plexiglass, setting up an eerie sound. A guard came for her and she started screaming at the top of her lungs about Cecily's days being numbered. Cecily clutched her throat. She'd met many people in her lifetime, but she'd never before met anyone like Ruby.

Cecily knew hate was wrong, that as a Christian you were to pray for and love your enemies, but Ruby had stolen the most important people in her life from her. It was impossible to form up any compassion for that evil woman. And yet, the sickness was there for Cecily to see. A sickness born of hate. Cecily wouldn't sink to that level.

Cecily couldn't face Glenda or anyone right now. She needed to be alone. She drove to the graveyard and sat on a stone bench that had worn with time but was still sturdy enough to hold her. She gazed upon the tombstones and the lush green wildness around her.

She wondered who had put the bench here. Wondered if it was Justin Moore, who had loved the Philly wife who wasn't contented here until after he had died. Or was it Hannibal, who had loved Sissieretta at a time the country wasn't ready to accept their union?

Cecily sat there for almost an hour before she rose and went to her car. Then she drove to her apartment for the baby gift she'd purchased in Santa Barbara. She debated what to write on the card. Then she signed it *Ryan and Cecily*. Not everyone needed to know what was happening between them.

She wrapped the gifts and placed them in the pretty gift bags decorated with teddy bears and balloons, and drove to the hospital to see Delcia and baby.

When she arrived, Delcia was feeding the baby. Cecily placed a smile on her face and tapped lightly on the door.

"Is it all right for me to enter?"

"Of course it is," Delcia said smiling down on her baby.

As Cecily took a seat close to the bed, a lump caught in her throat. Tears brimmed over. "You too look absolutely adorable," she said.

Delcia patted her hand. "Look at you. Even though I should feel like I tussled with a truck, I feel wonderful."

"You look it."

She finished feeding the baby and carefully laid him on her shoulder and rubbed his tiny back.

"As soon as I get home, I'm going to let you hold him."

"Well, you know you have a ready sitter," Cecily assured her.

Delcia chuckled. "You're going to take that back one day."

"I don't think so."

The baby burped and Delcia held him close. Then the nurse came to get the baby and the women were alone.

"I bought something for you and the baby," Cecily said.

"Oh, I love gifts. I'm going to leave this one so that Carter and I can open it together." Then she began to rip the paper from her gift. She opened the box, peeled back the tissue paper to reveal a stunning lavender gown.

"Cecily, it's beautiful. I didn't expect anything for me."

Cecily waved away her appreciation. "The new mama deserves something, too."

"It's going to be weeks before I can wear it."

"I'm sure it will fit."

"I wouldn't dare wear something this beautiful now."

"Nonsense," Cecily said. "Wear the gown. It'll go beautiful with your coloring."

Delcia held out her arms. "Oh, come here, you."

Cecily left the chair and went to her. Delcia hugged her tightly. Cecily squeezed her back.

"You're the best sister."

"Thank you," Cecily said, letting Delcia go and sinking into the chair she'd vacated. "So are you." She suddenly felt too weak to stand.

Cecily suddenly realized that her marriage to Ryan involved more than the two of them. If their marriage dissolved, she wasn't losing only Ryan but his family as well.

# Chapter 18

Ryan had missed Cecily for lunch at the tea shop and again when he visited Delcia in the hospital. His mind was so clouded with his conversation with Cecily the night before that he hadn't thought about a gift for Delcia and the little tike. But he was pleased that his wife had purchased one for them. The gift gave him hope. She still thought of them as a unit. She was willing to work as hard as he was to make their marriage work.

This marriage was made of glue that was much sturdier than elusive love. People who married for love discovered later that love wasn't enough.

When Ryan arrived home, tired from a sleepless night, he thought to start on supper. As soon as he entered the kitchen a note propped on the salt shaker sent a sinking feeling to the pit of his stomach. With dread he picked it up. Cecily wrote that she needed distance to think about her future. Ryan nearly exploded. "Her future? What about *our* future," he said as he paced the confines of the room to bring himself under control before he went after her.

Although after fifteen minutes his stomach was a little steadier even if his temper was still on edge, he decided he

Clay shrugged.

"Well, no sense in speculating. He'll be here soon enough."

Clay looked worriedly at her as she started back to work. He resumed his seat and they talked a few minutes. Then other workers began to arrive and he joined Harry on the front porch.

Ryan was acting as if nothing unusual were happening. He was as solicitous as ever. He called her several times each day. He shared lunch with her after the lunch crowd at the shop. And he slept with her each night, refusing even to consider her sleeping someplace else, which included another bedroom.

With a lack of sleep and with her nerves turned inside out, Cecily was turning into a basket case.

On Monday Ryan, Cecily, Emery, and Glenda went out on one of Emery's boats to a secluded cove and moored. Ryan declared it was his favorite fishing spot.

It was a warm day and before Cecily and Ryan sat on the dock to fish, they walked the shores in search of clams. The water was still too cold to swim, but near the shore the marshland mud was thick with clams. Donning gloves, they took their buckets and began to dig in the mudflats. They talked about inconsequential things as they dug. During a lull, Ryan ran a dark muddy finger down her nose.

"You scamp," she told him, wiping the mud with the back of her hand.

"You were too quiet over there." At his mischievous grin she just loved her heart turned over.

By trying to put some distance between them, Cecily was trying to save her heart but that moment she realized nothing could save her. He had already captured her. What on earth was she going to do?

"You only made it worse," he told her, grinning up at her. Then he frowned. "What's wrong?"

"Nothing." But he knew. She could tell that he did.

"Come here," he said. But she shook her head and

stepped back. She felt the rejection even more when she was cuddled up so close to him that she could hear the ticking of his heart.

She glanced at the sound. "Think we have enough yet?" she asked to break the strained atmosphere.

"We have plenty. Cecily—"

"Don't say anything. Let's just . . . let's go back and do some fishing." She picked up the hand rakes while he gathered the bucket and they took the trek back that seemed longer in the changed atmosphere.

Ryan stroked her arm and gathered her muddy hand in his. "I never meant to make you unhappy."

"I know."

"We'll make this work," he assured her.

Cecily remained silent and Ryan felt like a heel that he couldn't give her what she needed so desperately. He should have lied. But he didn't want their marriage based on lies. Only he couldn't imagine his life without her. He and Cecily had what it took to make a marriage survive. If only she wouldn't get hung up on the words and instead would concentrate on what they meant to each other.

Although weekday tours of the lighthouse wouldn't begin until summer, Harry still came over some mornings for breakfast and coffee. He liked to sit on the front porch to watch the ocean waves and the seagulls flying overhead. The front porch had quickly turned into a gathering place and more often than not Cecily would find a group of old men deep in conversation. One had even taken up whittling duck decoys while they conversed for half the day. She thought Harry liked to talk to people more than anything else. Often by one o'clock the group had dispersed.

Cecily was sitting on pins and needles. She was waiting for Mr. Burtrell. Emery and Glenda were in the kitchen and were almost ready to go upstairs to Glenda's apartment and Cecily was in the process of locking the doors when an older gentleman wearing a neatly trimmed beard and mustache came into the tea shop.

Cecily looked at him hopefully. "I'm sorry but we're closed," she told him.

But her heartbeat accelerated when he said, "I'm looking for Cecily Edmonds."

"I'm she. Are you Mr. Burtrell?" she asked. The voice seemed somewhat different, but it could have been distorted over the phone.

The man frowned at her. "Cecily is older than you. She must be close to sixty."

"Why would you think that? My mother was sixty. Certainly you wouldn't expect her daughter to be that old." There was something strange about this conversation. "You are Mr. Burtrell, aren't you?"

"Burtrell? 'Fraid not," he said.

"My apologies. How may I help you?" Glenda and Emery emerged from the kitchen laughing at something. Glenda was often in good humor lately, and it gladdened Cecily's heart that her aunt was so happy. They had made a timely arrival.

She continued to watch the man, who now focused on the couple who'd just emerged. The shop was closed. They were isolated and Cecily was beginning to feel uneasy about this man. If he wasn't Mr. Burtrell, what did he want with her?

Then she thought about the e-mail messages she'd received weeks ago. She had completely forgotten about them because they had stopped coming. She'd thought the message Ryan had sent had done the trick.

"Cecily," Glenda said.

"Yes?" Cecily responded but she didn't take her eyes off the man.

Glenda approached her, then gasped, carrying her hand to her throat. She grabbed for Cecily, but the man captured Cecily's arm and brought a sharp knife to her neck.

"Oh, my God! Eddie don't," Glenda said, when Cecily was snatched out of her hands.

"What is it, Glenda?" Emery came rushing over.

"It's him! It's Eddie!"

Fear snaked up Cecily's spine. She thought back to the

evil man who had murdered Glenda's fiancé. This must be the same man who now had an arm around Cecily's throat.

"So is this your daughter, Glenda? Even better."

"She's my employer, not my daughter," Glenda hastened to explain.

"You're a good liar. A mother wanting to protect her baby chick. I saw you coming out her apartment in New York."

He rubbed his chin against Cecily's face and squeezed Cecily tighter. Her skin crawled.

"By the looks of her, you must have been pregnant when I killed your lover," he said to Glenda. "We had a good thing going on the Internet before she dumped me like the others. Keeping track of you has been so much easier with computer. Isn't that right little miss tea shop owner?"

"Look, why don't you let her go? This has nothing to do with her. She isn't Glenda's daughter. Glenda doesn't have any children," Emery said, approaching him with his hands spread out.

"You're Glenda's lover now. I've seen you with her. I saw you Monday. A nice cozy little group you made. Too bad I didn't bring a gun, I could have gotten you all."

Emery stepped forward again and Eddie squeezed Cecily tighter, backing up two steps. "Stay where you are," he warned. Then he spoke to Cecily. "Your husband's going to be a mite upset but so was I when Glenda took my wife and child away from me."

"I had nothing to do with that," Glenda said.

"If I nick her right here, she could bleed to death in front of your eyes." He held the knife to her neck.

"Haven't you done enough?"

"Not nearly enough. I found my wife, by the way. Her and the kid."

"Oh, Lord," Glenda moaned.

"She got away. You won't." He cut Cecily's arm and she screamed. The pain hurt like fire, but after the initial scream, Cecily sucked the pain in.

Emery and Glenda came forward with their hands out.

"Uh, uh, uh. . . ." the man said and pressed the point at

Cecily's throat. "Get back. Now!" he said when they didn't respond quickly enough.

Glenda and Emery continued to talk to him but Cecily wasn't listening to the words. Fear held her in its grip. She knew what this man was capable of.

The man's grip was so tight around Cecily's neck that she couldn't move but she felt the warm blood streaming down her arm. She wondered if she would ever get to see Ryan again. In the face of this horror, Ryan's refusal to say he loved her didn't seem like such a gigantic issue after all. If she died, perhaps it would be better if he didn't. She wouldn't want him to suffer. But he would feel guilty and she didn't want that, either.

What on earth was she thinking about? She couldn't just give up.

But then she felt the knife in her side and stifled a scream. She saw Emery and Glenda approaching again. The man was saying something. She hurt so badly. She realized the knife wasn't at her neck any longer. She didn't have to pretend when she started sliding toward the floor. Suddenly she sank all her dead weight on him. The move was unexpected and he loosened his grip but she felt the point of the knife in her again—deeper this time. And then she was on the floor. She could feel the blood pouring out of her and wondered if she was dying.

She saw Glenda's mouth moving over her. She heard noise in the background. Time seemed to crawl. It seemed forever before once again she was on a harried drive to the hospital. But once she arrived, they immediately shipped her via medivac to Morehead City. It seemed the knife had pierced her liver.


Cecily was recovering. She looked pale and nearly lifeless in the bed. But she was still breathing. Thank God. Ryan put a trembling hand on her hand and squeezed.

When he'd seen the medivac fly toward the hospital, he never imagined that his wife would be on it. Or how easily it was for him to realize that what he felt for her wasn't something as lukewarm as *liking* her or just wanting to spend his life with her. He realized for the first time that what he felt was an elemental and powerful love. When life put him on the precipice, there was no pretending, there was no confusion. He loved his wife more than life itself. She gave him purpose, a reason to enjoy the day, not just exist in it.

As he sat on the chair beside her bed he watched the IV drip into her vein. He looked at her still form with deep-seated fury that that fool had kept hatred in him for thirty years.

That man would suffer no more because during the struggle with Emery, he'd died by his own knife. It had cut an artery. Ryan tried not to carry hate in his heart. Intellectually, he knew it was wrong. But the man's death was a fitting justice as far as Ryan was concerned.


"I love you," Ryan said to Cecily. She was still in intensive care, but he felt he had to tell her now.

"You promised you wouldn't lie." Her voice sounded hoarse and weak.

"I'm not lying. I do love you."

Cecily turned her head away from him. After refusing to say the words for weeks, even making an issue out of the fact that he didn't love her, how could he convince her now that he did?

"You look like hell. You should go home and get some rest," she finally said.

"Do you really think I can rest when you're not okay?"

She fell silent again.

He scooted his chair close to the bed. Leaning over her, he stroked her brow, wondering how to convey to her she'd unlocked his heart and soul. He finally settled on the simple truth—what was in his heart.

"My life wouldn't have been the same without you. You complete me, in the very best way."

She smiled, but he could tell she still didn't believe him.

"Ruby and Eddy were both filled with hate to the degree that they refused to look at what was good around them,

Cecily. Ruby had a daughter. She had husbands and a brother. She could have put the past behind her and opened her heart to the wonder of what she had. Instead she'd built up a legacy of hatred in Hazeline. Those people close themselves from love, from living any kind of decent life.

"Cecily, I was doing the same thing. I let what happened between LaToya and me close my heart to loving you. I knew I needed you. I knew you were the one for me, but I was afraid to open my heart completely to love. I was only living on the fringe of what could be the best that we could share together.

"When I almost lost you, LaToya wasn't important any longer. The money I lost wasn't important any longer. Only you and the fact that I really love you but was afraid to name it. I'm telling you now that I love you more than I've loved anyone."

Tears spilled from Cecily's eyes, running down the side of her face.

Ryan could finally tell that she believed him and his heart lightened. He was still distressed realizing that she could have died without knowing how much he treasured and loved her. Ryan kissed the salty tears away. She felt warm and real. He closed his eyes to hold in his emotions; then he gazed directly into her eyes. He needed her to witness the sincerity of his words. "I'm going to take very good care of you, my love. Trust me."

Cecily lifted a hand and caressed the side of Ryan's face that was prickly with stubble. Clearly he hadn't shaven since she was injured. Her heart ran over with love for this man and with the assurance of his love.

"I trust you," she said. "I'm going to take very good care of you."

# Epilogue

In June the tea shop was overflowing with customers and Cecily was working half days. She felt perfectly fine but Ryan and Glenda feared she was returning to work too soon, so at noon she disappeared upstairs to her old apartment for a nap. Afterwards she went downstairs where she'd discovered one of the employees hadn't shown up for the afternoon shift, so she worked through the heavy afternoon crowd. The nap had revived her and she was able to hang in better than even she thought she would.

Since it was the beginning of June, the schoolkids weren't out yet and the heavy beach crowd hadn't yet arrived. College kids had completed their semester in the beginning of May and plenty of them had thrown up tents.

Glenda and Emery set a wedding date in October. She wanted to wait until they could take a honeymoon together. And she wouldn't be rushed.

Two hours later, a replacement arrived and Cecily left the shop.

The temperature had lowered making the hot day bearable. Holding her mother's diary in her hand, Cecily walked along the beach and sat on her favorite piece of driftwood, taking in the sweeping view of the ocean. Mr. Burtrell had delivered her mother's package that included a diary along with photos of the past. As the seagulls squawked overhead, Cecily read her mother's secrets of so many years. Today she didn't bring bread for the seagulls to eat as she usually did. She watched them as they flew gracefully over the water.

Cecily used some of her recuperating time to write down stories the islanders had told her. She was planning to write the history of the island. She planned to get as much as she could while the older ones were still alive.

After a half hour, she realized she wasn't alone. Ryan approached her as he jogged along the coastline. He looked strong and handsome in his cut-offs and sleeveless shirt.

Ryan kissed her, then settled on the log beside her and perused her closely.

"You're looking well," he said. "Like an islander."

She closed the diary and smiled up at him. "I feel wonderful."

"What are you reading?" he asked.

"My mother's memoirs."

Ryan didn't worry any longer that she'd want to return to New York. She'd settled in as comfortably as if she'd been born and raised on Coree. His only worry was restraining her impatience. She was accustomed to keeping busy. So busy in fact that she barely took the time to enjoy the roses, as his mother would say. She wanted to work a full schedule. Push to fly right back into life full force. He'd had a time of it keeping her from getting bored. His family had pitched in. His dad dropped in to tell her stories, or coaxed her into sharing a cup of tea on the porch, although he wasn't a tea drinker. Uncle Harry had latched onto a fresh ear to listen to his war stories that everyone on the island had heard so many times they could recite them as well as he could. Willow Mae would regale her with her prize-winning recipes even parted with her clam and conch chowder that Cecily now served in the tea shop. His mom would talk about the children and Cecily's mother.

And Ryan cooked, cleaned, and just made sure Cecily

knew she was well loved. He only hoped she realized that slowing down could be nice, too.

"It's getting darker," Ryan finally said.

Sure enough she could see the light flashing from the lighthouse. "At least we won't have a problem finding our way," she said.

"That's for sure." He stood and pulled her up with him and Cecily carried her sandals as they strolled along the water. The tides had risen and Cecily found her toes sinking into the wet sand.

"Looks like we're going to have a full moon tonight," Ryan said.

Cecily immediately looked toward the window her mother had spoken of. Sure enough the light glimmered at an angle, casting a surreal shadow on the window. If Cecily were the whimsical type she'd think she saw two lovers embracing. She sighed, thinking at one time her mother and father had shared such an experience.

"Tired?" Ryan asked as he swept her off her feet into his arms. Cecily screeched; then she circled his neck with her arms and leaned up and kissed him.

"Never," she said. But he deepened the kiss. A laughing matter had suddenly turned serious. Her body slid along his as she stood, but he closed his arms tightly around her. For a time, they were two lovers on the beach. And it seemed as if her parent's scene from the lighthouse had been transported to them.

When Ryan released her with promises for later, she glimpsed the window again. The ephemeral image had disappeared. But the memory hadn't vanished from her mind. Perhaps what she searched for was within her. Cecily no longer dreamed of love and the special someone to share her life with. She lived a life dreams were made of.

Dear Reader,

I hope you enjoyed revisiting Coree Island with Cecily and Ryan. Ryan was first introduced in *Shattered Illusions* with Delcia and Carter's story.

Look for my next novel, ***Courage Under Fire***, July 2003 as part of the "At Your Service" military series. ***Courage Under Fire***, set in Washington, D.C., and Germany, is a story of rebuilding shattered trust.

Readers like you help me to continue working with the craft I love. Thank you so much for your support and for so many kind and uplifting letters.

I love hearing from readers. Please visit my web page at *www.candicepoarch.com*, or write to me at:

P.O. Box 291
Springfield, VA 22150

With Warm Regards,
Candice Poarch

## About the Author

Reared in Stony Creek, Virginia, best-selling author Candice Poarch portrays a sense of community and mutual support in her novels. She firmly believes that everyday life in small town America has its own rich rewards.

Candice currently lives in Springfield, Virginia with her husband and three children. A former computer systems manager, she has made writing her full-time career. Candice is a graduate of Virginia State University and holds a Bachelor of Science degree in physics.